QUEEN'S BOUNTY

The Ursula Blanchard Mysteries from Fiona Buckley

THE ROBSART MYSTERY
THE DOUBLET AFFAIR
QUEEN'S RANSOM
TO RUIN A QUEEN
QUEEN OF AMBITION
A PAWN FOR THE QUEEN
THE FUGITIVE QUEEN
THE SIREN QUEEN
QUEEN WITHOUT A CROWN *
QUEEN'S BOUNTY *

* *available from Severn House*

QUEEN'S BOUNTY

Fiona Buckley

CRÈME de la CRIME

This first world edition published 2012
in Great Britain and the USA by
Crème de la Crime, an imprint of
SEVERN HOUSE PUBLISHERS LTD of
9–15 High Street, Sutton, Surrey, England, SM1 1DF.
Trade paperback edition first published
in Great Britain and the USA 2012 by
SEVERN HOUSE PUBLISHERS LTD.

British Library Cataloguing in Publication Data

Buckley, Fiona.
  Queen's bounty.
  1. Blanchard, Ursula (Fictitious character)–Fiction.
  2. Great Britain–History–Elizabeth, 1558-1603–
  Fiction. 3. Detective and mystery stories.
  I. Title
  823.9'14-dc23

ISBN-13: 978-1-78029-024-9 (cased)
ISBN-13: 978-1-78029-527-5 (trade paper)

All Severn House titles are printed on acid-free paper.

Severn House Publishers support The Forest Stewardship Council [FSC],
the leading international forest certification organisation. All our titles that
are printed on Greenpeace-approved FSC-certified paper carry the FSC logo.

MIX
Paper from
responsible sources
FSC® C018575
www.fsc.org

Typeset by Palimpsest Book Production Ltd.,
Falkirk, Stirlingshire, Scotland.
Printed and bound in Great Britain by
MPG Books Ltd., Bodmin, Cornwall.

For
Liz and William
and
Anne and Ian

With special thanks to Ian
who gave me one of the central ideas of the story

ONE
Family Matters

I don't believe in witchcraft. Nor does my husband Hugh or my good servant Roger Brockley or my gentlewoman Sybil Jester. Fran Dale, my maid, who is actually Roger's wife, thinks there may be something in it, but Dale is inclined to be credulous. As for that aged hanger-on of mine, Gladys Morgan – I have never been sure. Gladys, being old, unprepossessing and poor, lacks influence on account of just those things, and resents it. Pretending to have supernatural abilities has sometimes been her way of commanding respect, or even fear. Where pretence blurs into belief, I don't know.

Oh, very well, let us be quite honest. There are times when even people with the strongest minds lapse into credulity, a little. In the noon of the day, when the household is all round you and you are busy with mundane tasks, then it's easy enough to say *I don't believe in witches*. But at dead of night, when winds and raindrops and ivy leaves tap on windows, when houses creak and whisper to themselves, and even if you light a candle, it only makes a little pool of brightness, with formless shadows fleeing and flying beyond its edges: are any of us quite so certain then?

Probably not. Still, for the most part, I maintain that sorcery is nonsense, which is why, when Gladys Morgan was convicted of causing death through witchcraft and condemned to be hanged, I moved heaven and earth, and Queen Elizabeth of England, to save her.

I had an advantage, because the queen is my half-sister, though few people are supposed to know it. In fact, more people know it than either I or Elizabeth really wish, but it's rarely mentioned aloud, by anyone. Her mother was Queen Anne Boleyn, and her father was King Henry the Eighth. My mother served Queen Anne and was seduced by King Henry, and so I came into being. It gives me the right, in an emergency, to go to the queen. I did so, and Gladys was reprieved, just in time.

She was lucky, for she'd been accused of witchcraft before. An earlier accusation was the reason why she came into my household at all. There is a strong streak of Sir Galahad in Roger Brockley. Like me he decided that Gladys had been victimized because she was aged, ugly and rude, so he rescued her.

But it was true that she had a repertoire of imaginative curses that she would hurl at people who annoyed her, which was all too easy to do. After she came to us, her habit of cursing outraged more than one vicar, and then an unkind fate made some of her ill-wishes apparently come true. Also, she was a gifted herbalist, and nothing annoys a male physician more than a female brewer of potions whose medicines work better than his. There were plenty of people to bear witness against her. Hence her narrow escape on this last occasion.

Afterwards, she became quieter and better behaved. I worried about her though when, in the year 1570, Sir Edward Heron became Sheriff of the County of Surrey. He was a conscientious man who wished to perform his duties properly, but he not only believed in witchcraft, he also hoped that in the county under his jurisdiction he would succeed in stamping it out.

Hugh and I met him for the first time at Cobbold Hall, the home of the Cobbold family, seven miles from Hugh's West Surrey house, Hawkswood. Hugh, who had been born at Hawkswood, knew the Cobbolds well, and as it happened, Anthony Cobbold knew Heron. Heron, like us, was a guest at the wedding when their elder daughter Alice was married.

'This is a bigger affair than I expected,' Hugh said to me as we got out of our coach. Surrounded by the other wedding guests, who were mostly on horseback, we had just jolted back from the service at St Peter's Church in Woking, a couple of miles away. The guests had almost filled the church, though St Peter's was quite big, surprisingly so for a place like Woking, which was little more than a well-grown village. However, despite its dignified name, Cobbold Hall wasn't particularly large. It was attractive, certainly, built of warm red-brown brick topped by black and white timber and plaster, with a thatched roof and a formal garden with a dovecote, but its rooms were not spacious. As we entered, I wondered how such a crowd could be fitted in. Anthony Cobbold, the bride's father, welcomed us at the door and announced that the feast in the dining room was not yet ready. To begin with, would guests please go into the parlour?

'He should have said would we *cram* ourselves in,' Hugh whispered in my ear.

The modestly sized parlour itself was pleasant, south-facing, with the sunshine of late June streaming through its leaded windows. There were glossy oak floorboards underfoot, and the air was scented by garlands of roses, strung in loops between the ceiling beams. The room was also well supplied with settles and padded stools. Between these and the crush of guests, there was hardly an inch of floor space left free.

'However will they seat us all for the dinner?' I said. 'I had no idea that the Cobbolds had such a wide acquaintance. I hardly know anyone here!'

Though Anthony Cobbold and Hugh had been friends since they were boys, our two households had not met often during the last few years, and we hadn't encountered many of their current social circle. It was some time since Hugh's worsening rheumatism had made him reluctant to travel away from home, even by coach. The seven miles between us and Cobbold Hall had become more and more of a barrier. But a wedding was a special occasion. For that, Hugh had said that he must make the effort. Now, we found ourselves amid a crowd of strangers.

Somewhere, though I couldn't see them, musicians were tuning up. As we pushed our way further in, we saw that a low platform, draped in a carpet, had been placed by the window. On it, in two high-backed chairs, sat fair-haired Alice, in ivory brocade, with a glittering new wedding ring on her left hand, and her bridegroom Robert, an amiable-looking young man in a pearl-grey doublet. Smiling people kept squeezing through the crowd to congratulate them.

A few feet away from the platform was a table where wedding gifts were being received and arranged for display by Alice's younger sister Christina. Aged seventeen and dressed for the occasion in crimson velvet with a farthingale and a pretty, lace-edged ruff, Christina was firm of jaw, with strong eyebrows, brown hair and brown eyes as bright as a squirrel's. Just now, those eyes were very alert, watching to see that the table wasn't jolted in the crush and that no one made off with any of the gifts. Such a thing was most unlikely, in this hand-picked company, but Christina visibly enjoyed being in charge.

'We are so glad you could come,' said Jane Cobbold graciously, making her way through to greet us. 'I saw you in the church, but you only arrived as the service began and I had no chance to welcome you before.'

'The roads were muddy,' said Hugh. 'There's been so much rain lately. We came by coach, and it stuck twice. My rheumatism won't let me ride a horse these days.'

'At least the sun has come out for your daughter's wedding,' I added.

'Well, the coach kept the mud from your skirts, Mistress Stannard,' said Jane, visibly studying the detail of my tawny overdress and cream brocade kirtle. She was a soft-featured, garrulous woman with big, earnest blue eyes and a habit of imitating other women's dresses and jewellery.

When I married Hugh, I had accepted his friends as mine, and therefore, because he and Anthony had known each so long, I had accepted the Cobbolds. But they wouldn't have been my choice, and when Hugh began to say that the journey to Cobbold Hall seemed to be getting mysteriously longer and more difficult, I hadn't tried to persuade him otherwise, or urged him to invite them to Hawkswood instead. At least, I didn't mind Anthony, for he was always polite even though he looked intimidating. He was tall and black-haired with a pointed beard and piercing dark eyes, and my maid, Fran Dale, after her one and only glimpse of him, had said in a hushed voice that all he needed was horns and a tail to look just like Satan. I had laughed at her. Anthony Cobbold was harmless enough, I said. But Jane . . .

Try as I would, I couldn't like Jane. She was both talkative and tactless, and also I had noticed that she usually agreed with anyone who expressed a point of view with any degree of vigour. I had heard her say, 'I feel just the same,' twice in five minutes about two opposite opinions expressed by different people, who were, in fact, arguing with each other.

In addition, if I didn't take to Jane, she hadn't taken to me either. Hugh, introducing me to his neighbours, had been kind enough to be proud of my somewhat unconventional past, but with Jane, this was a mistake. Hugh had let the Cobbolds know that I had been involved in private and sometimes adventurous enquiries for the queen, and also that I had eloped with my first husband by getting out of a window at night and sliding down a roof. Anthony had been amused, but the effect on Jane was to make her look at me, whenever we met, as though I were slightly dangerous, like a barrel of gunpowder that might explode at any moment. My championship of Gladys hadn't helped.

However, to please our husbands, we put up with each other. So now Jane was uttering platitudes about muddy skirts, while I replied with similar platitudes about being glad that the sun had shone for her daughter.

'And how is your own daughter, Meg?' Jane asked. 'You should have brought her with you; why ever didn't you? I hope she is in good health?'

'She's perfectly well. But the invitation didn't mention her,' I said.

'Oh, what of it? You could have brought anyone you liked. Surely you know that!'

I hadn't known it at all but decided not to say so.

'And tell me, what about Gladys Morgan? How does she fare? We had to admire the way you saved her when she was convicted of witchcraft. Such loyalty to your dependants! The whole district was talking about it when you brought her home.' The words were admiring, the tone less so. 'I hope it's turning out well. I would be afraid of harbouring such a one, I don't mind telling you.'

No, I know you don't mind. You've said all this, several times before. I clenched my teeth to stop myself from actually speaking my thoughts.

Jane was racing on. 'After all, can you be sure she won't drift back to her old ways? They say that when the devil gets hold of someone, he never lets go. Sir Edward Heron – the new Surrey sheriff; we know him quite well and he's here as one of our guests – was saying as much only the other day . . . Oh, here he is. Anthony is bringing him over.'

'We should be most interested to meet him,' said Hugh suavely, while I controlled my annoyance and made myself smile.

Anthony Cobbold was accompanied by a man even taller than himself, with a long neck and a beaky nose. Whereas Anthony, as became a bride's father, was resplendent in a russet velvet that suited his dark colouring, his lanky companion was all in black.

'Anthony met Sir Edward last year when they were both on a coroner's jury,' Jane whispered. 'A man of great integrity, Anthony says, and a firm upholder of the law, and particularly severe on witchcraft. He has a chaplain who preaches against it, and there have been several witchcraft trials since he took office. Quite rightly, I dare say. Oh, I think you once told me you didn't believe in such things, Ursula, but I'm sure you're wrong about that. You'd best keep Gladys Morgan away from him.'

Anthony and his companion arrived beside us. 'Ah, Hugh Stannard and Mistress Ursula. Sir Edward, these are our friends the Stannards. You will have heard of them, no doubt.' He dropped his voice. 'Acquaintances of the Secretary of State, Sir William Cecil; I believe they expect a visit from him shortly. Mistress Ursula . . .'

'I will address her as Mrs Stannard,' said Heron. 'I prefer the short modern terms of Mr and Mrs. The honorific *Mistress* is suitable for young unmarried girls, but when used for mature people, it has to me an old-fashioned ring, and I can't help but equate *old-fashioned* with Popery.'

'As you wish,' Anthony said. 'Mistr— Mrs Stannard is . . . well, related to the queen, you know, though it isn't mentioned too openly. Ursula, Hugh, this is Sir Edward Heron, County Sheriff.'

Hugh bowed. I curtsied, stifling a regrettable urge to laugh because the name Heron was so completely right for a man with long legs and neck and that sharp curved nose. There was even, I thought, something a little predatory about his cold grey eyes.

I gathered, as we stood talking to him, that Jane had not exaggerated when she said he was severe on witchcraft.

'I am finding my new post onerous in many ways,' he informed us, 'although I expected that and it has given me the means to take certain matters in hand. There has been much laxness, I fear. Because I respect the queen and she has said that she does not seek windows into men's souls, I try not to interfere with what people do in the privacy of their homes, but open Popish practices are too often winked at and they have increased since that wicked Papal Bull last month, telling Catholics not to obey Queen Elizabeth. And as for witchcraft – why, every other village seems to have a witch and even to be proud of it! Sorcery is a terrible thing and needs to be rooted out. In the short time since I have been in office, I have brought six cases to justice, and all were found guilty and hanged.'

'You are sure they really were witches?' Hugh asked mildly.

'Oh, undoubtedly. There was a woman who publicly cursed some small boys who were stealing her apples, and one of them died that same week, falling out of a tree in another garden. And after an informer had warned us, we raided a house in Woking one night and found the most shocking rites in progress: a black-draped altar, an upside-down crucifix attached to it, and three couples copulating on the floor. I look for real evidence, I assure you. I do not allow the old custom of swimming suspected witches and saying that the ones that float are guilty. I regard such things as superstition. I deal in facts. There was no doubt at all what was happening at that Woking house. Several times my men have raided suspect houses and found some shocking books – full of instructions on how to make magical brews with the most repulsive ingredients, and how to create various, well, *things*, which can be put to evil use. I order those to be burned, or most of them.'

'What happens to the rest?' enquired Hugh with interest. I wondered if, like me, he was having a private vision of Sir

Edward Heron poring over dubious literature secretly, by candlelight, at dead of night.

'I keep some – under lock and key, of course – for when I am training young men for my staff. I let them see the books, briefly, so that they can recognize them. I'm careful, of course. I discourage any signs of unhealthy interest.'

'What happened to their original owners?' Anthony asked.

'They were all among those hanged, and good riddance,' said Heron. 'The Bible says *thou shalt not suffer a witch to live*, does it not? My chaplain, Mr Parkes, preached on that text only last Sunday.'

I flinched inwardly, though not on account of the house with the black-draped altar. That sounded horrible, blasphemous if nothing worse, but to me, the story of the orchard-raiding boys was far more alarming. Lads who go apple scrumping are liable to fall out of fruit trees now and again. They hardly need curses to help them. But Heron was clearly ready to pounce on any indignant orchard owner who had shouted a few profane threats. I was sure he had hanged the innocent. We would indeed be wise to keep our Gladys away from him.

Anthony drew Heron away to be introduced to someone else, and Jane, clearly concerned that we shouldn't be left without anyone to talk to except each other, led a couple of middle-aged ladies towards us. One was tall and dark-haired, more handsome than beautiful, with an aquiline nose and shapely eyebrows and a firm mouth. Her skin was tanned, as though she spent a lot of time out of doors. The other, by contrast, was fairish, dumpy and small, with plump, smiling features. They were too dissimilar to be sisters, but they were dressed like sisters in identical dark-blue gowns. Jane introduced them as Mrs Jennet Ward and Mrs Margery Seldon.

'Like Sir Edward, they prefer the title Mrs in the modern fashion,' Jane explained. 'They share a house with their little maidservant Bessie, and they are both good musicians. They have been tutoring Christina in music. She is quite talented, they say.'

'We are both widows,' said Jennet Ward. She was the tall one. 'We offered to provide the music for this occasion,' she said, 'but Jane and Anthony had already hired a trio. The lute and the spinet are our instruments. We live in Woking, and we got to know the Cobbolds when we undertook to instruct their younger daughter.'

'Unlike Alice, Christina is very musical,' Jane said. 'She had lessons as a child, but she wanted to improve. We were pleased. The practising keeps her occupied. We have had some difficulties with Christina lately. She is unlike Alice in more ways than one! Now, Alice has never been a worry to us. We found Robert for her, told her that she should consider him as a husband, and she thanked us and said she was agreeable, before she had even met him. Of course we made sure that the two of them were acquainted before the betrothal was announced, and luckily, they took to each other without any trouble. But it has all unsettled Christina, and there she is, thinking she's in love, though she knows nothing about it. Girls of seventeen are so easily led into foolishness by unwise examples.'

I knew that, without actually saying so, she was warning me that I might be an unwise example and should not talk to Christina about my first marriage. I didn't comment.

Jane swept on. 'I think,' she said, 'that we should get her married soon. I dare say you'll soon be thinking of a husband for Meg, will you not, Mistress Stannard?'

Confound Jane. She had obliquely warned me not to say the wrong thing and then done just that herself. Meg had a suitor, and they had been pressing to be allowed to marry soon, but . . . 'Meg is still a little too young,' I said. 'She's only fifteen.'

'Girls don't always grow up at the same rate,' said small dumpy Margery. Her mild voice was agreeable to the ear, and I didn't find her irritating even though she was talking on the same theme as Jane. 'Some are still children at fifteen, others are young women. We've brought our maid, Bessie, with us today – have you found a seat for her at the lower table, Jane? She loves celebrations, of any sort, and we indulge her. Now, she is sixteen but she's been grown up for years. There she is, over there, the little lass with the dark curls escaping from her headdress . . . She never seems able to keep her hair under control, or does she let it out on purpose, I wonder?'

'At the moment,' said Jennet dryly, 'she's found a young man to talk to so I dare say that *on purpose* is the right answer. We had better go and rescue him. Bessie works hard and cooks nearly as well as my dear Margery here does, but she is a shocking flirt and I fear may have gone further than flirting, on occasion . . .'

'Such a delightful pair,' said Jane, watching them go. 'And now, do come and meet the Emorys. They have a farm – Greenlease – three miles or so from here. My husband bought some very good sheep from Paul Emory last year. Paul . . . Cathy! Is your daughter Margaret not with you?'

'She has a cold,' said Paul Emory, who was dressed in a doublet and hose of fine dark-brown wool but had no ruff, only a voile collar, and had *farmer* plainly written on his weathered face. When I exchanged a handclasp with him I felt the calluses on his hands. He had brownish teeth, with several gaps, and I saw no laughter lines beside his pale-blue eyes. He struck me as having a dour air. 'Her trouble's not serious, but until now this has been a shocking bad summer . . .'

'We've wondered if we'd ever get the hay in,' agreed his wife. 'If only today's sunshine lasts!' She was as weather-beaten as he was and looked ill at ease in her tawny silk. She had a ruff but it was unfashionably small.

Hugh expressed agreement and said that he was glad that the hayfield on his home farm faced south. 'It's on a slight incline and gets a good share of the sunshine. What about yours?'

The conversation turned comfortably to farming.

'An enjoyable occasion,' said Hugh as the coach rolled homeward. It was seven miles back to Hawkswood. 'And we've made some new acquaintances. They did fit us all into the dining room, at least, but only by squeezing us shoulder to shoulder. I could hardly move my arms enough to cut my meat, and breathing was quite difficult! What did you think of Heron?'

'I didn't take to him,' I said. 'I didn't know what to make of some of the things he told us. Small boys do fall out of trees. Almost any rude old woman who shouted a few ill-natured things while chasing of them out of her orchard could be accused of willing him to have an accident. That was a nasty story, though, about the black-draped altar and all the rest of it.'

'There are people who believe they can raise demons by performing unsavoury rituals,' said Hugh. 'I've served on juries, too, the same as Cobbold and Heron. I've heard a thing or two. Black-draped altars and inverted crucifixes included. Nasty, as you say, but in my opinion not quite as bad as Heron thinks. From my jury experiences, I'd say that the people concerned are usually folk of no importance or influence. I suspect that their unpleasant gatherings are mostly a way of convincing themselves that they *can* wield power, of a sort. Others probably indulge in their goings-on to break up the monotony of very dull lives! I don't myself believe that anyone can whistle up the powers of hell, by that or any other method.'

'We've never really talked about this before, have we?' I said. 'We've always just been concerned with keeping Gladys out of trouble.'

'If I were a poor, unimportant man but found I could summon the powers of hell to do my bidding, well, I wouldn't stay poor and unimportant for long,' Hugh said. He turned his head and grinned at me. 'In return for my soul, I'd want my tame demon to give me money and position and beautiful women. Or I would have done, when I was young. All I'd want nowadays is a quiet life.'

'I agree with you there,' I said. 'I have had enough of exciting times.'

'I wonder.'

'Hugh?'

'You have been a secret agent for the queen and for Cecil. You've undertaken some dangerous missions and come through. You might well have developed a taste for excitement.'

'No, Hugh, that isn't so. Being with you, seeing the seasons change and guiding Meg's future, those are excitement enough for me now. I'm thirty-six. I've had two husbands before you; I've travelled; I've known danger and bereavement . . . Now I just want peace.'

I once heard someone say that there was a proverb to the effect that it was wise to be careful about the things you wanted, in case you actually got them. My own experience has been different. Again and again, what I want has *not* been what fate delivered. Quite the contrary.

I said: 'What do you think we should do about Meg? I suppose that lady – what was her name? Margery Seldon, that's it – I suppose she had a point. About girls growing up at different speeds. Meg is very grown up for fifteen. I have been saying that she should be at least sixteen before she was married. Now I'm not so sure.'

'Sir William Cecil is a family man. When he pays us his promised visit,' said Hugh, 'let's talk to him.'

TWO

Six Against One

'If I were you, I would say yes.' Sir William Cecil, Secretary of State, leant back in his chair. He and Hugh and myself were on the terrace at Hawkswood, seated round a small table and watching the young couple who were strolling in the rose garden just below. 'The young man has done his courting as he should and she's fallen for him, and in my view, she's chosen well. Let them marry. George Hillman is an estimable fellow. I doubt if you could do better for Meg. Why make them wait?'

'It's because she's only just fifteen,' I said. 'We have always felt that sixteen was soon enough. Haven't we, Hugh?'

The sunshine, having arrived at last, had held. It was a beautiful July day. Bees hummed busily among the blooms in Hugh's beloved rose garden, and the woodland to the east echoed with the call of doves and blackbirds. Meg, the child of my first husband Gerald, was at that moment bending her glossy dark head to enjoy the scent of a crimson rose, and the young man who so much wanted to marry her was flicking away a bee that had come too close. Hugh, though he was only Meg's stepfather, nevertheless looked on her as his own, and now he was studying her with a frown of affectionate anxiety between his brows.

'Originally,' he said, 'we thought she should have a year or two at court before she married. We've decided against that now, and it does make a difference. You are still definite about not sending her to court, aren't you, Ursula?'

'Yes, indeed,' I said with feeling. I knew too much about life at court. I had been a Lady of the Bedchamber to Queen Elizabeth. While there, I had also, as Hugh had reminded me on the way home from the Cobbold wedding, become embroiled in the world of diplomatic intrigue. I had been well rewarded for my secret work on the queen's behalf, but more than once my life had been endangered, and so had the lives of some much loved servants. I did not want Meg to go anywhere near the court.

'But that doesn't mean,' I said, 'that I want her to take the risks that go with early marriage. A girl can be harmed by having children when she is too young.'

'Meg is well grown,' said Cecil. 'And even if she had a child very quickly, she would surely be sixteen or nearly before it could be born. I don't think there is any special danger for her. She isn't immature in her thinking, either.'

'She's my daughter,' I said, and I know there was a touch of bitterness in my voice. 'I have done my best to keep her safe, but she knows a great deal of the world and its perils, simply because she knows of the work I have at times carried out. No, I agree, she is not immature.'

The glance Cecil gave me told me that he knew very well what I meant. He had thrust me into many of those perils, because for him his duty to the queen came before all else.

'So,' said Hugh, 'what, really, is your objection, Ursula?'

He spoke reasonably, as he usually did. Hugh, my steady, sensible third husband, who had shown me how happy a simple domestic life away from the glamour and pitfalls of the court could be, rarely attempted to impose his ideas on me. But he had a way of thinking things through and arriving at conclusions I couldn't argue with.

'I think,' I said, groping for words and not finding very good ones, 'that I would just like her . . . to be free for a little longer.'

'But she doesn't want to be free. She wants to marry George Hillman,' Cecil pointed out. 'Half an hour ago, they were standing here in front of us, hand in hand, asking your consent to wed next month. I am a father too,' he added. 'I have a daughter a little younger than Meg, and she also wants to marry. Mildred and I have been looking round for a suitable bridegroom.'

Once more, he gazed out into the rose garden. He sighed a little and eased the position of his left foot. It was bandaged and resting on a footstool. Sir William Cecil suffered from

gout, and the jolting carriage journey he had made in order
to visit Hugh's and my home at Hawkswood House in Surrey
had brought on an attack. I thought that he was probably
remembering what it was like to be young and healthy, and
envying the youthful pair now before his eyes.

I had been alarmed when, just before the Cobbold marriage,
he had sent word that he wished to visit us, because I feared
that he meant to persuade me into yet another secret undertaking.
However, he had taken his time over actually making the
journey, and it seemed that he really had come for social
reasons and to bring me a few items of news connected with
my last perilous assignment. 'In case,' he said, 'you're so
immersed in country life that the news doesn't reach you.'

He had much of interest to tell us, but when all that had
been talked over, I'd remembered Hugh's idea that we should
ask his advice on the matter of Meg and young Hillman. We
had done so. It chanced that Hillman was making a short stay
with us, and I fancied that the young pair somehow heard that
we had discussed them because the very next day they had
come to ask us for permission to marry at once, and when I
say *us*, I mean Cecil as well as Hugh and myself. They had
presented themselves when we were all together.

'I don't know what to say.' I think I sounded harassed. 'It's
true that Master Hillman has a comfortable home to offer her,'
I admitted. 'We visited it at his invitation early in May.'

'Riverside House, in Buckinghamshire,' said Hugh. 'Nearly
as big as Hawkswood, and with plenty of land attached. And
it needs a mistress.'

'Master Hillman is very much in love, if I'm any judge,'
said Cecil. 'But young men are impatient by nature, and if he
really needs a wife to take charge of his home . . . I said, he is
an estimable young man. Don't let him slip through your
fingers.'

'Do you mean,' I said, 'that he might go off and find someone
else?'

'I don't think he'd do that quickly or easily,' said Hugh. 'I
fancy he is in love with Meg. But it could happen. Sir William
is right.'

Behind us, a door creaked, and Sybil Jester, my good friend, who acted as companion both to me and to Meg, came through with a trayload of white wine, cooled in Hugh's underground store.

'Dale is feeling the heat,' she observed as she put the tray down on the little table. 'Brockley said she ought to rest and thought you wouldn't mind if she went to lie down.'

'No, of course I don't mind,' I said. Brockley was even more of a trusted friend than Sybil or Fran Dale, his wife and my personal maid. He and Dale – I still called her that out of habit – were the valued servants I had put at risk during some of my exploits. Brockley was courageous by nature, but Dale, though loyal and honest, was not particularly strong and not very brave either. I had often felt ashamed of the way I kept dragging her into alarming situations, though I never did so intentionally. The situations just seemed to happen. If she wanted to rest on a hot afternoon, the least I could do was allow it.

Hugh said: 'Sybil, Meg and Hillman told us today that they want to marry at once, instead of waiting until Meg is older. What do you think?'

Sybil would be on my side, I thought. I called Sybil my gentlewoman because she was educated and well spoken, even though she was actually the widow of a pie shop proprietor in Cambridge. She still owned the pie shop, which she had leased out and from which she drew a good income. She lived with me as my companion, but I did not pay her. She had refused to be paid.

She was sensible as well as educated, and middle-aged, with no high-flown romantic ideas. She had a striking face; it was as though her features had been compressed a little between her chin and the top of her head so that her eyebrows stretched unusually far towards her temples, and her nose and mouth were a fraction too wide. Yet the effect was not ugly; in fact, it was attractive in a common-sense kind of way; an excellent mixture.

'It's lovely to see them, isn't it?' she said, gazing at the couple in the garden, her dark eyes soft. 'They look so at ease together. And Meg is no foolish child; she's a young woman, in mind and body. I should say yes, if I were you, Mistress Stannard. Brockley was saying, only the other day, that it was a pity to hold them back. We saw them ride in from hawking, side by side and looking so *right* – that was how he put it. Dale and Gladys were both with us. Dale agreed with him, and as for Gladys . . . well, she cackled – you know that terrible laugh of hers – and said, ah, there were two people who didn't need love potions.'

Hugh and Cecil both burst out laughing. I gave up. Everyone but me seemed to be ranged on the side of young love. Even Gladys.

Since encountering Sir Edward Heron, I had fretted a good deal over Gladys. She was exactly the kind of old woman who might attract his attention. The reprieve I had won for her hadn't come until she was in the death cart, crying in terror, with a rope round her neck. I had been there. I would never forget it. I had nightmares about it sometimes.

Since then, Gladys had been careful, busying herself with dusting and plain sewing and giving a little help in the kitchen; sinking quietly into the background of the household. I hoped to goodness she would go on being careful and unobtrusive, but I did occasionally seek her opinion on this matter or that. Simply because she was old and had not had an easy life, she had a certain amount of wisdom. If such trustworthy souls as Hugh and Cecil, Sybil and the Brockleys, all thought I should consent to the young couple's plea, and Gladys agreed with them, then I was outnumbered and outmanoeuvred. It was six against one.

I gave in. 'Very well,' I said, with a sigh. 'And as our pair of turtle doves are no doubt anxious to know what we have decided for them and praying that it's the right answer, we had better tell them. Sybil, would you go and fetch them here? I suppose we can get something organized by mid-August.'

'I'll have to go back to Riverside to make sure it's in good order for when I bring my bride home,' George Hillman said. 'But before I go, Master Stannard, Mistress Stannard, I must talk to you about the relatives and friends I'd like to ask to my wedding, and you must tell me how big an affair you wish it to be. I shall be sorry to leave you, Meg, but I shall be back before long and then we won't be parted again.'

Meg gazed at him admiringly. Yes, I thought as they stood before us on the terrace, hand in hand, glowing with joy because we had said yes, they were a heart-warming sight. George Hillman was a fine young man; Cecil was right there. His crisp red-brown hair had the patina of health proper to a man in his twenties; his eyes, which matched them, were straightforward and smiling; his open, suntanned face was full of good humour. Meg would be safe with him.

As for my dark-haired, dark-eyed daughter (who was also suntanned; in summer Meg could never preserve a fashionable pallor), Sybil was right about her. Meg was a young woman and no mere child. I could do nothing but say: 'The time will pass quickly while he's away, Meg. We have a guest list to prepare, your bride clothes to make ready, a feast to create. We shall be busy. And I wish happiness to you both, with all my heart.'

Late in the evening, when Hugh and I had withdrawn to our chamber, which was above the terrace and therefore overlooked the rose garden, I glanced from the window, and there the two of them still were, enjoying the cool at the end of the long summer day, walking side by side among the flowers.

I turned to Hugh, and he said: 'There are tears in your eyes, my Little Bear. Why?'

'They're so happy. So young. They don't *know*!'

'Know what? Come here.' The bed curtains were open in the warm air, and Hugh, wrapped in a loose gown, had sat down on the edge of the bed. I went to him, and he slid an arm round me. 'What is the matter, Ursula?'

'They're looking forward to being happy. But one day, one of them . . . will have to watch the other die. As I watched Meg's father die. I sat and listened to him while his breathing grew fainter and slower. He was unconscious. I didn't want him to be conscious; not covered in smallpox sores like that. But while he was breathing, he was still with me. And then it stopped, and although all around me everything looked just the same, I knew it wasn't. All in a moment, my world had fallen apart. I was a widow, not a wife. I couldn't see where I was going any more. And one day—'

I broke off. Then I said: 'I shouldn't be talking to you like this. It's not fair. Gerald has been gone ten years. You're my husband now and—'

'I am fifty-seven, soon to be fifty-eight. You are still only thirty-six. One day, very likely, you will have to go through something similar with me. I realize that. I am not always in good health, and I know you worry about me sometimes . . .'

I nodded, looking at him gravely. Hugh had blue eyes, and when I first met him, some years ago, their colour had been very bright. I had noticed that lately it had faded somewhat. 'Yes,' I said. 'Perhaps that is in my mind as well as Meg and George.'

'One could say,' said Hugh comfortably, tightening his arm, 'that precious things are apt to be expensive. Loss, bereavement – I was widowed twice before I met you. I know all about them. But would you rather have gone all your life unmarried, with no love to warm you at night, and no Meg, either? And would you want that for her?'

'No, of course not! Of course I don't want her to miss . . . the lovely things of life.'

'Well, then. Take heart. Pray that when the bad time comes for them, whichever one is left behind, he or she will say, well, it was worth it and I'd do it all again. And by the way, I am not jealous of Gerald's memory. He was Meg's father, and it's right that you should remember him. I'm not jealous of Matthew, either, and he isn't even dead.'

Matthew de la Roche had been my second husband. I had lived with him in France for a while, and with him I had scaled the very heights of passion. But I had never known peace. He was an enemy to England and to Elizabeth, and she had stepped in. I had left Meg in England and been drawn back to my homeland because she needed me. Elizabeth kept me there. I was too useful for her to let me slip away. She had arranged that Matthew and I should each be told that the other had died, and unknown to me at the time, she had annulled our marriage as well. By the time I discovered that Matthew was still alive, he was married again and a father, and I was married to Hugh.

I said: 'I couldn't go back to him. I came to see that, eventually. He was always plotting, plotting, to do harm to England, to the queen.'

'But you did love him,' Hugh said soberly. 'And I'll never forget how touched I was when you told me that you preferred to stay with me. And now, Little Bear, come to bed and leave those two out there to their romantic transports. I think we can still manage some transports of our own.'

'They're behaving very soberly,' I said. 'Sybil's on the terrace, watching them, but I don't think they need watching.'

'Probably not. George is most unlikely to overstep the line, and certainly not in my garden. Come.'

We slid under the sheets. Hugh's arms wrapped me round, and heat began to glow between us. I abandoned myself gladly, without fear. He'd had two marriages before ours but he'd never sired children and to me this was a relief. I'd had a bad time with Meg and had nearly died in France, trying to give Matthew a son. The baby did die, poor thing. In Hugh's embraces, I felt safe.

We decided that Meg should be married from Hawkswood and not from our Sussex house, Withysham. I was fond of Withysham, which was mine, since Hugh had never laid claim to it, though as my husband he could have done so, but Hawkswood was by far the finer property.

Withysham had once been an abbey and still had a slightly ecclesiastical air about it. It was built of grey stone, with pointed windows, many of them narrow, so some of its rooms were forever dim. Hawkswood was a grey stone house as well, but it was full of light, with generously proportioned rooms including a fine great hall with a minstrels' gallery and big, modern mullioned windows that Hugh had had installed.

The house also had two parlours, one big and one small, and a little downstairs room with linenfold panelling that Hugh used as a study. There he had a desk, a writing set, a supply of paper and a small abacus, and there we worked together while preparing plans for the wedding. There was much to do. After George had left for Riverside, we found ourselves deep in consultation for a couple of hours on most days.

On the last day of July, the matter under discussion was the final guest list. 'George only wants to bring ten guests,' I said, picking up the sheet of names he had left with us. 'He hasn't much family – just two cousins, one with a family, and some friends.'

'And on our side . . .' Hugh had been making notes. 'You'll want the Hendersons – they used to look after Meg for you whenever you had to leave her, didn't they? Meg's Uncle Ambrose, I suppose, with his wife Anne. They are her kinfolk, after all, on her father's side. Do they have children?'

'Two girls in their teens,' I said. 'We'd better invite the girls to be bridesmaids. It would be polite, though neither Meg nor I have ever seen them. I hope they're pretty!'

'Bridesmaids,' said Hugh thoughtfully. 'But doesn't Meg want Christina Cobbold to carry her train?'

Meg and Christina had not met often, but they had become friends, just the same. Meg had been disappointed over not being invited to Alice's wedding, because it meant missing a chance of seeing Christina. Jane Cobbold, I thought crossly, was a muddlehead. It was just like her not to make it clear that we were free to bring Meg – or Sybil, for that matter – if we wished.

'So that means,' said Hugh with a chuckle, 'that we have to have the Cobbolds, and therefore we'll have to leave the Ferrises off the list.'

'Oh, the Ferrises!' I said with exasperation.

It was an absurd situation which caused quite a lot of amusement in the Woking area and beyond, but it also had a serious side. Other people might laugh at it, but the Cobbolds and the Ferrises did not.

The Ferrises lived in a handsome house called White Towers, not all that far from Cobbold Hall. Hugh in his youth had known the grandfather of Walter, the present Master Ferris, slightly and Walter's father quite well, but the friendship between Hawkswood and White Towers had faded after the older men were dead. For a good thirty years now, Hugh of Hawkswood and Walter of White Towers had just been acquaintances. For one thing, the Ferrises were Catholic and Walter took religious differences more seriously than his forebears had.

I had only met him twice. The first time had been five years earlier, when Hugh and I were first married. We had received a civil invitation to dine at White Towers. We had tried to return the compliment, but the Ferrises were just about to leave for a visit to kinsfolk in the north, and somehow it had never happened. Then, the following Christmas, we came across Walter and his family at a big gathering in Guildford, the county town. But that was all.

I wasn't sorry. I didn't like the Ferrises much more than I liked Jane Cobbold. Walter's wife Bridget was a good-looking woman, but she had a stiff, cold manner that I found off-putting, and on both occasions she was accompanied by a very vocal lapdog, which interrupted conversation with its yapping. Walter was simply commonplace, dull to talk to, and humourless. Both times, we had met their son and daughter, who were then in their teens. In their parents' presence, they were so respectfully silent that they had left no impression on me at all, but I remembered wondering what life in the Ferris household could be like, if the young people were so colourless.

What had left an impression on me, as it did on the whole locality, was the socially inconvenient state of affairs between the Cobbolds and the Ferrises. The two families could not appear on the same guest list, ever, and those whose duty it was to convene juries knew better than to summon Walter Ferris and Anthony Cobbold to the same one.

'I wonder how many generations it will last,' I said. 'And it's all because the paternal grandfathers of Walter Ferris and Anthony Cobbold fell in love with the same girl and quarrelled over her. One really would think it would be forgotten by now!'

'Oh, there was more to it than that,' Hugh said. 'I suppose you've never heard the full story. I rarely bother to talk about it. It irritates me too much. And the rest of the locality have taken it for granted so long that other people don't talk about it either. The two grandfathers were apparently ardent gamblers. They decided to have a race on horseback, and the loser would withdraw his suit to the young lady. Anthony's grandfather lost but accused Walter's grandfather of cheating by nobbling the Cobbold horse.'

'How?'

'By bribing one of the Cobbold grooms to give the poor

animal a bucket of water just before the race. I believe it! I can remember Walter's grandad quite clearly, and even in old age he had mischief in his eyes and an iron determination to have his own way at all times. The story came out because the little daughter of the bribed groom saw her father take the bucket into the stall and, later on, prattled about it. The result of that was a furore and a duel – no one was killed, but both men were wounded, though not seriously.'

'Did one of them marry the girl who caused it all?'

'No, the young lady very sensibly refused to have any more to do with either of them. Her parents found her someone else, and the two rival swains found other brides. But they hated each other from then on. Since then, ricks have been mysteriously burned and gates have been opened at dead of night so that cattle have got out of their fields and eaten crops . . . and thirty years ago, Walter Ferris's father was murdered though no one was ever arrested for it.'

'Murdered! And the Cobbolds were suspected?' I said.

Hugh sighed. 'Anthony's father was suspected, to be precise. Nothing was proved. Walter's father went out one day to ride round his home farm. His horse came back without him, and he was found lying at the edge of a wheat field, stabbed. Because he didn't die in bed of some well-attested illness, the Ferrises were quite likely to accuse a Cobbold, with or without any evidence. Maybe things would never have come to such a pass if the two families didn't live only two miles apart. It's so easy for them to get at each other. Mind you, it probably *was* Anthony's father who did it. The Ferrises were very likely right.'

'What a dreadful story.'

'It's an uncomfortable situation,' Hugh said. 'Not that it matters too much to me. I'm happy to be on friendly terms with the Cobbolds and keep the Ferrises at arm's length. Walter Ferris will get into trouble one of these days. He and his family turn up now and then at the Anglican church to conform with the law, but everyone knows that their steward is also a Catholic priest and says Mass for them in private. Not that that's the reason why Anthony Cobbold hates them or vice versa. The hatred comes from the old feud. They traditionally loathe each other, and that's that.'

'Oh well,' I said. 'We'll just have the Cobbolds, and never mind about the Ferrises. Who else? Oh, shall we ask those two ladies – Mrs Seldon and Mrs Ward? We met them at the Cobbold wedding, if you remember. The ones who are skilled at music. I took to them. I'd like to know them better.'

'By all means,' said Hugh, with a grin. 'And their flirtatious little maidservant Bessie, too, the one who loves celebrations. We'll have all three.'

'Then there's Aunt Tabitha and Uncle Herbert. I suppose I had better invite them. We're on reasonably polite terms now.'

'Invite them and hope they won't come?' said Hugh, still grinning.

'More or less,' I said with regret.

'They can't be ignored,' Hugh said reasonably. 'They may not have been so very kind to you and your mother, but they did shelter her when she came home from King Henry's court in disgrace, and they did look after you, until you climbed out of a window in the middle of the night and ran off with the young man they wanted your cousin Mary to marry.'

'They sheltered us,' I agreed. 'My mother and me. But no, they weren't kind. I think that's why my mother died so young. And I'm sure that Gerald was happier with me than he would ever have been with Mary. However, it's all a long time ago and we've made it up since.'

'You can't blame them for being annoyed about your elopement!'

'I don't.' Fleetingly, I remembered that night, and how I had scrambled out of a window, slid down some sloping tiles and a creeper and dropped the last few feet into Gerald's waiting arms. My uncle and aunt had been understandably furious. However, fences had been mended since then. Our relationship would never be warm, but it was now civilized. 'Put them on the list,' I said. 'Oh, and Sir William Cecil and his wife. We can ask them if they want to bring any of their children. I think that's it. Now we have to settle what Meg should wear. I described Alice Cobbold's gown to Meg, and she says she wants ivory damask too, but she'd like a pale-blue kirtle and sleeves, and she wants gold embroidery and a gold net for her hair. I can buy the net and the right kind of materials, all ready embroidered, in London.'

'Is it legal? I mean, there are laws about who is entitled to wear gold,' Hugh said, momentarily doubtful. Then he saw my expression and laughed. 'Well, it ought to be legal for Meg. You were once a Lady of the Bedchamber to Queen Elizabeth, and not only that.'

Quite. Meg was Elizabeth's niece.

My parentage was another reason why Elizabeth had kept me in England and cut me off from Matthew. I could have been a valuable hostage, if France and England had ever gone to war.

But all that was in the past. The only significance my royal connection had now was that it conferred on me and on Meg the right to pack our hair into gold nets and wear gold embroidery, if we could afford it.

I leant back and stretched. 'Meg must have plenty of trousseau gowns, and there will be a great deal of sewing to do. Sybil and Fran and I can do much of it, but we'd welcome extra help. And I think we should have extra hands for the kitchen, too. I must send Roger Brockley to Guildford and Woking to get it cried in the streets that we need applicants. Hugh, I find I'm enjoying all this. I shall like being the mother of the bride.'

'I thought you would,' said Hugh, laughing.

I looked out at the grounds. The rose garden was past its best, but there were still bushes in bloom. Beyond lay the formal knot garden which was also our herb and kitchen garden, and beyond that I could glimpse the orchard, where a good crop of apples and cherries was ripening. In spring, their blossom was a marvel of which I never tired.

Over to the right, to the west, beyond a small poultry yard, was a paddock where some of our horses were grazing. I could see Roger Brockley at the gate, with one foot on its lowest rung, leaning over it to pet his cob, Brown Berry. He was very fond of the cob, and Berry always came to his call. My dappled mare, Roundel, was more skittish, and even Bay Gentle, Meg's sweet-natured three-year-old mare, sometimes, when out at grass, teased us by being difficult to catch.

To the east, with a gate opening from the knot garden, was a beechwood, and beyond that was an ornamental lake where lilies grew in summer. Our home farm fields and cattle pastures lay beyond the lake, and I knew that our cows were there now, glossy with good grass and the sunshine on their backs. All was serenity and prosperity.

It had been in danger the previous year when, due to an unfortunate investment in a merchanting venture that failed when two ships were lost at sea, Hugh found himself in serious debt. The enquiry I had undertaken then had led me into danger but in the end had been successful and was so well paid for that the debt was cleared. Hawkswood was made safe, and I was as glad of that as Hugh was. I was content to be retired into country life, now that last year's frightening Catholic rebellion in the north was over.

The fate of the ringleaders was the news that Cecil had brought to me. They had fled into exile. Thomas Percy, Earl of Northumberland, was in Scotland, and his ferocious wife Countess Anne was in the Netherlands. And although the Pope had issued an alarming Bull telling English Catholics that they must turn traitor to Elizabeth or risk damnation, it hadn't caused any further risings. People like Walter Ferris were more open than they had been about their Catholic observances, but the authorities had sensibly not interfered too much, but as far as possible left things to settle.

The country was at peace, and as I had now decided that it was right to let Meg marry her George at once, I was at peace as well. All unaware of the evil that by then was already on its way towards me, a finger stretching out from the past, from someone who did not intend to let me enjoy my peace. Or even my life.

THREE
The Extended Claw

The wedding day was to be Wednesday, the twenty-third of August. As we made ready, the house hummed with excitement. Meg was so radiant that I could hardly believe in my original objections. They seemed churlish now.

Our well-publicized need for extra servants produced results. Two excellent assistant cooks, a married pair called Joan and Ben Flood, joined our kitchen. Whereupon, our chief cook, a large and highly gifted individual called John Hawthorn, and his skilled young assistant Abel Forde, at once set about teaching the newcomers their most elaborate recipes, so that at the wedding feast exciting food could be served in quantity. John liked to instruct and regretted that in the ordinary way he rarely had an opportunity to create his more exotic dishes. This was his chance both to show what he knew and to transmit it. Indeed, he became so inventive and enthusiastic that when we had to decide on the subtlety which would be a display feature at the top table, he and I had an argument.

'It is a marvel, madam, and I know how to do it, for I was taught it, and I helped to do it several times before I came here. It is a model, in good, thick, stiff marchpane, of a stag, with golden antlers if possible, but the antlers can be made of wood and gilded with paint. The stag's body is hollow and is filled with red wine. One leaves a hole between the antlers, to be plugged with more marchpane when the wine is in. That must be done just before serving, for fear that the wine will soak through the marchpane if there is any long delay. The stag has an arrow sticking out of its side – a golden arrow, or what looks like one. When everyone has had a chance to admire the model, the arrow is pulled out, and the red wine flows like blood, and all who are near enough may hold out their wine cups to be filled . . .'

'No, Hawthorn. It isn't the kind of scene I want for my daughter's wedding feast. I would prefer a marchpane model of Hawkswood House.'

'We could vary it and use a model of a crossbow bolt,' said Hawthorn yearningly.

'*No!*' I said. 'A marchpane house, if you please!'

'But, madam . . .'

'*No*, Hawthorn!'

I had reason, later, to be glad I had said no, especially to the crossbow bolt.

Hawthorn got his revenge by presenting me with an astonishing list of the ingredients he required for the feast and the startling quantities in which he required them. When I visited London to buy gold net and embroidered damasks for Meg, I also had to order numerous spices, some of them hitherto unknown to me. We used merchants in Woking and Guildford for such things as flour, sugar, salt, lamp oil, candles and ordinary dress materials, but extraordinary spices were beyond them.

They were expensive, too. 'Marrying off a daughter seems to be a costly business,' Hugh remarked. 'Just as well there's only one of her, Ursula, my love.'

To help with Meg's trousseau, we also acquired a young sempstress and embroideress called Dorothy Beale. Dorothy was no more than eighteen, and she was a skinny, undersized, mousey-haired little thing, but she had magic in her thin fingers. Oddly enough, she had come to us from the Ferrises, the family we couldn't invite along with the Cobbolds.

'Well, they've not had much work for me lately, and when I arst if I could look round for another place, they said all right,' Dorothy told me when she presented herself to be interviewed. 'They've given me time off for lookin' round. They treat me well enough, but I do like bein' busy.'

I gave her some work to do as a test and, after seeing how skilled she was, snapped her up.

'I never thought there could be so much detail in planning a wedding,' Fran Dale said to me as we were cutting out sleeves for one of the trousseau dresses. The big hall table, which was ideal for major sewing projects just because it was so large, was strewn with pieces of material, bobbins of silk, and embroidery designs. We had eaten dinner in the larger parlour and would have supper there as well. 'But dear Meg will look like a princess in that wedding gown,' Dale said. 'I've never seen such lovely damask.'

'Where's Meg now?' I said as I began to cut out the second sleeve from a length of tawny satin. 'I asked her to come and help us.'

'I believe Mistress Jester and Dorothy wanted her to try on the wedding dress again. They've finished making the ruff that goes with it. I think it was so right to decide on a small ruff. She's just a young girl, after all. They wanted to do the fitting before the day got too hot. It wouldn't do to have sweat stains getting on to the damask.'

'It's hot already,' I said and laid down my shears to go and open the side door to our main courtyard. I paused in the doorway to look at the activity outside. A cartload of fresh rushes had just come in, and Roger Brockley, standing four-square with his hands on his hips, was overseeing the business of unloading.

Brockley's position in the household was unusual. Long ago, he had been a soldier, and after that, for a time, a groom. Since then he had been my companion through many adventures and eventually, before my marriage to Hugh, had become my steward at Withysham, my Sussex home. He had done well as a steward, since he was a dignified-looking man, straight-backed, with a high, intelligent forehead, lightly dusted with gold freckles, and he had a calm demeanour.

However, after my marriage to Hugh, Brockley chose to resign as Withysham's steward because Hugh and I would often be at Hawkswood and he wished to be where I was. Now, Withysham had a new steward, while at Hawkswood we had Adam Wilder, a grey-haired widower in his fifties, who had been in Hugh's service for years. Brockley had reverted to being my personal manservant, though he would also act as a courier or an escort, oversee deliveries, or do anything else which presented itself as necessary, and he still helped out in the stables on occasion. In any case, he always looked after Brown Berry himself.

'He's my horse and comes to my whistle if he's out in the

field; I don't want anyone else looking after him,' he had told
the other grooms.

He was a straight-faced man who did not often smile, and
yet a strong vein of humour ran below his surface. He was
conventional and was often scandalized by the unusual tasks
that I carried out, but his adventurous instincts would take
over as soon as there was need of them. I valued him highly.
There had been a time when he and I had come dangerously
close to being more than lady and servant or even comrades,
but that was far behind us now. Now, we were simply friends.

As I watched, the unloading finished and Brockley entered
into earnest discussion with the man in charge of the cart,
probably ordering a further delivery before the wedding date.
Our lake could supply some of the rushes, but not enough,
though the sweet herbs to mix with the rushes would come
from our garden.

I could trust Brockley to see that all was done as it should
be. I was turning away when our two guard dogs, Hero
and Hector, set up a noisy barking, and I saw that a horseman
had arrived at the gatehouse and was talking to our gatekeeper.
A moment later, the gatekeeper stepped back and the rider
came on into the courtyard. My first impression was that both
horse and rider looked tired. As soon as it was allowed to
stop, the horse let its head droop, and the rider descended
from the saddle as if he were thankful to be out of it.

Brockley went to speak to him, beckoning a groom to take
the horse. Then, seeing me in the doorway, he brought the man
towards me.

'A courier, madam. Master Twelvetrees from Norwich. He
says he has an errand to you.'

'Bartholomew Twelvetrees at your service, madam. I'm a
Norwich man, earning my living as a messenger,' said the
newcomer. He was a big, tow-headed young man with a broad,
sun-reddened face. He was plainly dressed in brown, with a
linen collar open at the throat. I recognized the up and down
cadence of East Anglia in his accent.

'I was hired by a man off a ship that docked in Norwich
two days ago,' he said. 'He give me this for you.' He held out
a small scroll with a seal. 'He said it was urgent.' He added,

with an air of embarrassment: 'I'm sorry that's a bit dirty. Getting my saddlebags off the horse, at an inn, I dropped one and it weren't done up proper and this here letter fell out. The inn yard was muddy, like.'

Offering the scroll to me, he pointed out the smear of dirt and flicked at it vainly, with a broad forefinger.

'I expect the inside is all right,' I said. 'Don't worry. Two days?' I looked at him sharply. 'You can hardly have been out of the saddle. You were probably tired when you dropped your saddlebag. Who was the man who hired you? Where did he come from?'

'The Netherlands, he said, madam,' said Twelvetrees. 'Said he had to get back at once. He paid me in advance. I got a reliable reputation, and someone recommended me to him.' He spoke with a pride that I found rather endearing, and he radiated reliability. Most messengers wouldn't have bothered to point out the dirty mark.

I looked at the scroll. The mark was on the outside and didn't matter. My name and direction were written there, but it hadn't touched them. The seal was unbroken, which was more important. It was a plain seal, however. There was no device stamped into it. Someone did not wish to advertise their identity. But it had come from the Netherlands. The first sense of unease came to me then, a small, cold coiling in the pit of my stomach. I would read this in privacy.

'Look after Master Twelvetrees, Brockley,' I said. 'I'm taking this to the study.'

After a brief word of explanation to Dale, I made for the study and there opened the letter. It had no outer wrapping but had simply been rolled up and sealed, and it was written on ordinary paper, not parchment. I frowned as I broke the seal and unrolled it, and I glanced first at the signature. The guess I'd instinctively made had been right.

The chill inside me intensified. I sat down to read.

Five minutes later, Hugh, who had been in the rose garden cutting off dead blooms, came in and found me. 'Ursula? Brockley says a messenger's brought you a letter from the Netherlands. He clearly doesn't like the idea of messages to you from there.' He studied my face. 'And by the look of you,

he was right. Ursula, you're as white as paper and your eyes
. . . your eyes are hazel, but when you're ill or upset, they
look like pools of ink. They're like that now. What in God's
name is wrong? What's in that letter? Who sent it?'

I handed it to him. 'It's from Anne Percy,' I said.

'Anne Percy . . . The Countess of Northumberland?'

'The exiled Countess of Northumberland,' I said grimly.

He looked at the letter again and then, slowly, read it out:

*To Mistress Ursula Stannard, bastard sister of the usurper
and heretic Elizabeth and enemy to the true queen of
England, Mary Stuart, greetings. In the north, greetings
is a word with another meaning. In the north, to greet
means to wail and weep. In that sense I wish you many
greetings and long, lasting until your death.*

*When in the north those who are faithful to Mary
Stuart and to the true religion rose to fight for them, and
met with so fierce a resistance from the usurper's forces,
it was largely through you that the last hope of turning
the tide in our favour was lost.*

*Because of you, my husband is now a prisoner of the
heretics who have so much influence in Scotland and I
fear they will sell him to Elizabeth. Because of you, I too
had to flee to Scotland, riding hard although I was with
child. My daughter was born in Aberdeen, far from her
home. She has never seen her father, nor has he ever
seen her.*

*Now she and I are in exile in Bruges, dependent on
the charity of King Philip of Spain for money on which
to live. I see no future for us.*

*I hold you to blame, you and your manservant Brockley,
who between you destroyed both my hopes and my dignity.
I have the right to vengeance. It is the only hope of joy
that I still possess. You and he have done as much as
your vixen of a sister to keep our sweet Mary from her
lawful throne. For Queen Mary's sake, I have placed a
bounty on your head. There are those whom I will gladly
reward if they bring you down. King Philip will pay
the reward on my behalf. He has promised.*

*Oh yes, Mistress Stannard. If you thought that here in
exile I have no claw that can stretch out to reach you,
you are wrong. I know those who will act for me, gladly
and without question. Soon, trouble and dread will overtake both you and your servant (or is he your lover?).
And when they have wrung the last juices of hope and
happiness from you, death and damnation will complete
my vengeance.*
    Anne Percy, Countess of Northumberland

The handwriting of the signature was noticeably the same as
that on the rest of the letter. It hadn't been dictated to a
secretary. In the grip of a deeply personal rage, Anne Percy
had penned it herself.

Hugh had read it in even tones, even the suggestion (I
silently thanked God it was not true) that Brockley and I were
lovers. But I stood trembling. Ill will rose from that sheet of
paper like a stench. For the first time, I understood why Gladys
Morgan's curses had frightened people to the point of hounding
her and even demanding her death. Curses carry hatred and
malice, and they do have power. At this moment, they were
shrivelling my very bones. Hugh put a hand on my arm. And
then we realized that Brockley was in the doorway. 'How long
have you been standing there?' Hugh asked him sharply.

'Your pardon, sir. I didn't think I should interrupt you while
you were reading aloud. I heard most of it. If I shouldn't, I'm
sorry, but—'

'I would have told you anyway,' I said. *Most of it, anyhow.*
I wouldn't have embarrassed Brockley by telling him quite all
of it. I also knew that he must have heard the phrase I would
have omitted, and that he would never refer to it.

He showed no sign of embarrassment now, but said calmly:
'I'd like to say some words of reassurance.'

'I wish you would,' I said. My voice shook.

'Madam, I find it hard to believe that, away in the
Netherlands, Anne Percy has any means whatsoever of carrying
out these threats. All those who knew her, who were loyal to
her, are exiled or dead or afraid to put their heads above any
battlements. I think she is simply full of anger and resentment

and wishes to frighten you. A matter of wounded pride, I fancy.'

Brockley suddenly grinned, his rare, broad grin that made his lightly freckled face look boyish and far younger than his middle-aged years. 'I would remind you, madam, of how the countess looked when we caught sight of her through that kitchen window, just as we made our escape from Ramsfold.'

'Dear God, yes!' Suddenly, my heart lightened. 'Hugh,' I said, 'I've told you how when Brockley and I were in the north last year, we were imprisoned by Anne Percy in a house called Ramsfold. You know that we escaped from the cellar where she had put us, but she and her henchmen came on us and chased us into a kitchen. We'd thrown pepper into their eyes to put them in check . . .'

'How very resourceful of you,' Hugh said. 'I don't believe you've told me those details before. You just said the two of you had escaped from the cellar. You said that the other man in your party – Carew Trelawny – had stayed free and dropped the cellar key to you through a grating and had your horses ready. But Trelawny was killed when you were pursued, and that upset you so badly that you didn't want to go on talking about it.'

'No, I didn't,' I agreed. 'That was tragic, and I remember, I did find it distressing to talk about it when it was still so raw. But Trelawny did more than get hold of a key and saddle our horses. He gave us advice. He was the resourceful one! He told us to do something that he called *using what's there*. Turning anything handy into a weapon. That's how we came to think of throwing the pepper. And some pewter plates as well. And because we did that, we managed to hold up the enemy for long enough to let us get away through the kitchen, and we set a trap there before we rushed out of a door to the open air and got to our horses. We poured olive oil on the kitchen floor and balanced some things over the door our pursuers would come in by. Using what was there, you see. And the countess was caught by the trap . . .'

My sudden lightness of heart had faded when we spoke of Trelawny, whose death had been a bitter blow to all his companions, but now it returned. I found myself laughing. Brockley was laughing too.

'Anne Percy's a well-dressed, commanding woman,' I said. 'With a clear, commanding voice. Much aware of her dignity. And vindictive. Brockley and I were roughly handled when she had us in her power. When we were escaping, we caught a glimpse of her through a kitchen window, sitting on the floor with a colander on her head and cold pottage splashed all over her. It was one of the loveliest sights I've ever seen,' I added reminiscently.

'You certainly never told me that!' Hugh chuckled. 'No wonder Anne Percy hates you. I know that type of woman. The colander and the pottage probably infuriated her nearly as much as the part you played in defeating the rising and driving her into exile. But I fancy Brockley is right. There is nothing she can do to you now. This ugly letter –' he flicked it disdainfully – 'is nothing but an attempt to disturb your peace. The lady is in exile and dare not emerge from it. I've been wondering why her courier came from Norwich. Dover would be the natural port of entry for her messenger. But I fancy Dover is being watched. Wouldn't you think so, Ursula?'

'Very likely,' I said. 'Anne Percy isn't the only one who fled abroad after the northern rebellion was put down. There were quite a number, all resentful. There are few people left now in the north who could be of use if any of the exiles wanted to stir up trouble from a distance, but there are one or two people in the south, in London, that they might try to contact. For instance, Mary Stuart actually has an ambassador at court – the Bishop of Ross. Yes, I fancy Dover is being very carefully watched, but Norwich, perhaps, is less so. So she sent this letter via Norwich, as a precaution.'

'So either she or her messengers, or both, are nervous,' said Hugh. 'And I see that the lady is reduced to writing on mere paper, without a wrapping.'

He turned the letter over, showing the grimy smear on the back of it. 'I doubt if King Philip of Spain is being overgenerous with his pension, and if he has agreed to reward someone for harming you and Brockley, I suspect he doesn't think he'll ever have to pay. He has a parsimonious reputation. Don't be afraid, Ursula. You're here with us. You're an Englishwoman,

my wife, preparing to give her daughter a joyous wedding.
I'll burn this.'

I said: 'No, don't do that. Give it to me. I shall put it in
my document box. Just in case I need it one day.'

'How could you need it?' Hugh handed it to me but looked
surprised.

'I don't know. But . . .' It was difficult to find words for
something so nebulous. 'If – somehow – trouble is made for
me, it might prove that I'm the victim of malice.'

'As you wish, Ursula. But I think Brockley is right. These
threats have no teeth.'

They were both wrong. The claw that Anne Percy had
extended was very real indeed. Its sharp tip was already in
my house. Her vengeance had begun.

FOUR
An Air of Disturbance

At the time, I let myself be reassured. Besides, the wedding preparations were demanding. Rooms must be made ready for guests, Meg's trousseau must be completed, the dishes for the feast finally chosen. The excitement had already stimulated John Hawthorn into culinary creativeness, but unfortunately it also stimulated him into fits of temperament, during which he positively needed someone to quarrel with, just as a swordsman needs a partner to practise on. Several times, I had to settle arguments involving him. With all this on my hands, it was not so very difficult to let Anne Percy's horrible letter slip into the background of my mind.

Brockley was bound to tell his wife Fran Dale about it, and I told Sybil Jester, from whom I had few secrets and who would probably have learned of it from Dale anyway. But I told them that it was to go no further. Above all, no one was to mention it to Meg.

At least one item on the list of preparations was no trouble. We had plenty of room for the influx of guests' horses. We had extensive stables, but Hugh had given up riding now, and since our near escape from having to sell Hawkswood to get ourselves out of debt, we had reduced the household. We had fewer men on the place and fewer horses, too. There were two heavy horses for the farm, my dappled mare Roundel, Brockley's cob Brown Berry, Meg's mare Bay Gentle, and two sturdy geldings which could be ridden if necessary but were mainly there to draw Hugh's coach. There were plenty of stalls to spare as well as the paddock, which was big enough for several horses.

Guests began to arrive, though to my relief they didn't include Aunt Tabitha and Uncle Herbert. We had duly invited them but received a polite answer to the effect that their health wasn't good enough to withstand the journey from Sussex, even in a coach. We sent civil regrets and hopes that their health would improve, and left it there.

Cecil had sent word that he and his family would not be able to come either, because of commitments at court, but he sent gifts: a ruby pendant for Meg and a matching brooch for George to wear in a hat. George Hillman, along with his cousins and friends, rode in three clear days before the wedding, in a noisy, merry cavalcade. Meg ran out to meet them, and the moment George got off his horse, she was in his arms and being enthusiastically hugged, amid hearty cheers from his companions.

'Good God. Prise those two apart!' said Hugh. 'Tell them to wait just a few more days! When the ceremony's over, they can embrace to their heart's content, in private.'

But he was laughing, and so was I. I was happy for Meg, and who was Anne Percy, after all? An exile far away in another country, a minuscule figure in a remote corner of my mind. Towards evening on the next day, which was a Sunday, Anthony and Jane Cobbold, with their daughter Christina, arrived on horseback, and Anne Percy's corner became more remote than ever. For the Cobbold party was anything but merry. From the moment they rode into our courtyard, it was clear that something was very wrong.

Some people, especially the more ardent Protestants, did not travel on Sundays. 'But we attended at St Peter's this morning and thought it no harm,' Anthony Cobbold said.

'We were all ready and didn't want to delay. I said to Anthony, the sooner we set out and get to Hawkswood, the better,' said Jane cryptically.

Not one of the three was smiling, least of all Christina.

Christina Cobbold was not precisely pretty. Her small square jaw and strongly marked eyebrows suggested an unfeminine determination somewhere in her character. But she did have attraction, mainly her animation and her shining hair and the brightness of the brown squirrel's eyes. And since she was Meg's principal bridesmaid, to be entrusted with carrying the bride's train, she should have been very animated indeed, full of happy eagerness.

Instead, the strong eyebrows were drawn together in a frown and her lips were compressed, and as she curtsied to me and Hugh and murmured greetings, I saw that her eyes were not bright but clouded and the lids a little reddened.

Meg was beside me. 'Show Christina to her room,' I said to her, and as the two girls disappeared inside, I turned to Jane. 'Is Christina well? She doesn't seem . . . quite . . .'

'At Alice's wedding, I mentioned to you, did I not, that we'd been having difficulties with her?' Jane said. 'I told you she was fancying herself in love. *That's* the difficulty.'

'Greensick,' said Anthony lugubriously.

'Who's she in love with?' asked Hugh with interest.

Anthony, tall, intimidating Anthony Cobbold, emitted something like a despairing groan. Jane said bitterly: 'Of all people on earth, she's gone and fallen head over heels with . . . Oh, how could she, knowing how her father feels! I don't feel it so much for myself because I wasn't born a Cobbold, but it's upset Anthony badly and that's enough for me. If only we'd been more watchful! We went to the midsummer fair at Woking – before Alice's wedding; there were things we wanted to buy – and there was such a crowd, and tumblers giving a show and pedlars shouting their wares, you know what these fairs are like, and somehow we became separated from Christina, and by the time we found her again, she had met this young man and watched a bear-baiting with him and the harm was done.'

'Harm?' I asked.

'Yes! It was young Thomas Ferris, Walter Ferris's son!'

'A *Ferris*!' Anthony rolled his eyes heavenwards.

'Christina had told him her name,' said Jane, 'but he hadn't told her his, and she didn't know Thomas Ferris by sight. She didn't understand who he was until we informed her, and by then, would you believe it, it was too late! It seems that he took to her on sight and didn't as much as blink when she said she was called Cobbold, and before we found them, she'd taken to him as well! Just like that! Then and there, at the bear-baiting. Even if he weren't a Ferris, it wasn't right, to go talking and . . . and *taking to* . . . a strange young man like that. It wasn't proper. Or maidenly. We have always tried to

impress on Christina that women should be modest; that a
lady shouldn't talk too freely to men or involve herself in
men's business.'

Her eyes, meeting mine, told me that she considered me to
be deficient in all these virtues and that she might even be
wondering if I had contaminated Christina.

'By the time we got to them,' she said, 'they'd already made
a plan to meet again, secretly, though we didn't know that
then, of course. We learned later that he'd got her to agree to
the secrecy by saying that her parents might not want her
meeting someone they didn't know. We took her away from
him and told her who he was, but she tossed her head and
said she didn't care. Didn't *care*! We were appalled. But we
had no idea then that they meant to see each other again.
We didn't find that out until *after* they had met clandestinely
three times – *three*!'

'We received a most unpleasant letter from Walter Ferris,'
said Anthony glumly.

'Yes, one of his grooms, out exercising a horse, had seen
Christina with Thomas, walking in a field.' Jane tumbled the
words out in her indignation. 'And then it seems that Walter
Ferris challenged Thomas about it and got out of him that he
and Christina had been meeting. Three times!' Jane repeated,
in tones of horror.

'It was a most offensive missive,' said Anthony. 'I will leave
out the strong language. It ordered – yes, *ordered* – us to put
a stop to this nonsense. It's apparently intended that Thomas
should marry a girl called Margaret Emory, whom he's known
since childhood. I think you met her parents at Alice's
wedding?'

'Yes,' Hugh said. 'Though Margaret herself wasn't there.
The Emory family know both you and the Ferrises, it seems.'

'Neither we nor the Ferrises expect our neighbours to take
sides. That's probably the one thing we agree about,' Anthony
said. 'Sir Edward Heron is acquainted with both our families,
and so are you, of course, and it's the same with the Emorys.
We know them, and Margaret too. She's a nice enough young
wench. Well, the letter went on to say that there could never
be an alliance between a Ferris and a Cobbold. It also said

that he – Walter – did not wish to harm Christina, as our feud had always been conducted between men, but if he were to find my daughter in the company of his son, I would myself pay for it. Just as my father had killed his, he would kill me. Even if he hanged for it. An explicit threat.'

'But we don't want our daughter mixed up with a Ferris any more than he wants it,' Jane said. 'So we spoke to Christina about it. And she tried to deny it. She tried to lie to us.'

'We showed her Walter Ferris's letter,' Anthony said, 'and I threatened to use my stick if she didn't speak the truth, and in the end, she admitted that she'd been pretending to have errands of this sort or that, somewhere in our grounds, and then slipping off to keep her wretched trysts.'

'So immodest!' said Jane with energy. 'Why, she had the impudence to say she had fallen in love with Thomas Ferris, and he with her, and she wouldn't promise not to see him again, even if her father did beat her. As you should have done, Anthony; it would have been best for her in the end; it would have put a stop to all this before it went any further. But you are too good-natured to do such a thing or allow me to do it. I suppose that's a virtue in you, but oh dear . . .' For once, Jane Cobbold ran out of words.

'I have never struck my daughter. I can't do it,' said Anthony. Unexpectedly, he added: 'My mirror tells me that I look intimidating, but I am not quite so good at matching my actions to my looks.'

'So,' said Jane, 'all we can do is watch her and see she doesn't disobey us. And now she's sulking, because here at Hawkswood she'll have no chance of slipping away to see this wretched boy Thomas. Oh, what can one do with headstrong young people who won't heed their elders?'

As I had once been a headstrong young person who didn't heed her elders, I thought it best to say no more than: 'Oh dear.'

'A Ferris. Of all people on earth. And they're Catholic, too,' said Anthony. '*And* pretentious. I always want to laugh when I ride past their house. It has a squat little tower sticking up at each end and some fancy crenellations, and they call it White Towers just as if it were a palace and they were princes!

The Emorys say that it has a private chapel. I understand that it's so small it almost counts as a cupboard, but the Ferris steward, Maine, holds Masses there. The Emorys are Catholic too, you know. They're more circumspect about it than the Ferrises – or I wouldn't be as friendly with them as I am – but Paul Emory once admitted to me that he and his family have once or twice heard Mass in the Ferris chapel. He described the place to me. I told him he should be careful.'

Since my Uncle Herbert and Aunt Tabitha were Catholic as well, I now felt doubly relieved that they weren't coming to the wedding. I had also learned, only the previous day, that Joan Flood, one of our two temporary cooks, came from a Papist family, though she herself was prepared to worship in accordance with the law.

Indeed, the religious preferences of the Floods had caused one of the arguments John Hawthorn kept getting into. Fran Dale truly detested the old religion, though not without reason, as once, when we were travelling in France, she had come near to being tried for heresy. On hearing of Joan's origins, she had told Hawthorn that we shouldn't keep her on – which would of course mean not keeping her husband Ben on either. Whereupon, Hawthorn retorted that although when Ben first came he hadn't known how to make spun sugar, he had learned faster than anyone Hawthorn had ever trained in the past, while Joan was better than he was himself at making marchpane shapes, and he, Hawthorn, did not personally care if either of them were Protestant, Catholic, followers of Mahomet or members of a coven.

'Right in the middle of the hall, I was, when Fran Dale accosted me,' he had said, 'and there was old Gladys Morgan, who looks like a witch even if she isn't one, mending linen and cackling like a hen laying an egg when I said the word *coven*. Dale just flounced off, muttering. Mistress Stannard, I'd take it kindly if you'd tell Dale to mind her own affairs and leave my kitchen staff alone. We want to do well by you and Mistress Meg, and this kind of wrangling over who believes what won't do. Beliefs don't make any difference to marchpane and spun sugar!'

I had soothed him, assured him that he would keep the services of Ben and Joan until the celebrations were well over, and had a few quiet words with Fran Dale. I now found myself hoping that the Cobbolds wouldn't enquire into the religious affiliations of my cooks. For the moment, I contented myself, once more, with an anodyne remark. 'How worried you must be about Christina. I *am* sorry.'

Supper was a strained meal. Christina took hardly any part in the conversation and ate very little. As she left the hall afterwards, with me a step or two behind her, Gladys Morgan came up to her, saying that she didn't look well and asking if she would like a valerian and chamomile posset, mixed in wine, to help her sleep. Christina promptly backed away from her, visibly repelled, and said: 'No!' very rudely.

I was close enough to hear, and I was annoyed. Gladys did have a cackling laugh, knowing eyes, teeth that resembled brown fangs, and a questionable local reputation. But these days she was reasonably clean and neat and polite. I expected visitors to Hawkswood to be reasonably polite to her in turn.

Gladys not unnaturally went off in a huff, and I turned to Christina. 'You know, my dear,' I said, 'you could just have said *no thank you*. It wasn't kind to bark out a refusal and shy back as though you thought Gladys might bite. You've hurt her feelings.'

'I'm sorry.' Christina looked at me quite wildly, as though I had bitten her myself. 'I'm sorry, but my mother wouldn't like Gladys Morgan to make possets for me. Mother says she's a witch and that witches are dangerous. The sheriff, Sir Edward Heron, says they're dangerous, too. He and my father have made friends, and he often visits and talks about witches and how we should always take care to have nothing to do with them. He makes me frightened, and Mother says a special prayer every night, because Sir Edward says that it's at night that witches work their evil. He says they are women who make pacts with the devil and slip out at night to ride the skies on broomsticks. Mother closes the bed curtains so that the moon can't see in – the moonlight is a treacherous light, she says. She calls it the witches' lantern and says it can bring madness if it shines on someone sleeping. Sometimes my father says he feels stifled at night.'

Christina almost laughed but it turned into a sob. 'She'd be so angry with me if she thought I had been given a potion by someone who's been found guilty of witchcraft, and oh, why is everything I do *wrong*?'

She picked up her skirts and ran away, rushing up the stairs, presumably to the sanctuary of her room. I turned and found Hugh beside me. He had been listening as well.

'Are you really angry with Christina, or are you on her side, at heart?' said Hugh.

'I do have a fellow feeling for her,' I said. 'And her mother and Sir Edward have obviously been scaring her with their talk about witches. I really did *not* take to Edward Heron. But she need not have been quite so rude to Gladys.'

'She's upset her parents by falling in love with Thomas Ferris,' Hugh said. 'Maybe she doesn't want to quarrel with them in two different ways at the same time. So she tries to do as she's told when it comes to avoiding witches, and then *you* pounce on her!'

I sighed. 'Perhaps I shouldn't have said anything. I'll apologize to Gladys quietly. I'm bound to be in sympathy about Christina's love affair, you know. After all, I eloped with Gerald.'

'This is different. The Cobbold–Ferris feud is long-standing and deeply entrenched, and Christina and Thomas are young fools if they think they can defy it,' Hugh said. He glanced over his shoulder, but Christina's parents were still in the hall, talking to Meg. 'We mustn't encourage her, Ursula. Anthony is my friend, and I have to respect his wishes in this, whatever my private opinions. So must you. I hope she won't upset Meg, though. After all, she's supposed to be a bridesmaid!'

'I know. I won't say anything unwise to Christina. But it's a sad situation for her. Meg's marrying a man she's in love with, while Christina isn't going to be allowed to.'

'Yes. I really think,' said Hugh with some feeling, 'that I'll be glad when this wedding's safely over!'

'So will I!' Together, we started up the stairs. 'I was enjoying it at first,' I said, 'but now – if it isn't one thing, it's another. Hawthorn keeps quarrelling with people, and that extra delivery of rushes hasn't arrived. I'll have to send Brockley to Woking tomorrow to find out why. And now there's all this trouble with Christina. There's an air of disturbance in the house, somehow.'

'Then let's forget it all for a while and go to sleep,' said Hugh. 'And be thankful that we're not young and silly any more!'

Matters improved somewhat the next day. Other guests joined us. Meg's Uncle Ambrose came first, with his family. Ambrose was tall and arrogant as ever, though he looked older than when I had last seen him, his dark hair and beard turning grey. He was always one for dressing well, but I wondered how he could bear to wear such a heavy doublet in this warm August. His wife and daughters, however, were all pretty and very alike, with soft browny-gold hair and blue eyes. The girls would make charming bridesmaids.

Rob and Mattie Henderson came next, the couple who had fostered Meg when I was in France, years ago. I hadn't seen them for a long time, either. Mattie was still her good-natured self and had hardly changed, but Rob, like Ambrose, was greying, and he complained as he dismounted that these days more than an hour in the saddle made his back ache. Then, in the afternoon, Mrs Jennet Ward and Mrs Margery Seldon arrived on hired horses, with their pert little servant Bessie perched behind Jennet. I was pleased to welcome them, for somehow they brought an air of bright normality with them.

Bessie was like an excited small dog, running here and there to find her way round the house, flirting with our rather good-looking second groom, Simon, and giggling with the other maids. Jennet and Margery were cheerful and serene, full of harmless small-talk about other weddings they had attended, and what a pretty bride Meg was going to be, and the latest gossip from Woking. Jennet had brought her lute, and I let Margery try out my spinet, and that evening they entertained us with music. I was glad we had invited them.

Also, our new sempstress, Dorothy Beale, was proving to be a really excellent aide. That morning, by chance, she had walked into Meg's room with some completed work to find Christina there, in tears, being soothed by Meg. Dorothy then came in search of me, found me in the linen room, and offered a helpful suggestion.

'I think the young lady, Mistress Christina Cobbold, is what my mam used to call overwrought, madam, and it's worrying Mistress Meg, and that's not right, just before the wedding. She's been upset because of something to do with not being allowed even to see some young man she wants to marry. Gladys says Mistress Christina said no to a calming medicine, and it's a pity because she knows a good recipe for one. Madam, if it's not wrong of me to say so, I think Mistress Christina might drink one if she knew it wasn't Gladys that made it for her.'

'I dare say,' I said. But I took the point. I made a valerian and chamomile posset, in accordance with Gladys's favourite recipe for the purpose, but I assembled all of it myself, even picking the herbs personally, and took it to Christina. I found her in her room, alone, and still crying. She turned sullenly away from me at first, but after a little persuasion she drank my offering. By dinner time, there seemed to be a result. She sat with Meg, and the two girls appeared to be talking and smiling in a natural way.

Also, the missing cartload of rushes arrived in time to save Brockley from going to Woking, and before midday, the last of the embroidery on Meg's gowns was finished. There were still some final touches to be put to the bridesmaids' dresses, but that could be left until the morrow, and when Dorothy asked for a little time off to visit an aunt in a village called Priors Ford, three miles away, I was agreeable.

'She's the only family I've got, madam,' Dorothy explained. 'She give me a home when my mam died, and me only ten! My dad, he'd walked out when I was a baby; I don't even remember him. Auntie was that good to me.'

'You've more than earned it,' I told her. 'Go as soon as dinner's over. Get some fresh air. We'll be busy again tomorrow, but we can spare you this afternoon.'

When we were abed that night, Hugh, who had looked very tired at supper, fell asleep at once, but I was restless. The air was sticky, and we had left the bed curtains open, but I was still too hot, and details of our preparations kept churning in my mind. Had I remembered to tell Fran Dale about . . .? Had I reminded Brockley that . . .? Would Hawthorn's subtlety turn out well? Had we ordered enough wine? Had I . . .?

Moving carefully so as not to disturb Hugh, I slipped from the bed and walked softly to the window. I pushed it open and leant out to breathe the cooler open air. It was a bright night, with a full moon. I leant my elbows on the sill, thinking about Meg, with love and with some sadness. Soon now, she would ride away with George to begin her new life at Riverside House in Buckinghamshire. We had been parted before, for a considerable time when I was in France with Matthew, but I had always minded. Now the parting would be for ever.

No, that was wrong. Buckinghamshire wasn't Ultima Thule. I would visit Meg, and she would visit me. When she had her children, I would go to her. *Dear God, take care of her at those times. Don't let it be for her as it was for me . . .*

My train of thought broke sharply. I had glimpsed movement below me. Someone had slipped out of the house and was hurrying swiftly along the terrace. As I watched, a dark figure, wrapped in a hooded cloak, ran lightly down the steps from the terrace to the rose garden. The cloak caught on a thorny rose bush, and the figure stopped to release it, turning round to do so. Its hood slipped back, and for a moment, in the moonlight, I saw its face quite clearly. I think I had already half-recognized the walk and the shape of the shoulders. It was Christina Cobbold.

Slipping through the garden after dark, alone? Christina Cobbold, Meg's principal bridesmaid. Christina Cobbold, who was in love with Thomas Ferris and had already had three clandestine meetings with him.

Hugh was deeply asleep. I had no wish to disturb him. Quickly but silently, I pushed my feet into a pair of shoes and unhooked my cloak from where it always hung on our bedroom door. It was the custom of the house to keep a number of cloaks of various sizes in a small alcove in our entrance vestibule, so that anyone going out, perhaps in a hurry, could simply take one, but Hugh and I preferred to keep our own in our room. I swung mine round me and hurried noiselessly out.

The gallery outside our door was dark, but the stairs down

to the hall were only a few steps away and the hall below was moonlit. I could see my way quite well. I went down, treading lightly, hastened through the hall to a door that opened on to the terrace, and let myself out.

How far could Christina have got by now? Still making as little noise as possible, I ran down the steps to the rose garden and stopped to listen. No sound. The silvered hush around me was undisturbed.

I had never in my life been prey to the fears that haunted so many people, such as Jane Cobbold and Sir Edward Heron. In this respect, I have to speak well of Aunt Tabitha and Uncle Herbert. They had no superstitious beliefs in fairies or witches, and spoke of such things with mockery. I had never been taught to fear the dark; in fact I had never done so once I was past the age of five.

But now, suddenly, that very fear, not of any real danger, but of things unseen, came upon me. Heron's unpleasant description of orgies conducted in the presence of altars draped in black and crucifixes blasphemously turned upside down came back to me, and so did the vicious ill will of Anne Percy's menacing letter, rising up in my mind like a poisonous toadstool. Whether or not rites with black-draped altars had power, and whether or not ill-wishing could bring real harm to anyone, those who indulged in such things intended evil. Evil was real, even if demons were not.

And evil was stronger by night. The whole world knew that. I stood looking uneasily round me and for the first time ever experienced the fear of wicked things that steal about their business after sunset. I looked up at the moon, with the smudges that make it look so much like a witless face. Jane Cobbold believed its light was treacherous and shut it out from her bed.

It was ridiculous. I had often been abroad at night, often alone, and at times in very real danger. But in my mind I could hear the words that Christina had repeated to me, about women who make pacts with the devil and slip out at night to ride the skies on broomsticks. Around me, the rose bushes were dark anonymous shapes in the moon-shadows, strange entities, lacking the colour and detail that made them friendly by day.

Even the queen, my sister, believed in the world of spirits. She regularly consulted a magician and astrologer called Doctor Dee. Who was I to say they were both wrong?

Something rustled and then ran across the garden in front of me. I jumped and only just managed not to squeal, and then the moonlight picked up a sharp nose and a pair of gleaming green eyes as the creature halted and turned to look at me. It turned away and fled, and my last glimpse of it was a whisk of a bushy tail. It was nothing more unearthly than a fox.

I pulled myself together. What was wrong with me? Too much emotion because of Meg, perhaps. Loving her, fearing to let her pass into someone else's power, to face the dangers of childbirth – which I knew all too much about – had softened my brain. Anne Percy's letter had frightened me too, more than I wanted to admit.

But none of that should make me afraid of rose bushes and a scuttling fox. The biggest danger I faced now was bumping into a bush I hadn't seen and getting myself pricked by its thorns. Even Christina was daring the hazards of the night, whatever her mother might have told her.

I was myself again. I moved on. The paths were gravel, but they had grassy edges which were a great nuisance to Hugh's gardeners, who had to scythe them regularly. They were useful now, however, since I could walk on them and keep my footsteps noiseless. I paused again. Which way?

I hadn't found Christina in the rose garden, and as it had no side gates, she must have gone through it and on into the herb and kitchen garden. This did have side gates, leading into the wood on the left and on the right to the fowl-yard and paddock. I hurried forward.

The division between the roses and the herb and vegetable garden was a row of lavender bushes, but there was a pretty wooden archway over the entrance, with climbing roses on it. From beyond it, the aromatic scents of herbs on a summer night came to meet me. In the arch, I paused again to listen and this time heard voices, very low, somewhere to the left. I stepped through and turned that way, towards a corner where a bay tree grew. And there I found them. A single shaft of moonlight had filtered through the branches and revealed them, standing in each other's arms. 'Christina?' I said.

They sprang apart. 'What? Who . . .?' Thomas Ferris stepped forward, out of the shadow. I had not seen him since he was in his teens, and all I remembered of him was a skinny youth, very subservient to his father and with nothing to say for himself. But now, though I recognized his features, I was amazed by the way he had filled out. He had grown tall and broad, even though, as I knew, he was still only twenty-two. He was much bigger than Walter.

Christina moved after him and took her stand beside him, looking petite by contrast, sturdy though she was. 'Mistress Stannard?' she said.

'Yes. I followed you from the house, Christina.'

'What business was it of yours?' demanded Thomas angrily.

He was trying to sound intimidating, but despite his inches, young Master Ferris was no phantom of the night. After my foolish fright in the garden, he was positively reassuring. 'You're trespassing in the Stannard garden, and that is certainly my business,' I said. 'And as for you, Christina, I'm ashamed of you. Is this the way to repay our hospitality? To respect Meg's friendship?'

'We wanted to be together,' said Christina, shaky but obstinate. 'Thomas managed to get a note to me yesterday, to arrange this meeting.' That, presumably, was what had brought her out of her sulks, and not the valerian and chamomile potion at all. 'There's no harm in it,' Christina said. 'We weren't doing anything we shouldn't. We—'

She stopped short, and both she and Thomas turned sharply. From somewhere in the wood, just beyond the fence, there had been a rustling and the crack of a twig.

'I've just seen a fox,' I said. 'That's him, I dare say, making a pounce. You both have the jumps, haven't you? A sign of guilty consciences, no doubt.'

'I don't have a guilty conscience!' said Christina angrily. The woods were silent now. 'Neither of us do. Thomas needed me! His note explained. So I'm here for him, and no, I *don't* feel ashamed.'

'Needed you?'

'My family has experienced a tragedy,' said Thomas. 'I have a married sister, Lucy, living just over the Hampshire border. Or rather, I had. My parents were sent for, the day before yesterday. Lucy had fallen ill with smallpox. My mother came home this morning, in a dreadful state. Father's still there, helping Lucy's husband to arrange the funeral. She died at dawn today.'

'Thomas was fond of her,' said Christina. 'And he wasn't allowed to go and see her, though he's had the disease himself, and even his own mother hasn't comforted him or let him try to comfort her, all because his parents are so angry about him and me! What have I ever done that makes me into a monster? Well, if his own family won't give him a few kind words, I will!'

'You already have, love.' Thomas's voice changed when he spoke to her, went from aggressive to gentle all on the instant. Christina drew closer to him, pressing herself against his side, and his arm went round her.

I groaned inwardly, but my duty was plain. 'Christina,' I said, 'your parents are our friends and are here as our guests. Master Stannard and I *cannot* connive at this sort of thing in opposition to their wishes. You must come back to the house with me at once. As for you, Master Ferris, I am sorry for your loss and I mean that sincerely, but you should still not be tempting a young girl like Christina to creep from her room and meet you like this in the dead of night. And you, Christina, should not have agreed to it. Both of you should have more sense of responsibility.'

'Did you?' asked Christina. 'When you climbed out of a window to run off with Meg's father?'

'Who told you that?' I demanded, unwisely. I should have said *don't be impertinent* and left it there, but she had caught me wrong-footed. I felt as though my unconventional past was catching up with me.

'Meg did. She said you fled with her father one night and got married against the wishes of your guardians.'

'The circumstances were different from yours,' I said repressively. 'I have no intention, however, of explaining them to you.'

It would have been a complicated explanation, anyway, though a true one. I had been escaping from an unhappy home and the bleak prospect of life as an unwed dogsbody. Christina had two loving parents who, I was sure, intended to plan a happy future for her. But this was not the time to go into all that.

'Christina, my love,' said Thomas, turning to her as though I were not there, 'I think I should go. We will meet again soon, I promise.'

He kissed her, adjusted his cap, gave me an ironical bow, and then stepped away. A moment later, I glimpsed his figure at the gate into the wood and heard a horse whicker in greeting. Then, briefly, I heard the sound of hoof beats, which faded swiftly out of hearing.

'We are not going to be pushed apart by a silly, ancient quarrel!' said Christina, defiant too, standing rigid.

'At the moment,' I said, 'you are bound for bed and sleep, and the day after tomorrow you will be your friend Meg's principal bridesmaid. I shall not tell your parents about this escapade, not this time, but if you do such a thing again, don't count on my silence, or that of my husband. I shall have to tell him about tonight, naturally. We shall be watching you. Now, come with me.'

FIVE

Spectre at the Feast

Next day, Christina was pale from lack of sleep, and though she was clearly trying to appear normal, I could see that she was miserable. I could only hope that she would be more like herself on the morrow, for the wedding. I had other concerns, too. Everyone had tried hard to make sure that all preparations were complete, but there were last-minute hitches and alarms.

Dorothy, although we needed her to help with the brides-maids' dresses, disappeared during the morning without permission. On returning, just in time for the midday dinner, she said that on the previous day she had found her aunt unwell. 'I just ran over to see how the poor soul is. I found her better; it was naught but a cold, but she ain't young and she's on her own and I was worried.'

'You should have asked!' I said angrily. 'We didn't know where you were or when you'd be back, and Mistress Jester and Dale and I have seen to the bridesmaids' dresses without you. Well, don't do such a thing again, that's all I can say.'

Meanwhile, Brockley had to rush to Woking after all because John Hawthorn suddenly decided that he needed more sugar and more almonds for the special subtlety and I had need of some silk thread and an extra roll of linen. Brockley brought everything back with him, but he arrived home in what was so obviously a put-about state that I asked him what was wrong.

'It was nothing, madam. Nothing that need worry you, anyway.'

'*What was it, Brockley?*'

Brockley sighed, realizing that I didn't mean to let go. 'I was nearly arrested, madam.'

'Nearly . . . Whatever for? What happened?

'Before I started home, I took a meal at the Lion Inn, madam, and left Brown Berry in the stable there. I unsaddled him and took off the saddlebags with my purchases in them, and hung them up. There are hooks for that. It's a respectable place; no one goes into the stable that shouldn't. Everyone who's got saddlebags just leaves them there. I made sure the bags were strapped shut. If anyone knocked against them, I wasn't going to have the things I'd bought falling out the way that letter did, which the Norwich courier brought. But when I'd eaten and came back to saddle up, someone had been interfering with my things.'

'You mean something had been stolen?'

'No, not that, as it turned out. But I saw straightaway that someone had been at one of my saddlebags, because although it was still strapped shut, the strap was fixed at the wrong hole. I mostly use the same one, and there's a mark on the leather. I saw that the mark was on the hole below, and that wasn't how I'd left it. Of course, I thought: *thieves.* But when I looked into the bags, nothing was missing. Something had been added! There was a little drawstring pouch I'd never seen before, very pretty, with gold embroidery and little white beads on it, and when I had a look inside, believe it or not, there was a rope of pearls in there.'

'Had someone put it in your saddlebag, thinking it was his?' I asked.

'Maybe. There were other saddlebags there. But it's lucky I found it. I took it straight back inside the inn and handed it to the landlord, and just in time, because in came a fellow – I don't know who he was – shouting that a rope of pearls had been stolen from him. It belonged to his mistress, he said. He'd come to Woking to collect it from a jeweller after it had been restrung. He left his horse and his bags at the Lion while he went on foot to fetch it, and when he came back with it, he'd put it in his saddlebag. He was sure that a man who was just bringing a brown cob in had seen him do it. It was in a pretty bag that caught the light, he said. He'd had a bite to eat and then gone to saddle up for home and thank heaven he'd had the sense to check his saddlebags because the neck-lace was gone! And then he pointed at me and shouted, "That's him, he saw me put that pretty pouch in my saddlebag, he's the thief!" In fact, he tried to lay hold of me. I had to grapple with him to get free, then and there, in the entrance hall of the inn!'

'Brockley!'

'The landlord promptly produced the pouch and the pearls, of course, and said that far from being a thief, I was an honest man who had brought it to him the moment I found it, and please would this fellow stop shouting. Here was the jewellery safe and sound in its pouch, and he ought to be thanking me, not pointing fingers. Well, the wretched man did thank me,' said Brockley, 'though none too gladly. I've never in my life had anyone say thank you to me, for anything, with such a scowl! I apologized to the landlord for the disturbance, though it was hardly my fault, and then I walked out – and I checked both my saddlebags all over again to make sure I hadn't got any more little strangers in them. Then I came home. But it was a near thing, madam.'

'I should think so. Thank heaven for your sharp eyes, Brockley.'

'Madam . . .'

'What is it, Brockley?'

'That letter. From the Countess of Northumberland. It threatened me as well as you.'

'You think it was an attempt to get you taken up for theft? That the pearls were put in your saddlebag deliberately – it wasn't a mistake?'

'That man said I'd seen him put the pouch away in his own bag. I hadn't. He wasn't in the stable at any time when I was, so I couldn't have seen him put anything away anywhere. I didn't make a to-do at the inn. I didn't want to upset the landlord any more. But that fellow was lying.'

'He *could* still have been mistaken,' I said. 'Perhaps he confused you with someone else who *was* there when he was.'

'Brown Berry was the only brown cob. There were three other animals there – one grey pony, one big chestnut and a little bay mare.'

'Look, Brockley, I don't know what to make of all this. I shall tell Master Stannard and Sybil, and I suppose you'll tell

Dale, but warn her not to gossip. I don't want talk, and people imagining things. But just in case – keep your eyes open and take care, at all times.'

'As you wish, madam.'

When I went to bed that night, I was exhausted. Anne Percy and her letter were no longer confined to the back of my mind. They were in the forefront of it once again. I had a grim, persistent feeling that trouble was on its way.

I did occasionally experience premonitions that turned out to be true. I sincerely hoped that this wouldn't prove to be one of them.

It did, of course.

At Hawkswood, the kitchens consisted of one big room, where there were two hearths and an oven for cooking, and several smaller ones which were mostly used for storage and the messier kinds of food preparation. One of them, however, was set aside for baths. We kept a big wooden tub there, because it was handy for the kitchen fire and the pails of hot water didn't have to be carried too far.

On Meg's wedding day, two big cauldrons of water were heating on the kitchen fires at dawn, and when they were ready, the tub was filled, the heat adjusted with cold water, a bottle of rose water was poured in, and Meg was brought downstairs to be ceremonially bathed.

During the process, the room was full of steam and somewhat congested, since Meg's helpers included myself, Sybil Jester, Fran Dale and all three bridesmaids – Susanna and Kate, the daughters of Meg's Uncle Ambrose, together with Christina. Christina was the last to present herself for her bridesmaid's duties, and was brought along by her mother (who, I noticed, had dressed for the occasion in a tawny gown and cream kirtle that were copies of the dress I had worn when we met at the Cobbolds').

Christina was still pale and looked as though she had been crying again, but she made the effort to smile, and once in the bathroom she made herself useful, helping to wash Meg's back and fetching the warm towel when she got out of the water.

When we had finished, and Meg's dark hair had been rubbed as dry as possible, we wrapped her in a woollen robe and took her back upstairs to her room, where, despite the summery weather, a fire had been lit so that her hair could finish drying quickly. With that done, Dale brushed it, until it shone with the blue highlights of a blackbird's plumage, and braided it. Between us all, we put Meg into her cream and blue wedding dress, and finally Dale coiled the gleaming braids into their golden net.

Then we sat her on the bed and told her to keep still while the rest of us put on our festive gowns. By then, the clock that we kept in the hall said eleven. It was time to set off.

The ceremony would be at the church in Hawkswood village. It was a good mile away and most people were to ride, though Hugh and I would use our coach. The bridegroom and his friends, who had been ordered to remain together in his room until it was time for them to set off, went ahead with most of the guests. When they were out of sight, the bride's party started out. The steward, Adam Wilder, was staying at the house to oversee the preparations for the feast, but Roger Brockley was going to attend. He had asked for the privilege of going on foot and leading Meg's mare.

Meg, a competent rider, protested about this, but Brockley overruled her. A bride, he had said, was a precious being and must be safeguarded as she went to meet her bridegroom, as though she were made of bright jewels in a casing of thinnest glass. Accordingly, even though Bay Gentle well deserved her name, she must be led at a walking pace with a strong hand on her bridle. Brockley would brook no argument, even from me – not that I offered any. I was touched by his care for my daughter and told her firmly to accept his protection with grace. Which, bless her, she did.

When we reached the church, the horses were hitched to the fence round the churchyard and everyone went inside. Meg, Hugh and the bridesmaids came last. Meg held Hugh's arm, and immediately behind her, gravely and carefully, with no hint of sullenness now, came Christina, leading the bridesmaids and carrying Meg's blue brocade train.

The church had been decorated with flower garlands, and

it was full of sunshine, streaming through the stained glass windows on the southern side. As I took my place near the front, I saw George Hillman look round to see Meg coming towards him, and the quality of his smile was balm to me.

Because, joyous though this occasion was supposed to be, I still found myself, every now and then, fretting because Meg was still so young and George Hillman was about to take her away from me. I was as sure as I could be that he would look after her, but I felt almost as though I were angry with him. If he ever mistreated her, said a small fierce voice inside my head, he would have me to deal with, and heaven have mercy on him then, for I would have none.

Dr Fletcher, the placid middle-aged man who was Hawkswood's present vicar, was waiting to begin. He was new to Hawkswood. His predecessor had testified against Gladys Morgan when she was tried for witchcraft, and had tried to stir up local feeling against her when we brought her home after her pardon. He had been a fiery individual, much given to ranting sermons about the evils of sorcery and Popery. When he was excited, he was apt to lean over his pulpit, thump it with his fist, and let his voice shoot up half an octave. Hugh had persuaded – well, paid – him to seek a transfer elsewhere. His replacement, the Reverend Hubert Fletcher, was a reasonable, peace-loving soul, and we had all become fond of him.

He smiled at Meg as she stood before the altar, and Sybil, at my side, murmured that it was nice, wasn't it, that these days weddings could take place at the altar instead of at the church door in the old-fashioned way.

Dr Fletcher cleared his throat. 'Dearly beloved . . .'

The service commenced.

The thing was done. My little dark-haired daughter had become Mistress Hillman. A gold ring shone on her left hand; stars shone in her brown eyes. Back at home, the kitchen staff would be putting the final touches to the feast. Brockley would not lead Meg's horse on the way back because she would be riding beside her bridegroom. All round us, there was a cheerful babble of laughter and talk.

I wanted to cry, but I knew I must not. I talked animatedly

to Hugh and Sybil as we returned to the house, which had acquired festoons of flower garlands during our absence. Fresh rushes and herbs had been laid in the hall as well. Indeed, the effect in the great hall was overpowering.

'They've overdone the herbs among the rushes,' Hugh said, wrinkling his nose. 'What in the world have they mixed with them? That isn't rosemary that I can smell.'

'I think it's mint,' I said. 'But I don't think we can do anything about it now.'

'A pity. I like to smell my dinner as well as eat it!' said Hugh. He added, glancing at me: 'Little Bear, you don't look as happy as you should, or sound it, either. What's the matter?'

'I feel I'm losing her,' I said. 'Losing Meg.'

'You won't feel like that when she gives you a grandchild. Come. They're waiting for us to sit down.'

Hugh had hired musicians to play during the feast and the dancing that would follow, and the meal began to the sound of drum, spinet and guitar. I looked with admiration on the efforts of John Hawthorn and his aides. The centrepiece of the top table, where Meg and George were seated in state, was a two-foot square marchpane model of Hawkswood House, as I had requested. Hawthorn and Joan Flood had made it between them, and it was a great credit to their skill. Little Bessie, at the lowest table, stood up to see better as it was brought in and let out an audible: 'Oooh!' and I heard admiring exclamations from Mrs Seldon and Mrs Ward.

Hugh nudged me. 'Look hard at Bessie. She was wearing a looser dress yesterday. But now – do you see what I see?'

'What do you mean?' I whispered, and then, with a shock, I realized. 'God's teeth! She's—'

'Gone a little further than flirting,' said Hugh. 'Four months, at a guess. I wonder if Jennet and Margery have realized?'

The feast began with soups and various pies, followed by fruit tarts, all accompanied by light wine or ale. Then, after a pause during which a red wine was brought round, the musicians fell silent so that Adam Wilder could step into the hall with a trumpet and blow a fanfare to introduce a procession carrying the roast meats which were the central item. We did not make a habit of serving feasts like this; indeed, our usual fare was inclined to be plain, and sufficient rather than extravagant. This was a striking departure from the norm. Meg looked across George to where Hugh was seated on the other side of him and said: 'All this for us!'

'My pleasure,' said Hugh, bowing towards her.

As host and hostess, Hugh and I did not stay in our seats all the time, but each in turn made the rounds of the tables, asking if everyone was happy, if the food was to their liking, if anything were needed. When I reached Jennet Ward and Margery Seldon, I murmured that I hoped Bessie was enjoying herself and added, cautiously: 'You're feeding her well; she's plumper than when I saw her at the Cobbolds.'

'Is that a hint?' asked Jennet, though with a smile. 'It's all right. We know. She's been a careless lass. It was a pedlar she met at the May Day fair in Woking, long gone on his way. But we shall look after her.'

I told Hugh, when I returned to my seat, 'They know about Bessie. She will be all right.'

'I'm glad,' he said. 'I wouldn't like to think of a young thing like that turned out with nowhere to go and a child on the way. We'd have had to offer her shelter ourselves in that case.'

Hugh was a good man. In marrying him, I had chosen well. I gave him a smile which said so, and he smiled back.

Wilder, who had continued to play the trumpet while the meat dishes were disposed on the tables, stopped when all were in place, and the kitchen staff hurried away to fetch the accompaniments such as the beans, the rice, the onions, extra bread and a choice of sauces. Hawthorn's assistant, Abel Forde, however, came back almost immediately, empty handed and at a run, made for Wilder and said something urgently into his ear. Wilder's eyebrows rose, and he put his trumpet down on a sideboard. He was far too dignified to run as Abel had, but he left the hall with rapid strides.

I caught Hugh's eye. He shook his head, puzzled. Lower down the hall, Brockley had risen to his feet and was looking towards the door to the entrance vestibule. And now, we could all hear the sound of raised voices out there.

George Hillman said: 'What's happening?'

Adam Wilder reappeared, still striding fast. He made straight for us. 'Sir, Madam, Master and Mistress Hillman, a . . . a gentleman has called unexpectedly . . . Well, it's Master Walter Ferris, and he is anxious to come in; he has something to say, publicly . . . I said I was not sure if this would be acceptable, but he is insistent and . . .'

He certainly was. Brockley had gone out into the vestibule to investigate the situation and was now returning, backwards and expostulating because he was being, literally, pushed by the nondescript-looking Walter Ferris. Nondescript or not, he was making himself felt by thrusting at Brockley's chest with the butt end of a hefty staff, and as he came through the door, he used the staff across my good Brockley's chest, thrusting him aside so roughly that Brockley staggered backwards and bumped into the sideboard where Wilder had left his trumpet. It fell to the floor with a clang. Someone emitted a snort of laughter, and at the top table, everyone came instinctively to their feet: Hugh, myself, Meg, George and the vicar, Dr Fletcher, who had come back with us from the church and been given a place among the principals.

A puzzled and indignant muttering broke out among our guests, and dear, placid Dr Fletcher said: 'Well, I never!' which for him was the equivalent of anyone else's shriek of outrage.

Ferris marched to within a few feet of our table and then stopped, staring at us. He had the kind of eyes which have no definite colour. At that moment, I thought they were like pebbles seen through water. He was not dressed as a wedding guest, but had a buff jacket and hose, with an informal, open-necked shirt. He might have been his own gamekeeper. He still held his staff at an aggressive angle, although there was a curious incongruity in the fact that under his left arm he was carrying a bundle that was big enough to be awkward.

Hugh, white with anger, said: 'Master Ferris! What is the meaning of this?'

'The MEANING?' said Ferris, so loudly that the muttering among our guests faded out. If his person was insignificant, his voice was not. 'It has come to my notice,' Ferris thundered, 'that my son Thomas last night had a secret assignation here upon your premises, Master Stannard, with Christina Cobbold, daughter of Anthony Cobbold, whom I see sitting there among your guests!' He pointed dramatically to his left, where Anthony and Jane Cobbold, along with Christina and the other bridesmaids, had been placed immediately next to our top table.

Anthony at once jumped up, shouting: '*Nonsense!*' but Ferris ignored him.

'I am aware that this assignation took place and that what I say is true!'

Anthony gobbled, unable to make himself heard. Christina was scarlet, biting her lip, while her mother was looking at her in horror. Hugh seemed to have been flabbergasted into silence.

'I am bewildered and appalled,' boomed Ferris, 'by my son's obstinacy in persisting with this improper love affair and in refusing the excellent match we have planned for him. But he is young and young people can be vulnerable. For instance, to such as YOU!'

To my astonishment, he pointed a forefinger at me. I stared at him, agape. I saw Sybil, who had slipped out of the room just before his arrival, probably to visit the privy, reappear briefly in the doorway and then vanish once more, as if frightened away.

'YOU ARE A WITCH!' bellowed Walter Ferris. The reverberations of his voice shook the flower garlands. 'Do not deny it! You harbour and consort with the witch Gladys Morgan! She has been tried for witchcraft and found guilty and would have hanged but for the too generous mercy of our sovereign lady Queen Elizabeth . . .'

'This is most unseemly!' Dr Fletcher for once raised his own voice and actually managed, for a few seconds, to overcome the tirade. 'What are you about, sir? The solemn joy of a wedding should not be interrupted in this fashion!'

'It certainly shouldn't!' Hugh came to life again and exploded. 'This is outrageous! Whatever your purpose here, Master Ferris, I suggest that you and I withdraw to discuss whatever it is, in private. I cannot allow you to—'

'BUT THE VERDICT STILL STANDS!' Ferris overcame

the opposition once again. 'The woman Gladys Morgan is a convicted criminal!' His forefinger stabbed at me again, and he let his voice drop to an insinuating tone. 'Yet you protect and care for her. Why? I think, because you are of her sisterhood.'

By ceasing to bellow, he had given others their opportunity. Gladys Morgan shouted: 'Here! Who's this fellow, and who's he calling a convict?'

At the same time, Rob Henderson shouted: 'Is he drunk?'

Meg's Uncle Ambrose replied by bawling: 'What on? A whole barrel of Geneva?'

'Drunk, nothing!' That was Brockley, exuding disgust. 'Ought to be chained up in a madhouse!'

Hugh, crimson now instead of white, pounded the table with an angry fist. 'This is *intolerable*! Leave my house at once, Master Ferris! How dare you invade it in this disgraceful fashion and fling insulting accusations at my wife and at a member of our household and—?'

'I AM GOING!' Ferris was thundering again. 'But not until I've finished what I came to say! Thomas, foolish boy, told me that last night, Christina, on beholding him, cast herself into his arms, exclaiming that she had grieved at being separated from him, and that she had been given a calming potion, made by Mistress Stannard. By YOU!'

Again that accusing finger picked me out. 'A calming draught? Was it? Or did my besotted son pay you to give Christina Cobbold a love potion that would fasten her passions on him and bind her to him yet more closely?'

I choked out: 'What? Are you out of your mind?' but I don't think anyone heard, least of all Ferris, whose voice still dominated us all.

'Thomas has not yet admitted it, but I read the truth in his eyes. Perhaps she was beginning to understand that Thomas was not for her and so he planned to bewitch her. As she had already bewitched him, though perhaps –' Walter Ferris smiling as he made a joke was an extraordinarily uncomfortable sight – 'not with a magic potion. What did you charge my foolish son for your services, Mistress Stannard?'

'What are you talking about, Master Ferris?' He had paused

as if he expected an answer, giving me a chance at last to splutter out an audible protest. 'You must indeed be mad or drunk! I never—'

But I couldn't finish. He was off again. One might as well have told a thunderstorm or a charging bull to stop.

'Perhaps the potion was made with the help, the advice, of the witch Gladys Morgan. I suspect that it was. And on those grounds, madam, I base my accusation. I say that YOU are guilty of the crime of witchcraft too!'

He paused once more, with an air of triumph, and Dr Fletcher burst out: 'That is a most offensive and unjustified accusation. Hawkswood is a respectable and God-fearing household, and you should be ashamed! You have forced your way into a feast to which you were not asked and flung shameful accusations at people who have done you no harm. Master Stannard!' He turned to Hugh. 'Surely you have menservants enough to remove this man?'

'What better disguise for a witch than to appear respectable and God-fearing?' demanded Walter.

There were indeed a good many able-bodied men in the hall, and Dr Fletcher's words had started a ripple of movement among them, but the reiteration of *witch*, that word out of nightmare, had a strangely paralysing effect. It hinted of demons behind the faces of dull, ordinary women, all the more dangerous because they are invisible; detectable only by their works. In the moonlit garden only two nights ago, I had learned that we all have those fears, somewhere within us. Even able-bodied men, it seemed.

Then, amazingly, Ferris nodded towards Meg and George and, in a perfectly normal tone of voice, said: 'Ah, the newly-weds. Honest newly-weds, these, marrying in accordance with the wishes of their elders, as all young people should. I congratulate you and wish you happiness together. As one day I shall wish happiness to my son Thomas and Margaret Emory, the young lady to whom he is lawfully promised. He shall marry her, and no other. Meanwhile, since anyone who attends a wedding feast should bring gifts, I have brought some for you.'

He stepped right up to the high table, elbowed some dishes

out of the way and put down the bundle he'd had under his arm. Then he bowed, twisted on his heel and strode out. He left the hall door open behind him, but we heard the crash when he slammed the outer door as he swept out of the house.

Brockley, half-rising from his seat, caught my eye and said: 'Madam, should we have the dogs see him off?'

I shook my head, and Hugh said: 'Not if he came on a horse and it's still standing in the courtyard. We can't have the dogs nipping at its hocks, poor beast. The horse isn't responsible for this . . . this scandalous scene.'

He sounded dreadfully shaken. His flush had faded, and his complexion had turned yellowish, while his lips had taken on a blue tinge that I did not like. He had sunk back into his seat. I got up and moved quickly behind him, pressing my hands down on his shoulders. 'Hugh. It's all right. He's gone.'

'And what a figure I cut as master of this house!' said Hugh, choking on the words.

'That doesn't matter. Forget it.'

'I would like to point out,' said Dr Fletcher, who had also seated himself again but now leant forward to speak to Hugh, 'that even if your good lady supplied a dozen love potions for the benefit of young Mistress Cobbold, she didn't break the law. Witchcraft is not illegal unless it's undertaken for the purpose of murder. There have been no deaths. Ferris is a foolish man, bellowing nonsense. Now, this is your daughter's wedding feast. It must proceed. What kind of wedding gift did your unpleasant guest bring her and her groom, I wonder?'

George was already pulling the strange bundle, which seemed to be wrapped in coarse black cloth, towards him. Meg helpfully cleared some extra space by moving more dishes out of the way, and George unrolled the cloth, revealing a pile of golden brown velvet, which he held up. 'A cloak! An expensive one, too.'

'There are two.' Meg pulled out some more velvet, moss green this time. She shook it out. 'Yes. Another very fine cloak. I think it's lined with silk.' Then, as she examined it more closely, her young face stiffened. 'But it isn't new! There is scuffing inside the collar, and the lining's been torn and mended!' She pointed to the place. 'George, is the one you are holding a new one, do you think?'

George was frowning. 'No, it isn't. There's a lot of rubbing at the neckline – it's very well worn, I'd say. What an insult! What does the man take us for? Does he think we're an old clothes stall in a cheap market?'

'The wretched things are still velvet,' said Hugh tiredly. 'They can go into the alcove with the other old cloaks that everyone uses. They'll be warm at least. Take them away, Wilder.'

The garments were removed. Then, with a visible effort, Hugh stood up, and I stepped back, releasing his shoulders.

'Dr Fletcher was right,' Hugh announced. 'The feast must continue, despite this deplorable interruption. I fear that my neighbour Master Ferris really is either insane or intoxicated. Either way he shall not disturb our revels any further. I ask you all to see that you have wine or ale in your goblets or tankards, and to raise them in a toast to my foster-daughter Meg and her bridegroom George, to wish them joy.' He picked up his own goblet, and raised it high. 'To Meg and to George!'

We all reached for our goblets and raised them. I saw Sybil creep back into the hall and to her place, and pick up her own glass. Everyone was trying to recreate the normal world.

In vain, as far as I was concerned. The hatred in Walter Ferris's eyes had been unmistakable, and for some reason, it had been aimed far more at me than at his traditional foes, the Cobbolds. I was terrified.

SIX

The Unexpected Onslaught

The feast went on. Hugh, with that well-timed toast, John Hawthorn and his helpers with a further array of excellent dishes, Adam Wilder with his dignified announcements of every new course, the musicians in their gallery: all combined to wrench the occasion back on course as though it were a ship in a heavy sea, being kept to her heading by a squad of brawny steersmen. Everyone stayed put and continued to eat.

Gradually, the atmosphere settled. I did my best to push my fear away. When the feast was over, everyone withdrew to the parlours or to tidy themselves in their rooms while the hall was cleared for dancing. Then we went back to it, the musicians struck up a merry tune, and George led Meg out on to the floor.

A buffet supper was to follow the dancing, but while the tables were being set, I caught Sybil's eye, beckoned to Fran and the two remaining bridesmaids and Meg's Aunt Anne. We gathered round Meg and took her upstairs. Behind us, we knew that George's cousins and friends were similarly gathering round him.

For this night, Hugh and I were occupying a spare room, because our usual bedchamber was the best one, and tonight, the newly-weds were to have it. Rose petals were strewn over the coverlet and new candles placed in all the holders. A tray of cold meats, bread rolls, fruit, and jugs of wine and milk, had been placed in the room as well. The young couple would have their supper in private.

We undressed Meg, put her affectionately into the bed, kissed her, wished her luck, and left her. Presently, back in the hall, we heard masculine voices and laughter overhead and knew that George had been escorted to his bride. After a while,

his entourage came down to join us, and supper began. I ate
very little. Half my mind was with Meg, my little, young Meg,
and what was happening up in the nuptial chamber. The other
half was remembering Walter Ferris's pointing finger and his
ugly accusations.

I think the same was true of Hugh. It seemed a long time
before the goodnights were finally said. Uncle Ambrose had
drunk too much and fallen into a stupor. Brockley, Adam and
the valet Ambrose had brought with him carried him to bed,
but we didn't feel we could go to ours until everyone was
settled. When at last we retired, Hugh looked exhausted.

However, he fell asleep easily, and his deep, steady breathing
reassured me. But for me, sleep was elusive. Dawn was
breaking before I slipped into an uneasy doze. In the morning,
Hugh seemed rested, but I was heavy-headed and late to the
hall for breakfast.

The morning sun was already growing hot. Uncle Ambrose
and his family and the Cobbold party were all to leave that
morning and had broken their fasts before I ever came downstairs. When I did, I found them preparing for departure. Out
in the courtyard, horses were being saddled or laden with
packs or harnessed to wagons. Ambrose looked as though he
had a headache, and his too-elaborate doublet was causing
sweat to run down his temples.

'How can he *stand* that doublet?' Hugh whispered to me.
'It's already scorching hot, and he's got padded shoulders and
fur trimmings!'

'Showing off,' I said. 'He's like that.'

'He's Gerald's brother. But surely Gerald wasn't . . .?'

'No,' I said. 'Gerald was quite different. Meg takes after
him.'

Gerald had been dark like Ambrose, but there the resemblance ended. He had been stocky, instead of tall, and far
more intelligent and sensible than Ambrose. Gerald never
drank more than he could hold (though his capacity was
certainly good) and wouldn't have dreamed of donning a
fur-trimmed doublet in August. I wished he could have seen
his daughter married. But that was not something I would
ever say to Hugh.

I finished my meal in time to wave goodbye to the Ambrose party, and then turned to assist the Cobbolds, who, having been much embarrassed by Walter Ferris's revelations about his son and their daughter, were now embarrassed again because they couldn't find Christina.

'We spoke to her severely last night,' said her mother in exasperation, standing in the courtyard with Christina's hat and cloak on her arm. 'And the end of that was that she ran off, crying. Now, this morning, we can't find her at all! The servants say she took breakfast early and then went outdoors. Oh, where *is* she?'

She was eventually discovered wandering disconsolately, all alone, in the herb garden, bareheaded, with her brown hair carelessly plaited and coming out of its braids. She must indeed have come out early, before it grew so warm, because she had snatched a cloak from the alcove in the entrance hall. In fact, she was arrayed in the green velvet affair that had been part of Ferris's objectionable wedding present.

Her parents, scolding, haled her back to the courtyard, removed the despised mantle, handed it disdainfully to one of our maidservants, planted a hat on their daughter's untidy head, bundled her on to her horse and took their leave. Jennet, Margery and Bessie went with them, to have their company part of the way to Woking.

As the tail of the last horse whisked out of sight beyond the gatehouse, the courtyard suddenly seemed quite empty. Hugh and I went back inside. The Hendersons and George's friends were sitting at leisure over an even later breakfast than mine, and I was glad to find that Meg and George were with them. One glance at their happy faces told me all I needed to know. There was an air of confidence in the way George held himself, while Meg looked mysteriously different – not older, but more adult – and the softness in her eyes whenever she glanced at George was a joy to see.

That first night had gone well, then. I was thankful. But now they must prepare for their own departure and the journey to Meg's new home in Buckinghamshire. They intended to be gone before noon and to dine on the way. The moment of parting was rushing towards me. We both cried a little when it came, and Meg, endearingly, also cried at having to leave her spaniel bitch, Marigold, behind. Marigold was feeding a family of young pups and to take her on a journey wasn't feasible, so she would stay at Hawkswood and become my dog. George had promised to find a new one for Meg. The Cobbolds had been interested in the pups, and on the previous evening, they had asked to have one of them as soon as the litter was old enough.

'Perhaps training a puppy will take Christina's mind off romantic assignations,' Anthony had said, with a snort.

The goodbyes were over at last. I watched my girl, sitting straight-backed on Bay Gentle, ride off through the gatehouse arch. As she did so, she turned, just once, to wave, and then she was gone. There was something gallant in that wave, but I knew well enough that before she had travelled much further beside George, the wrench would be over and she would be thinking of the new life that lay ahead. I wiped my eyes. I mustn't grudge that to her. Only now, of course, I was free to think about Walter Ferris and those lurid accusations.

It was no surprise to me that, soon after dinner, I was stricken with migraine.

I had always been prone to these agonizing headaches. Back now in our own bed, I lay still, because the slightest movement sent bolts of agony through my head. Gladys brewed me a remedy and Fran Dale brought it to me, but although it had often been effective, it didn't help this time.

Towards the end of the afternoon, Hugh came to me. He sat on the side of the bed and said bluntly: 'Is it Meg or Walter Ferris that brought this on?'

'Sir Edward Heron's the sheriff,' I said. 'What if Ferris takes his tale to him? We know the kind of views he holds! He was good enough to tell us, at the Cobbold wedding! Heron has a chaplain who thinks as he does, who preaches on texts like *thou shall not suffer a witch to live.*'

'Well, let me tell you one or two things,' said Hugh bracingly. 'You are not a witch, and no one can pretend you are. All Ferris actually has against you is that you gave Christina a posset to calm her when she was upset! You made it yourself, in the kitchen here, presumably in the presence of John

Hawthorn and Abel Forde and the Floods. They no doubt know what you put in it. Surely they took an interest when the lady of the house came to make a posset with her own hands?'

'Yes, they did. Hawthorn was amused, and Joan warmed the wine for me, and Ben helped me to chop the herbs. I just used valerian and chamomile with honey to sweeten the taste. That was all.'

'And Fran Dale was with you when you gave it to Christina. You both watched her drink it. All the absurdities about Thomas getting you to make it for her because it was a love potion, that's just Walter Ferris's crazed imagination. I think he really is crazed, you know.'

I tried to nod but thought better of it.

'Also,' said Hugh, bent on reassuring me, 'the verdict against Gladys was overturned by the queen herself, and Gladys, mercifully, has behaved properly ever since. Edward Heron won't be able to find anything against either of you, no matter how he tries. I will deal with him if necessary. So, I fancy, would the queen.'

'I couldn't ask her for help again, Hugh. I did it once, for Gladys's sake, but it isn't the sort of thing one can keep on doing.'

'I don't think you'd have to ask, Ursula. We'd only need to make sure your royal sister knew the situation. We could leave the rest to her. She owes you too much. Don't be afraid, Little Bear. The queen is your sister, and I am here.'

Shortly after that, my malady reached its usual climax. Fran Dale and Sybil were at hand and came at my call, but Hugh was there as well and it was he who held the basin while I threw up, with such abandon that it was a wonder I didn't turn myself inside out. Then, exhausted, I slept. By the next day I was myself again. All the same, I was still afraid.

But nothing happened. The rest of the guests departed. No riders bearing the sheriff's badge came pounding into our courtyard. No more menacing letters came from the Netherlands, either. The events at the marriage feast were gossiped about in the village, of course, for many of our servants had families

there, and the talk presently spread beyond the village because
gossip always does.

Much of the spreading was done by a father and son, Harry
and Eddie Dodd, the Hawkswood thatchers. These two had
clients for miles around and had the busiest tongues for miles
as well. Hugh always said that although women were traditionally said to be more talkative than men, the Dodds outdid
them by far. But because there was no more excitement, the
talk died down quite quickly.

I had of course told Sybil, who'd missed most of it, all that
had happened, and she duly shook her head over it but agreed
with Hugh that there was no evidence that anyone could use
against me, and as for Christina and Thomas, they were not
our responsibility.

A letter came from Meg, enthusing about her new home,
praising the excellent lady's maid that George had found for
her and saying that she and George meant to plant a rose
garden like the one at Hawkswood. She sounded happy. I took
comfort in that.

Everyday affairs moved in. I decided to keep Dorothy Beale
on, because despite her thoughtless rush to see her aunt in
Priors Ford, she really was very skilled and I wanted to over-
haul my winter gowns. John Hawthorn pleaded with me to
keep the Floods on as well. Hugh demurred at first, saying
that although they were good, they were also far from cheap,
but finally he agreed to retain them for a while. Christmas
was still a long way off, but we knew from experience that it
always crept up faster than expected and there would be any
amount of entertaining then. 'They can stay till the new year,'
Hugh said.

A little more than a week after the wedding, an invitation
came from Jennet Ward and Margery Seldon, inviting Hugh
and me to dinner on the morrow at their Woking home. Woking
was nearly as far away as Cobbold Hall, but Hugh, whose
health had improved, said that we would go.

It was a beautiful early September day when we arrived at
their home, which proved to be a large thatched cottage. Our
hostesses, however, had dressed as if to receive royalty,
Margery in pale peach silk while Jennet was dignified in rust

coloured brocade. The cottage had no spacious hall, no fine furniture, no Turkish carpets or tapestries to adorn its walls; no family portraits. What it did have included a comfortable living-cum-dining room scented with the polish that made the oak stools and benches shine, and numerous cushions in beautifully embroidered covers. There was also a shelf of books ranging from accounts of expeditions to the New World and serious works on English history, to Sir Thomas Malory's *Morte d'Arthur*, Geoffrey Chaucer's *Canterbury Tales* and several collections of poetry. There were gleaming pans on the limewashed kitchen walls, and musical instruments were everywhere. Jennet and Margery were clearly the kind of musicians who can get a tune out of almost anything.

Bessie was now noticeably pregnant. Margery shared the cooking with her, and while they were in the kitchen, clattering pans and dishes, we could hear Margery warning her not to stretch up to that high shelf, and to leave that heavy saucepan alone.

Jennet smiled at us. 'We intend to look after Bessie. The child will be brought up here – all going well, of course. That's in God's hands. I never had children, and poor Margery lost hers. She had two, but they both died when they were small. We're both over forty now and neither of us want to marry again, so we have no more chances to produce our own. We shall look forward to having Bessie's little one to watch over.'

'We will buy it a christening gift,' Hugh promised. 'Bessie is a lucky lass to have fallen into such kind hands.'

'Mr Ferris – Margery's late husband was his bailiff at one time – said just the same thing when he called on us last,' said Jennet.

She saw our surprise and added: 'It was a few days before your daughter's wedding. We wouldn't want him to call on us now, and he hasn't tried. We were so horrified at what happened! Had he been drinking, do you think? But the last time he was here, we told him that we were fond of Bessie and wouldn't let harm come to her. Do you know, it was his idea that we should invite you to dine? We wouldn't have presumed otherwise. Our house is so much smaller than yours and our circumstances very different. But he said he had heard that we were invited to your daughter's marriage feast and why did we not return the compliment afterwards? He was sure you would like our house.'

'Master *Ferris* said these pleasant things?' I asked, bewildered.

'Well, that was before his son met Christina Cobbold at Hawkswood, wasn't it?' said Jennet. 'It seemed to me that that was what set him off. That feud has been part of life hereabouts for generations! Ah. Here comes my dear Margery to announce dinner! Margery is gifted with herbs and flavourings, though I do most of the work in the garden.'

'We grow most of our own herbs and vegetables,' Margery said, setting a tray on the table. 'Jennet weeds them. Where do dandelions and thistles come from? They shoot up overnight, as if by magic.'

'We're proud of our herbs,' Jennet said. 'Margery is clever with herbal remedies. Some of our neighbours come to us regularly for her horehound linctus for coughs and her ointment for chapped hands.'

It was an excellent dinner, well cooked and served with an admirable wine. Afterwards, we all joined in singing to spinet and lute. Bessie sang too and proved to have a very sweet voice. We gathered that the two ladies earned quite well from giving lessons in music and singing, and that, in addition, each had property outside Woking which they rented out: a smallholding in Margery's case, and some pasture and woodland in Jennet's. They reared chickens as well as growing herbs and vegetables, and Jennet, who turned out to be the one who had embroidered the cushion covers, taught embroidery as well as music. It seemed to be a happy household, and by no means poor.

When we had tired of singing, we partook of a last glass of wine before going home. Bessie had finished the washing up and been sent to bed by Margery, who told her she needed her sleep. Hugh had wandered over to the bookshelf.

'And when you're not playing music, or doing embroidery, or tending your hens and your garden, you read,' he remarked, scanning the titles. 'You have wide tastes.' He pulled out the *Morte d'Arthur* and stood leafing through it. 'This is a very fine edition of the King Arthur legend – beautiful printing. Tell me, is one of you very serious, with a liking for travel and history, while the other likes legends and poetry? And if so, which is which?'

Jennet once more gave us her smile. It emerged only now and then, but it lit up her good-looking but austere face as though the sun had come out to transform a rocky landscape. 'We both have wide tastes,' she said. 'We are trying to teach Bessie to read, though it's quite an undertaking. She isn't a good pupil. But it would be useful to her; anyone ought to be able at least to write their own name and do labels for jars of preserves, so that when you've left them on a larder shelf for months, you can still tell plums from cherries.'

'We never do well with cherries, for some reason,' Margery remarked. 'The birds always get them. They seem to go for the cherries more than the plums; I don't know why . . .'

Hugh turned from the shelf with a slim book in his hand. 'Mrs Ward, Mrs Seldon,' he said. His voice had changed. From light and friendly, it had become very grave. 'I have just found this. It had slipped, or been put, sideways on behind the other books. I saw it when I pulled out the book about King Arthur. What is it doing here?'

'What is it?' asked Margery, setting down her glass.

Hugh was turning the pages. His mouth had taken on a shape of distaste. 'It's an old book – over half a century old, by the printing and the kind of paper. It's a handbook of instructions for making some very strange things. Such as, for instance, a spancel and a hand of glory.'

Margery looked puzzled. 'What is a spancel? And I've never heard of a hand of glory!'

'I've heard of them,' said Hugh, staring at the page before him, 'and this book contains instructions for making them. A spancel is a tape made of a dead man's skin, taken from the outline of his body – difficult to do, I should think, if it means cutting in and out between fingers and toes . . .'

'But whatever for?' said Margery.

'It's used in witchcraft,' said Jennet. 'I've heard of it too. And the hand of glory is the left hand of a hanged man, with—'

'Ugh!' said Margery. 'Please don't go on.'

Hugh turned back a page or two. 'It's here. The hand, in use, is fixed upright, and to each finger and to the thumb is attached a candle made of fat from the man the hand belonged to.'

'*Ugh!*' said Margery again.

'Did you know this book was here?' Hugh asked quietly.

I had sat silent throughout this exchange. After all, we did not know Jennet and Margery well. I found myself looking at the two of them, at Margery's round, ingenuous face, at Jennet's countenance, so grave and yet with that underlying charm that showed only in her rare smile. They were both so attractive in their different ways. But did the faces truly reflect the minds behind them, or did they hide something very different? There had been too much talk of witchcraft lately; Ferris's accusation at Meg's feast had shocked me more than I knew. To my horror, I caught myself wondering. Doubting.

But then: 'No!' said Jennet and Margery together, in tones so appalled that I was reassured.

'Of course we didn't know!' Jennet's indignation rang true.

'I would urge you to get rid of it, at once.' Hugh closed the book and laid it down on a nearby stool. 'If such a thing were found in your house . . . you can imagine what might be said. I advise you to burn it.'

'Mr Stannard,' said Margery, 'the kitchen fire will be banked for the night, but can easily be woken. Please would you burn the book for us? I don't – I really don't – want to touch it. Do you, Jennet?' Jennet shook an emphatic head. 'Neither of us knows how it got there,' Margery said earnestly. 'That shelf is emptied and cleaned every spring and that . . . that *thing* certainly wasn't there last time. Please, Mr Stannard!'

Hugh obliged. After that, there seemed no more to be said. We bade the ladies farewell, promised that we would never mention the mysterious book, now turned to ashes, to anyone else, and took our leave.

Our senior groom, Arthur Watts, usually acted as our coachman these days, since his predecessor, John Argent, had died during the winter. We had left Arthur with the coach and horses at a nearby inn, which had stables. He had already harnessed up when we returned to him that evening, and we set off for home at once. As we jolted along – if only there were a way to cushion the ruts in a road – I said to Hugh: 'If Jennet and Margery are telling the truth, someone planted that book on them. But why?'

'God knows,' said Hugh. 'But it's what anyone might say, who had such a book and had kept it hidden, and then had to explain it away because someone else had found it.'

I remembered my moment of doubt. 'Hugh, you don't think those two nice women could possibly . . .?'

'It seems very unlikely, but we shall probably never know. I don't think we'll pursue the acquaintance, though. Forget it, Ursula. The book's gone. That at least has been done.'

'The things in it were revolting! I'd never heard of a spancel or a hand of glory either, and I wish I hadn't heard of them now.'

'Don't think about them,' said Hugh, and I was glad to feel the warmth of his hand, laid over mine.

We travelled on in silence. And then, as we came into the Hawkswood courtyard, a worried deputation, consisting of Adam Wilder, John Hawthorn and Roger Brockley came out to meet us.

I looked at their faces as I descended from the coach, and said: 'What is it? What's wrong?'

'It's Abel Forde, madam,' said Adam. 'Master Hawthorn here will tell you. Abel is ill.'

'He wasn't well yesterday,' Hawthorn said. 'Complained of a headache and didn't want to eat. Midday today, he said he was feverish and aching all over, and he's taken to his bed. Might be just a chill, but somehow I don't like the look of him. He's been throwing up, too.'

Jennet, Margery, Bessie, music and embroidery, good food and good wine and the accoutrements of sorcery went out of our heads at once. It is never wise to take chances with unidentified illnesses, in case they're contagious.

Above the outbuilding where Hugh's coach was kept, and reached by an outside staircase, were two rooms where visitors' servants could sleep. They were also useful if anyone developed an infectious malady.

'If he's that unwell,' I said, 'he'd better be separated from the rest of you. Get one of the rooms over the coach house ready. Make him as comfortable as possible, and I'll come and see him.'

'Should we call the physician from Woking?' Brockley asked.

'I'll see Abel first,' I said. 'Within the hour, if you please!'

When Brockley fetched me to the coach house, I found the invalid settled on a well-stuffed pallet with a light coverlet over him, a jug of water to hand and a basin on the floor at his bedside. He was flushed and sweat-soaked and quite clearly in a high fever. When I entered the room, he was moving uneasily and mumbling that his back hurt.

I had seen it all before.

There are things, details, that you don't forget, not if they concern the death of someone dearly loved, as my first husband, Gerald, had been. I had no fear for myself. As a small child, I'd had an illness which could have been either a mild attack of smallpox or the much less serious cowpox. I am inclined to think it was cowpox for it hadn't damaged my complexion. It was common among milkmaids, and as I did sometimes help with milking the cows at Withysham (it got me away from Uncle Herbert and Aunt Tabitha and was approved because it was making myself useful), I was quite likely to get the illness.

Whichever I'd had, my mother had told me that I was probably safe from smallpox for the rest of my life. I was sure that she was right, for though I had nursed Gerald, I hadn't caught it. Meg had had cowpox too, and I was thankful, for she hadn't sickened either. As a precaution, I'd sent her away as soon as I knew what was wrong with him, but she had been in contact with him at the start. Standing by Abel Forde's bed, I was afraid, but it was for him, not for myself.

I knelt down, murmured something soothing, and asked Abel to open his mouth to let me see inside. He did so, and I saw that his mouth and tongue were covered with small red spots. Gerald's mouth and tongue had looked exactly the same.

'You can close your mouth,' I said. 'Lie back and rest.' I stood up. 'I think I know what the trouble is,' I said to Brockley and drew him away towards the door. 'Have you had smallpox or cowpox, Brockley?'

'Smallpox as a boy, madam. Not badly. I'm not marked. And Fran's had it too.'

I nodded. Fran did have pockmarks, though they were not too noticeable.

Brockley said: 'Is that what Abel has?'

'I think so. I remember how it was with Gerald.' It hurt, even now, to remember Gerald's death; the ugliness of the disease which had destroyed his good looks so completely before finally destroying his life. 'We must make sure that no one comes near him who hasn't had one of the two diseases I've just mentioned. I know the queen has had the illness, and I know what treatment was given to her. Her doctor was more competent than Gerald's! We need red flannel . . . Oh, *damn*!'

Brockley looked shocked. He always did if a lady swore in his presence.

'We haven't got any,' I said. 'There's some back at Withysham, but not here.' It was used very often to make petticoats for the women servants, and at Christmas, Hugh and I always gave them new lengths of the material. We bought it in November. This was September, so we hadn't stocked up on it yet. 'Brockley, you'll have to ride to Woking in the morning and buy some. Buy plenty. We don't know who else may go down with this.'

'Red flannel, madam?'

'If someone with smallpox is wrapped in red material, it helps to bring out the rash, and people stand a better chance then. The queen once told me she thought it helped to prevent scarring as well. It's said to be useful for measles, too. This *could* be measles, but—'

'He's had measles,' said Brockley. 'We talked about it one day, comparing notes on childhood maladies.'

'Then this has to be smallpox. Saddle up first thing in the morning and go and get that flannel, Brockley! The Woking mercer, Bryant – I've often seen red flannel on that stall he puts outside his shop door. Try there.'

It was over six miles to Woking. The roads were dry, but all the same, Brown Berry must have toiled to cover the distance so fast, for next day Brockley was back within three hours, with one thick bundle of cloth on his back and two more sticking out of his saddlebags.

'I took all Bryant's stock, madam,' Brockley said, dismounting. 'He wouldn't have let me have it except that he has another consignment coming in tomorrow, by river barge. He said, what if this is the start of a local epidemic? If it is, there'll be a run on the stuff.'

'At least we have enough,' I said. 'Let someone else look after your horse. I want you to help Wilder wrap the flannel round Abel.'

It would be pleasanter for Abel, I thought, if those who had the task of stripping him and wrapping him in red flannel were men. But in the event, it was neither here nor there because poor Abel was unconscious.

We did all we could. He was swaddled in red flannel, and we also hung it over the one small window. We did our best to get nourishment into him in liquid form, coaxing him to swallow water and mulled wine and chicken broth; we made sure someone was always with him, day and night. The rash did come out, monstrously and horribly, but the attack was too severe. Two days later, he died.

By then, it was clear that Hawkswood had another casualty. Dorothy Beale had got it, too.

SEVEN
A Whisper in the Night

D isasters fell upon us like a hailstorm. No sooner had we got Dorothy into bed in the second of the rooms over the coach house, than a sad letter came from Meg's Aunt Anne. Uncle Ambrose had been seized with an apoplexy one hot afternoon and had died the same evening.

'His own fault,' said Hugh brusquely. 'Drinking too much and riding about in a heatwave, dressed for a blizzard!'

But Ambrose was family, whether or not I liked him, and I was sorry to have to pass such sad news to Meg. But I knew I must, so I reluctantly wrote a letter for Brockley to take the next day. He couldn't set off at once as he was on an errand to the Cobbolds. We had promised them one of Marigold's puppies, and as they were now old enough to leave their mother, Brockley had ridden off with a pup in a basket strapped to his back. He had looked thankful to be getting away for a while from the miserable atmosphere in the house, but he came home with a grave face and told us that Christina had smallpox too.

I dispatched him to Buckinghamshire the next morning with my letter to Meg and panicky instructions to let me know if she and George were well.

He was back by the following evening with the reassuring news that they were in perfect health and that, like Meg, George had had cowpox in his youth and had said it was common knowledge that this was a protection against the more serious disease. Hugh and I were relieved, but it seemed that any pleasant thing – a ride in the fresh sunshine for Brockley, and good news of my daughter's well-being for me – was instantly doomed to be buried under a further calamity. We woke next day to learn that our second groom, Simon, was feverish and so was one of our maidservants, seventeen-year-old Netta. And when I went to see them, yes, it was the pox.

Simon and Netta were the lucky ones, for they both recovered within three weeks, although they were noticeably marked. Netta cried dreadfully over her pocks. Simon, the first time he was fit enough to go to the well for water for the horse trough, found her fetching water for the kitchen and weeping into the bucket, where she had caught sight of her reflection.

He told her that her scars weren't as bad as she thought and were so commonplace anyway that no one would think anything of them, but at first, all she said, or sobbed, was that it didn't matter the same for a man. He soothed her, using, as he told me, the voice that he used for reassuring nervous horses. They became friends, and just before Christmas, they married. It was a happy union, and I like to think of that. At least one good thing came out of that catastrophic epidemic.

At the time, of course, all that lay in the future. At the time, we had three dangerously ill invalids on our hands. It was clear from the start, though, that Dorothy was far more ill than the other two. We put them all into the coach-house rooms, wrapped them in red flannel, kept them clean, and watched over them by day and by night. With Simon and Netta, the tide slowly began to turn. But with Dorothy, nothing checked the hideous progress of the illness. There came a moment when we knew that, as with Abel, Dorothy was not going to come through.

Looking back, I realize that for nearly a month, Hawkswood was ruled by smallpox. Dr Hibbert, the physician, came from Woking to see the patients, but he was little help. He agreed that we were already doing all that could or should be done, and that the outcome lay in the hands of God. He provided some medicine for reducing fever, but that was all, and we soon found that Gladys's herbal remedies were better than his anyway.

I rarely remember feeling so tired. There seemed no end to the nightmare. Simon and Netta might be mending, but Dorothy, though horribly ill, her whole skin a mass of oozing pustules, was not, and yet she did not slip away quickly as Abel had done, but lingered and lingered, and cried out in her distress. Finally, we cleaned and tidied a disused attic room in the roof of the house and carried her there, where she would not disturb the others. It meant that extra people were needed to look after them all but that couldn't be helped.

We formed a routine. Two maidservants who'd had the illness took charge of Netta and Simon, turn and turn about. Dorothy was cared for by Fran Dale, Sybil (who'd had cowpox) and myself, all snatching sleep as best we could.

Sybil and I usually shared the night watch. We would sit at a small table with a triple-branched candlestick on it, hour after hour, watching the light flicker on the sloping attic rafters. Every now and then, one of us would get up and give Dorothy some medicine, or a drink of milk or water; twice during the night we regularly moved her on to the floor and changed her sheets and nightgown, which were always stained with pus and excrement. We tried not to disturb her with talking, but we did exchange a few words now and then, in low voices, to keep each other awake, because exhaustion was our constant enemy. At dawn, before we could eat or rest, we would have to boil the dirtied linen and hang it out to dry. Hawkswood had good supplies of such things, but meeting Dorothy's needs was still a struggle.

After nine days, an evening came when we knew we must send for Dr Fletcher, if he were willing to come. He came at once, telling us not to worry about him; he'd had the pox in childhood. He gave Dorothy the last rites, Anglican style. She would no doubt have preferred Catholic ones, but they were illegal and Dorothy was scarcely conscious anyway. When he was done, he went away, promising to pray for us all, and we settled down for what we guessed would be the last night vigil at her side.

The hot weather was over. Summer was ending, the hours of darkness growing longer. The attic room had no hearth, but a small brazier had been brought in for warmth and we were glad of it. At some time after midnight, during the dead hours, rain began to rattle against the single dormer window. It was because of the rain that we didn't at first hear Dorothy trying to speak to us. Her mouth was full of sores, and she could only manage a weak and painful whisper. Then Sybil noticed

that her eyes were open and fixed on us, and that her mouth
was working. We sprang up and went to her.

'What is it?' I asked. 'Milk?' I was going to pick up the
mug of milk from the table by the bed, when a small hand,
as rough with pustules as a neglected ship's keel is with
barnacles, crept out from under the covers and clutched at my
wrist. Dorothy shook her head – slowly, because for her every
movement was pain, but definitely.

'Not. Milk,' she whispered. Every word was separate, an
effort in its own right. 'Confess.'

'Sweetheart, the vicar has been to see you, and you are
absolved of anything you have ever done amiss,' Sybil told her.

Another slow shake of the head. 'Not. Vicar. Mis . . . Mistress
Stannard. You.'

'You want to confess to me?' I said blankly.

'Yes. Master. Ferris. Sent me.'

'Dorothy, what do you mean?'

'Said. I must . . . tell him. Everything. That happens. Here.
What. People. Say. Do.' The halting murmur ended on a moan.
I held some milk to her lips. We had found that milk was the
drink that best soothed her painful mouth. She swallowed,
with difficulty, and then the hoarse account went on. Listening
to it was even anguish for us; God alone knew what it was
like for her.

'I asked to . . . visit. Aunt. No aunt.' Weakly, Dorothy shook
her head, repudiating the existence of an aunt. 'Met. Someone.
From Ferris place. Twice. Told about . . . Christina. Meeting
Thomas. How Master. Ferris . . . knew. Sorry. So kind . . .'

I said in bewilderment: 'But why? Why should Master
Ferris . . .?'

Again that slow shake of the head. 'Don't. Know. Paid. Told
me, get you, Mistress . . . give Christina . . . medicine . . .
any medicine. Said . . . don't ask why . . . but . . . all for the
Faith. Paid more. In advance. Money . . . useful.'

'All right. Don't try to talk any more,' I said. 'Just rest. You
may feel better tomorrow and . . .'

'No. Dying. Or. I wouldn't . . .'

But the faint, tortured voice was failing now. Her eyes
closed. The hand that still lay on my wrist fell away. She was

slipping back into unconsciousness. Just before dawn, she slipped further, into death.

'But why?' I said in bewilderment. 'What is the matter with Walter Ferris? We've never done him any harm, yet he bursts into Meg's wedding feast and hurls wild accusations at me – and now it seems that before that he planted a spy on us and paid her to tell him things and to get me, for some reason, to give potions to Christina! Not to poison her, just to give her any kind of potion! Where's the sense in that? It's so unreasonable. Perhaps Dorothy was just delirious.'

It was the afternoon of the next day. Dorothy still lay in the attic, covered with a sheet, and down in Hawkswood churchyard, the sexton was busy with his spade, preparing her last bed.

Sybil and I had laid her out and washed away the smell and the contamination and burned the old gowns we had used for our nursing duties. Some people said that such clothes could carry contagion. I had gathered Hugh, Brockley, Dale and Sybil together, and Hugh had led us all out into the rose garden, because, as Hugh frankly said, after the stench and the stifling air of sickrooms, we would probably be thankful to take in the fresh air and the scent of the last late roses.

Brockley, as confused as I was, said: 'Madam, you say that Dorothy seemed to be telling you that her aunt in Priors Ford doesn't exist. That's true. I rode over there this morning. I thought, well, better make sure. If Dorothy *did* have an aunt, someone should tell her what's happened.'

'Quite,' said Hugh. 'And you didn't find any aunt? Priors Ford is a tiny place, so I suppose enquiries weren't too difficult.'

'No, they weren't, sir,' Brockley said. 'The village is small, but it has an alehouse and a little church. I tried the alehouse first. Didn't Dorothy say to you, madam, that her aunt wasn't young and lived on her own?'

'Yes, Brockley. That's so.'

'I asked if there were any such women in the village, and the innkeeper said yes, two of them, but he'd never heard tell that either had a niece and neither's called Beale. Then I tried the vicar. He's a big fat man,' said Brockley disparagingly, 'with not enough to do in that little parish. No long rides for him, to get to parishioners miles away, and just as well, for he'd make the poor horse sag in the middle. He said the same as the alehouse keeper, and he'd never heard the name Beale, either. Said he'd know if either of the two women that live on their own had relatives called that. In my opinion, madam, it's true that Dorothy hadn't got an aunt there.'

'In which case,' said Hugh, 'the rest of her confession is probably true, and not the result of delirium. She used to work for the Ferrises, didn't she? But why Walter should behave towards us in such a way – I have no idea, none at all. When he interrupted the feast, it seemed to be because he was in a rage about Thomas meeting Christina here. But he apparently sent Dorothy to us long before that. I can't understand any of this.'

'Dorothy seemed to be saying that it was she who told Ferris about that meeting,' I said thoughtfully. 'Though how she can have known about it . . . Oh!'

'You've thought of something?' Sybil asked.

'Yes. When I came up with them, they were under that bay tree in the corner of the herb garden, only feet from the fence round the wood. We heard a rustling in the wood and a twig snapped. I thought it was an animal – something making a kill, maybe. I'd seen a fox that night. But it might have been Dorothy. Maybe she followed Christina too and was ahead of me. She could have slipped past them through the knot garden. They were so engrossed in each other, I doubt if they'd have noticed her despite the moonlight. She could have gone through the gate into the wood to spy on them from there.'

'Very likely,' said Hugh. 'Well, we can't ask her now.'

'I think,' I said, 'that we have every reason to ask Walter Ferris for an explanation, except . . .'

'I wouldn't want to go near him,' said Fran Dale. Fran's pockmarks always seemed more obvious when she was upset, and just now they were very evident indeed, and her protuberant blue eyes were scared. 'When he came here, shouting, he looked half-mad!' she said.

'But how else can we get to the bottom of this?' I asked.

'We'd better bury poor Dorothy first,' Hugh said.

EIGHT
Connections

I t was a quiet funeral, as Abel's had been. Afterwards, Hugh and I were not sure what to do next. It was all very well to say that we ought to ask Walter Ferris to explain his behaviour, but when it came to putting the idea into practice we recoiled.

'We *need* to ask him, but how can we?' I said to Hugh, on the third day after the funeral. 'Or rather, how can you? I wouldn't dare to go near Ferris myself, and if you call on him, he might well refuse to see you.'

'I could send a formal request to meet Ferris on neutral ground, I suppose,' said Hugh unenthusiastically.

We fell silent. We were sharing a settle in the smaller of our two parlours. It was our favourite. It had a window seat and cushioned settles, light-coloured panelling and a view towards the courtyard and the gatehouse, so that we could keep an eye on the comings and goings of the household and its visitors. We were on our own, for there was an unspoken arrangement that when Hugh and I were in the little parlour we would not be disturbed unless we called someone in, or something unusual made an interruption necessary.

Our quiet moment was ended that morning as Hero and Hector suddenly shot across the courtyard, barking. We turned to look out just as, with a clatter and a rumble, half a dozen horsemen rode in, followed by four matched bay horses pulling a heavy coach. The horsemen wore livery that we knew.

The cavalcade halted in the courtyard. Arthur Watts and Joseph, our youngest groom, came running from the tack room to silence the dogs and take the horses' heads. One of the outriders sprang from his saddle to open the coach door, and out came Sir William Cecil, Secretary of State, followed by his usual entourage of clerk and valet. Adam Wilder appeared from somewhere to greet him, and the little group made for the house – slowly, because Cecil was leaning heavily on his stick.

'Now what on earth,' said Hugh in astonishment, 'brings *him* here? He sent no warning.'

'And he doesn't like travelling, because of his gout,' I said, equally surprised. I knew that Cecil found it difficult enough following the queen from palace to palace along the Thames, with Windsor at one end of the line and Greenwich at the other, even though he could make those journeys the easy way, by barge. Accompanying the queen on her summer progresses, which meant lengthy journeys by coach, was an ordeal he dreaded. He made occasional social visits, like the one to us earlier in the year, but we hadn't expected him to repeat that for a long time. Whatever had brought him here now, unheralded, must be important. We waited, full of conjecture, until Adam Wilder brought our unexpected caller in.

I had known Cecil well for many years. I had great respect for his honesty and intelligence, and because of the pain he suffered from his gout, I also felt sympathy for him, just as I did for Hugh with his rheumatic knees. In Cecil's case, I also sympathized because his responsibilities as Secretary of State were so heavy. His long, bearded face was always serious, and between his eyes was a permanent line of worry that deepened every year.

But he had a ruthless side. He and the queen, once they had discovered my gift for intrigue, had not hesitated to use me. They had paid well for my services, but on occasion their treatment of me had been very ruthless indeed. As, for instance, when they deceived me and Matthew into believing each other to be dead.

They had their reasons, but I would never forget the shock when I learned the truth. Now I found myself quivering with anxiety, afraid of what this visit might portend. Before Cecil reached the parlour, I was bracing myself to say that whatever mission he wanted to send me on this time, the answer must be no. I wanted to stay here, in safety, with Hugh. I *would* stay here. I wouldn't give in. Not ever again.

Hugh and I rose, of course, as Wilder brought Cecil in. Joan

Flood followed with a tray of refreshments. Her work was supposed to be in the kitchen, but with Simon and Netta still abed, in need of care, and taking up the time of two maidservants, the usual household arrangements were in disarray.

Joan, who was good-natured, quite often did extra jobs to help. Wilder cast a professional eye over the goblets, the wine, the little meat pies and the dish of sweetmeats, expressed approval, thanked her for lending a hand, and withdrew, taking her with him.

'And so,' said Hugh, resuming his seat while I filled the three goblets with wine, 'where have you travelled from today, Sir William? You will dine with us, of course. Will you be staying the night?'

'I started out early from Hampton Court,' said Cecil. 'I'll return this evening. I doubt if you want overnight guests just at present. I am aware that you are having an outbreak of the pox.'

'We hope the worst is over,' I said. 'There have been two deaths in the household, but two other victims are recovering well. How did you know about it?'

Cecil sipped wine and considered me gravely over the rim of his goblet.

'Ursula,' he said, 'although you seem lately to have retired from public life, you have quite a history behind you, and then there is your relationship to the queen, which is more widely known than either she or I would really wish. We keep watch over you, more than you realize.'

'Indeed?' I said warily. I seated myself again.

'I don't mean that I have a paid informer in your house,' Cecil told me. 'I haven't.'

I was glad to hear it. Dorothy had been that, and one paid spy under my roof, I felt, was one too many.

'But there are those who, at my request – and unpaid – let me know of events here,' Cecil said. 'I know all about the outbreak of sickness, and all about the shocking scene at your daughter's wedding. Dr Fletcher, your vicar, sent me a full account of that, the very next day.'

'He is one of your informants, then?' I asked.

'With your well-being in mind,' said Cecil. 'He is not a

spy. He simply keeps me aware of Hawkswood news, as far as he can. I must ask you not to tell him that you know, and not to think the worse of him. He is a safeguard for you, not an enemy. Please don't take offence. You are valued, and both I and the queen wish to protect you.'

Hugh and I were both very still.

'Threats,' said Cecil, helping himself to a pie, 'were made against you on that day, Ursula, by one Walter Ferris, who burst into the midst of Meg's wedding feast in order to utter them. I have no idea why. But I am sorry to say that his threats look like coming true. I came to warn you.'

'But . . .' I began, and then stopped, bewildered.

'That's absurd,' said Hugh. 'All Walter Ferris could come up with was some nonsense about a soothing draught that my wife brewed for Christina Cobbold. She was one of the brides-maids . . .'

'I know. The Cobbolds are friends of yours, and they have a long-standing quarrel with the Ferris family,' said Cecil. 'Dr Fletcher informed me of that some time ago.'

'A ridiculous situation,' said Hugh, 'that has hardened over the generations, and no one on either side has had the good sense to shout *stop*. Ferris tried to pretend that his son, who is in love with Christina, had paid my wife to make the draught for her and that it was a love potion. But there are people here who can testify to its harmless ingredients and its innocent purpose. And love potions aren't illegal, anyway.'

'Nevertheless,' said Cecil, 'a complaint has been laid, with Sir Edward Heron, the Sheriff of Surrey. He got in touch with me at once. He is aware of your importance to the court, Ursula – and of your link with the queen. He is therefore hesitant about taking action against you. But the complaint isn't a mere matter of a love potion. It claims that you have caused death by witchcraft.'

'It claims – what?' I said blankly. 'What death? Whose?'

'There were the two deaths here, from smallpox,' said Cecil. 'And others have suffered the same disease, to the peril of their lives. One of them, according to Dr Fletcher, is Christina Cobbold. She is recovering, but her life was in danger for a time and she will be scarred.'

'But . . . people are always catching smallpox,' I protested. There was a cold, hollow feeling in the pit of my stomach. I tried to cling to common sense. 'What has witchcraft to do with it? Do you mean that Walter Ferris is accusing me . . .? But he wouldn't care a straw if Christina Cobbold *had* died, and he's probably delighted that she's going to be marked. It may cool his son's ardour!'

'Ferris isn't the one who laid the complaint,' said Cecil. 'That was Christina's mother, Jane Cobbold.'

'Jane *Cobbold* . . .! Look, Jane doesn't like Ursula particularly.' Hugh looked uncomfortable. 'When we were first married, the Cobbolds invited us to dine, and while Jane was showing Ursula round their garden, Anthony asked me how we'd met. I let out to him that Ursula had been on a mission for the queen at the time, one that brought her into danger. I was proud of you, Ursula. You were – you are – a loyal subject of the queen, and a courageous one. But I suppose Anthony told Jane what I'd said, and gradually, I realized that Jane, well, has attitudes that are different from mine.'

'She can't understand me,' I said. 'I think she believes that ladies shouldn't mix themselves up in political affairs, let alone dangerous ones. I fancy she feels I could be – perhaps am – an unhealthy influence where Christina is concerned! But that doesn't explain *this*!'

'Indeed it doesn't!' said Hugh. 'You have always been courteous to Jane and careful not to interfere in any way with Christina's ideas. You've never done anything to provoke Jane Cobbold into such extremes.'

I had never heard Hugh sound so nonplussed.

'With the Cobbolds and the Ferrises at daggers drawn as they are,' he said, 'the mere fact that Walter made such a threat ought to make the Cobbolds *not* want to make it. If you follow me.'

'Mistress Jane Cobbold is angry, just the same,' Cecil said. 'The gravamen of the accusation is that you, Ursula, together with a known witch, Gladys Morgan, who lives in this house, created the outbreak of smallpox by using witchcraft to conjure it up. As I said, Sir Edward Heron is hesitating. It's a serious charge, of a kind he usually pursues all too eagerly, but it's

quite true that smallpox is one of life's natural hazards. He
knows that. I understand, in fact, that Walter Ferris's daughter
died of it recently, in Hampshire.'

'Yes,' I said. 'I heard about that when I interrupted a secret
assignation that Thomas had with Christina. Ferris bellowed
about their meeting when he burst in on us, so I take it that
Dr Fletcher has told you about it.'

'Yes,' said Cecil. 'He did.'

'I disturbed the two of them in the garden,' I said. 'I ordered
Thomas to leave and I took Christina back indoors, but before
I did that, they insisting on telling me about Thomas's sister.
It seems that he sought Christina out for the sake of comfort.
His own family weren't offering him much. Thomas said his
father was still at his sister's home then, helping with funeral
arrangements.'

'Quite. You can hardly be linked with that death. It was
clearly natural, and that's one of the things that has made
Heron pause to think,' Cecil said. 'But there are the other
cases, which seemed to originate here, and also one of the
wedding guests, Meg's uncle, Ambrose Blanchard, has died
suddenly, of an apoplexy. It seems that Mistress Cobbold knew
of that and spoke of it to Sir Edward.'

'*How* did she know?' I demanded.

'I can't tell you that, but it's a fact. It's one more death that
could be put down to sorcery.'

'Oh, really!' I spluttered.

'Sir Edward does, passionately, consider that witchcraft
should be illegal in all its forms, not only when used for
harmful purposes,' Cecil said. 'He values his position, and he
doesn't want to get into bad odour with me or the queen, but
nevertheless, Mistress Cobbold's accusation is one he might
well decide to pursue if he has any further excuse.'

'He has no excuse at all!' said Hugh angrily. 'Ferris's charge
about the love potion is absurd, and I don't call either an
outbreak of smallpox or the death, in hot weather, of a hard-
drinking man from apoplexy very convincing evidence!'

'Nor do I,' said Cecil. 'But I think, Ursula, that you should
be on your guard from now on. If I didn't feel that so strongly,
I wouldn't be here now. Tell me, has Gladys Morgan done

anything of late that could bring her within the grip of the
law? The queen pardoned her once, but a pardon isn't a decla-
ration of innocence. Gladys Morgan is still a convicted
sorceress.'

'Gladys has behaved perfectly since her reprieve,' said Hugh.
'She has done nothing – *nothing* – that could possibly be a
reason for raking up the past.'

'She hasn't annoyed a local physician by prescribing for
his patients and jeering at his remedies?' asked Cecil, who
knew all the details of the charge which had once nearly
brought Gladys to the gallows. 'Or cursed anyone? If she has
dosed or cursed anyone who has since died, a new charge
could be brought against her, to strengthen the one against
you, Ursula. You have been her champion. That *could* force
Heron to act.'

I thought about the hair-raising curses Gladys had hurled
at people in the past and shuddered. 'Since we brought her
home, she hasn't done either of those things,' I said. 'Or
anything else.'

'Then I should think,' said Cecil, 'that any enquiry would
fall very flat, even if Heron were to set one in hand. I have
recommended him to say as much to Mistress Cobbold and
explain to her carefully that, for that reason, he can't justify
an enquiry. But I repeat, I urge caution on you. I feel there is
ill will here, directed against you, Ursula.'

I shook my head in puzzlement. 'I think so too, but I can't
understand it. Neither Hugh nor I have any quarrel with either
the Ferrises or the Cobbolds. Christina Cobbold and Thomas
Ferris did manage to meet while Christina was here, but that
can't be behind all this mysterious animus.' I told him about
Dorothy Beale's confession. 'She came here before Christina
and Thomas had their secret tryst. It's like a sum that won't
add up straight.'

Cecil sighed and shifted what was obviously a painful left
leg. 'I can't offer you an explanation. I came to tell you the
facts so that you would be prepared, if after all anything did
come of this attempt to blacken your name, Ursula. You see, if
there is a serious purpose behind it . . . and I have to say that
I smell one . . . then if this attempt fails, there could be another.'

I looked at Hugh, and he at me. He shrugged helplessly. 'I think,' he said, 'that it is time to dine.' He looked at Cecil. 'We hope that the outbreak of disease is over but . . . you have had the pox?'

'When I was three. I brought no one with me who has not had it. I fancy we can dine here with impunity.'

'You will be welcome,' I said, unhappily but graciously. This time, Cecil really did have my well-being at heart. I could not accuse him of ruthlessness now.

Cecil left after dinner. Afterwards, we told Sybil and the Brockleys – all of whom were agog with wondering why he had come – all that had passed between us. I didn't know what to say to Gladys. The news couldn't be hidden from her since it included a warning that she should be careful. But how on earth I was to explain that her questionable past now posed a threat to me? It would be like hitting her. Gladys was old. Her brush with the gallows had terrified her, and she had grown frailer in recent months. I quailed, imagining the hurt I would see in her eyes.

Brockley, who disliked her but had brought her into the household in the first place, said he would undertake to tell her and would do so in the morning. 'You should go out on Roundel to enjoy some fresh summer air while I do so, madam, and let the wind blow away your worries.'

I took his advice, but although the outing was pleasant, I came back as full of anxiety and bewilderment as ever. Hugh was in his study, playing chess with himself, and I too felt the need to occupy my mind with something intellectually demanding; something that would compel me to think about subjects less emotionally upsetting than Edward Heron, Ferris, Cobbolds and witchcraft.

Until three months before her wedding, Meg had had a tutor, and I had often shared her studies, as I had a liking for Latin and Greek, a taste I shared with my royal sister. I got out my copy of Homer's *Odyssey* and took it to the small parlour, where I sat down to read it. It was a better distraction than needlework. But I was not left quiet for long. Hugh appeared almost as soon as I had settled myself, and behind him trooped the Brockleys, Sybil Jester and Gladys, in a solemn deputation.

'What is it?' I said, alarmed.

I was addressing Hugh, but it was Gladys who answered, speaking out of turn as was her wont. 'I bin that upset. Didn't close an eye last night for fretting, I didn't. To think of you, Mistress Stannard, being accused of witchy doings, just because of being kind to me. Lot of nonsense, that's what it is, and I'd curse them as did it, except I promised meself I wouldn't curse anyone any more, not after what happened to me. But I'd *like* to! Accusing you of a thing like that . . .!'

'All right, Gladys,' said Hugh. 'We all feel the same. But no one's blaming you. There's nothing against you now, and we're going to protect you, just as we always have. It's right that you should be here in this room now, because you have been dragged into this, but what we're here for, Ursula, is something different. Sybil has had an idea. She told Fran Dale and Brockley here, and they came to me with it – Gladys seems to have joined them in mid-progress – and I said, at once, we must bring it to you.'

He said *mid-progress* with a smile, trying to make a joke of it, as though the four of them, walking to his study, were the equivalent of one of Queen Elizabeth's annual tours of her realm, but it didn't quite work. The situation was too serious for that.

'Sybil has an idea?' I said. 'What kind of idea?'

Hugh, with a gesture, invited everyone to sit, and they all disposed themselves on the window seat and the settles. Then he nodded to Sybil, who said: 'I didn't sleep much last night, any more than Gladys. And a thought came to me. It's so strange, Walter Ferris sending Dorothy to spy on you, and then coming here to attack you as he did, all for no reason that anyone can see; and now Jane Cobbold is being nearly as bad. Didn't you tell us, Mistress Stannard, that Cecil himself said there must be something behind all this? And then I remembered that letter from the Netherlands. From Anne Percy, the Countess of Northumberland, who is now in exile. You told me about it, if you remember, Mistress Stannard.'

'Yes. So I did. But what . . .?'

'Maybe she's the source,' said Sybil. 'Maybe Anne Percy, that we all thought couldn't possibly harm you, has managed it after all.'

'Anne Percy,' I said slowly. 'Sir William didn't mention her, and nor did we.' He probably didn't know about her letter, I thought, since I was sure that the busy Dr Fletcher didn't.

'Maybe,' said Sybil, 'it all stems from her.'

NINE
Out of Nowhere

'If you remember, madam,' said Brockley, 'I wondered the same thing, when I had that narrow escape from being arrested for theft.'

'Yes.' I looked at Sybil. 'Now that you've said it, it seems obvious.'

It did. It was as though some obtrusive animal, such as a dancing bear, had been wandering round the house and till now been unaccountably ignored.

And yet . . .

'I can't see *how*,' I said. 'I mean, I can't see how she could reach out from the Netherlands and be responsible for the things that Ferris and Jane Cobbold have done.'

'Nor can I,' Hugh said. 'And I am not one to imagine connections where no connections are. But there has been quite a succession of incidents, beginning with you, Brockley. That necklace *could* have got into your saddlebag through carelessness on someone's part but . . .'

'Anne Percy's letter threatened me, as well as the mistress,' Brockley said. 'I feel it was lucky for me that I found the little stranger in time.'

'Yes, indeed,' Hugh said. 'And – well, here is something else that most of you don't know. I'm wondering now if it's part of the same pattern. When we visited Mrs Ward and Mrs Seldon in Woking, I discovered a book in their house – a book about sorcery. They were, I think, truly shocked to find it there, and were grateful to me for burning it, which I did, in their kitchen fire. They have not wanted to welcome Walter Ferris to their house since that disgraceful exhibition here, but he used to call on them, and it was apparently his idea that they should invite us to their house.'

'Do you mean,' I said, feeling my way, 'that he could have

put the book there himself? And then tried to . . . to encourage
the friendship between us . . . so that if the book were discovered . . .'

'If they were accused of witchcraft,' said Hugh, 'their
associates might come under suspicion, too. Probably would,
in Heron's eyes. Ferris would only have to lay a complaint
against the two ladies, to start Heron off. Heron is apparently
doubtful about proceeding against you, Ursula. But if evidence
– such as friendship with a pair of witches – should come to
light, he might do so. It's similar to your necklace episode,
Brockley. You had a piece of jewellery planted on you; the
ladies Ward and Seldon had a book of sorcery planted on them.'

'But where can Anne Percy come in?' I said.

'I know.' Hugh frowned. 'A piece of the pattern is missing.
If there's a link between the former Countess of Northumberland
and the Ferrises, then what is it? Though there is one thing.
The Ferrises are Catholic, just as she is. It was a Catholic
rising that you, Ursula, helped to defeat.'

'The Cobbolds aren't Catholics,' I said. 'They wouldn't lift
a finger to oblige Anne Percy any more than they would to
oblige a Ferris! So how on earth can Jane Cobbold come into
it? She can't be in any kind of partnership with Ferris! I really
think that if a Cobbold saw a Ferris – any Ferris – drowning
in a river, he or she would just stand and watch. And vice
versa.'

'I know,' Sybil said quietly. 'I said all those things to myself
during the night. But if we are ever to find out what lies behind
this . . . this persecution . . . we must start somewhere. I can't
shake off the feeling that Anne Percy *is* the hidden cause. How
the Cobbolds come to be caught up in it, I can't guess, but
perhaps we'll find out if we probe.'

Fran Dale, sitting in the corner of a settle, said: 'It's all
dreadful. I can't abide such things. We all thought life was
going to be just peaceful for the future, with nothing more to
be afraid of. We've had so many frightening times in the past.
And now this!'

'I feel the same,' I said. 'But how can we find out if there
is any link between the Ferrises and Anne Percy? Apart from
their religion, I mean?'

'Cecil would know,' said Hugh. 'Sybil, I wish you'd thought of this before he left! We could have asked him. His records probably include family trees for all the great families in the land and details of their properties and their tenants and their friends. He could have looked it all up by now, and his answer could be on its way to us this very minute!'

'It's only twelve miles or so to Hampton Court,' I said. 'Brockley and I could set off to find him, this very day. If the court is still at Hampton, we can be back by nightfall, and if the court's moved on and he's gone with it, well, we'll just have to chase him until we catch up. We'd better prepare to be away for at least one night . . .'

'Easy, easy,' Hugh said. 'Tomorrow will do. I think we should put our question in writing. You never know; you might not be able to speak to him immediately – he could be caught up in council meetings or attending on the queen. He's a busy man. But a letter could be taken to him, and I expect he'd find a moment to read it and ask someone to look up the details we want. Yes, tomorrow will have to do. We have to write the letter first!'

Writing it was more difficult than either Hugh or I expected. Since Cecil knew nothing of Anne Percy's threats, they had to be explained, and he might well think he should have been told at once; that if the former Countess of Northumberland were trying to injure one of Queen Elizabeth's subjects (let alone relatives) in Queen Elizabeth's very realm, it shouldn't be hidden either from him or from Elizabeth.

We had therefore to express ourselves tactfully, to explain that we hadn't taken Anne Percy's threats seriously because we couldn't see how, living on what was probably a none too generous pension in the Netherlands, she could possibly attack us. But in view of recent events, we were beginning to think we might have been mistaken, and therefore, we would like to know . . .

'I can think of one other enquiry we could make,' Hugh said as he tore up the second unsatisfactory draft. 'What about that courier – the one who brought Anne Percy's letter to you? If the same man carried any message to Ferris – or the Cobbolds – that could be evidence of contact between them.'

'I suppose so,' I said doubtfully. 'If she sent the two letters – to Ferris and to me – at the same time. But they might have been sent separately, and then the Ferris one could well have been delivered by a different courier or even by Anne Percy's own messenger.'

'At a guess,' Hugh said, 'I should think that however many times the Countess sent a letter by way of Norwich, a local courier would have been used. I fancy the dear lady's household members wouldn't care for the idea of travelling through England in case they were recognized and seized. There were enough hangings after the rising to make them nervous! So if there was another letter besides ours, whether at the same time or not, and it came into the country at Norwich, Twelvetrees *could* have been the man who carried it onwards. Didn't he say he'd been recommended? He may be well known in Norwich. I think we could mention him. Where's the harm? Now, let's begin again . . .'

It was so difficult to get the wording just right that it took up most of the afternoon. In the end we reached what we felt was the best possible version, placed both our signatures at the foot and sealed the letter. I would leave in the morning, with Brockley as an escort. Hugh found our efforts tiring and, having stamped the seal, said he would go to our room and lie down. I was not tired, but the evening stretched tediously ahead. I tried once more to settle to reading Greek.

And was defeated within twenty minutes by an outbreak of domestic confusion.

We had three grooms, not counting Brockley. Arthur Watts, our official head groom (who was now our coachman), was a middle-aged, gnarled little gnome of a man, apt to be impatient with his underlings but endlessly gentle with the horses. His second in command was Simon, who was at the moment ill, and then came Joseph, the junior. Joseph had attended Dorothy's funeral, and it now transpired that he had been in love with her.

'He's doing his work, ma'am,' said Arthur, when Wilder had transmitted a request that I should go to the stable yard to talk to him, 'because I've seen to that, but he keeps crying while he does it and he can't see straight and the mess he's made of cleaning your Roundel's tack, well, I hardly like to say outright what I think of it. Bits of grass still stuck in the bridle and smears on the saddle; it's a disgrace. With Simon sick and Joseph as useless as if he was drunk – well, how am I to manage? I've only one pair of hands . . .'

'I'll lend him mine,' said Brockley resignedly when I had found him in the hall and explained the situation to him. 'Leave Roundel's tack to me.'

With relief, I did, only to be accosted, as I was returning to the parlour and my Homer, by a large and exasperated John Hawthorn.

'It's Joan Flood, Mistress Stannard. She's a kind, helpful woman, but she's too damned helpful, that's the trouble.'

Joan, it transpired, was now being helpful to the pox-stricken Netta. It had been agreed when we took Netta on that part of her wages should consist of some eggs and butter, and that every other Wednesday she should be allowed to take these to her mother in Hawkswood village. This would have been one of her Wednesdays, but as she was ill, Joan had kindly offered to do the errand for her, and at the same time to reassure her mother that Netta was being well cared for and recovering.

'Only, I still have supper to make, and when I want Joan to beat the eggs for the quiches, where is she?' Hawthorn had a meat cleaver in his hand, which he now brandished indignantly. 'Gone off to Hawkswood to comfort Netta's mother, *and* taken more eggs than she should have at that. Maybe there's some in the henhouse, but with half the servants sick-nursing, I only have Ben Flood and young Phoebe, who are doing the pastry between them, and the spit boy who's got to watch the fire, and little Tessie who's scared of going to the poultry yard because she's frightened of the cockerel. Dear God, how I miss Abel! I can't collect eggs *and* make quiche fillings *and* get the mutton steaks on the spit, enough for everyone, at the same time; I've only one pair of hands . . .'

Sybil and I went to the kitchen to beat the eggs ourselves and to shape some little marchpane fancies which Joan would normally have made. After that, we had a further absurd crisis when Tessie, our newest and most timid maidservant, only fourteen and small, tried to balance a trayload of glassware in one hand while opening the heavy hall door with the other and let all the glasses cascade off the tray to the floor.

'There isn't a whole one left!' thundered Wilder, and although he didn't actually clout poor Tessie he did make a threatening gesture, whereupon Tessie burst into tears. I felt like clouting her myself, but she was so terrified that, as a human being, I felt obliged to comfort her instead. I retired to bed feeling as though I had been put through a mangle and afraid I wouldn't be able to manage the early start I had planned. However, I slept soundly and woke to find that the day promised well, with a clear sky overhead and a little pale mist drifting from the direction of our lake. A waning moon still hung in the sky, and there was a trace of autumn sharpness in the air. It was pleasant riding weather.

And then, as Brockley and I were in the hall, at one end of the long table, breaking our fast with small ale, bread and honey and cold chicken legs, there was something else to disturb me.

Dale was sharing the early breakfast with us, and as ever when I was about to go off somewhere with Brockley, there was a look in her eyes that made me uncomfortable.

The time when Brockley and I had very nearly become more than lady and servant was far behind us. But though that tide had long since gone out, it had left its residue behind, as an ebbing sea leaves flotsam on a beach. Now and then, Brockley and I would find ourselves sharing a joke that others couldn't see, or referring to some past event, some danger or adventure that we had shared, and although I doubted whether Brockley had ever told her of that moment on the brink, Dale, who loved him, had read the clues.

For a long time, I knew, she had sheltered in the knowledge that I was married to Hugh and had given that side of my life to him alone. But during the adventure in the north, when we encountered the Countess of Northumberland, Brockley and I had had an extraordinary moment of rapport which had probably saved our lives but had also left a mark, an atmosphere. Love brings its own awareness. Since then, several times, I had seen the jealousy in her eyes.

Hugh himself knew perfectly well that he had no need to worry. My erstwhile husband Matthew de la Roche had been a far bigger threat, but I had chosen Hugh instead. After that, he was unlikely to lie awake over Brockley. But with Dale, it was different.

The problem was that I could not think of a way of lancing the boil. Simply to say: '*It's all right, Dale; I would never hurt you and nor would Brockley; your bond with him is safe,*' would be to admit that grounds existed for doubting that safety. So I ate my bread and honey and cold chicken in silence, aware of Dale's eyes watching me, with pain in them and even resentment, while I was quite unable to offer her any comfort.

Then we were out in the courtyard, mounting our horses. Brockley's sturdy cob Brown Berry turned his head as his master adjusted the girth, and nudged him with a hopeful muzzle, causing Brockley to delve into his belt pouch, produce an apple, and present it to him. I too had an apple for Roundel, but the mare waited politely for me to bring it to her attention.

'She's a lady. Now, Berry's just plain greedy,' Brockley said, rubbing the cob's ears affectionately.

We had a few spare clothes in saddlebags, in case we had to stay away overnight, but did not burden ourselves with food or water bottles. Twelve miles wasn't that far, and there were inns on the way, in any case. We set off, with Dale blowing a kiss to Brockley as we departed.

By this time, the morning had become warm. The mist was gone and so was the sharpness. Before we had covered the three miles to Priors Ford, we felt too hot, and we paused to shed our cloaks, roll them up and push them into our saddlebags.

Beyond the village, the land was mostly open heath, dotted with clumps of gorse, much of it in bloom. There were one or two spinneys but nothing one could call a wood. The heath was not much used for grazing, as the grass was coarse and mixed with thistles. A few donkeys were pastured there, on long tethers, but that was all.

'Not even sheep,' Brockley remarked. 'Going to waste, if you ask me.'

'It's common land,' I told him. 'But the Ferrises come here for hawking, I think. Hugh says they've always been fond of the sport, and I believe there's a patch of woodland inside their boundary fence, where they rear pheasants just for that. They beat the woods to send them this way and then go after them with goshawks.'

'Rough ground for headlong galloping,' Brockley said, regarding the heath with an expert eye and talking to me over his shoulder, since at this point the track was too narrow for us to ride abreast. 'The Hawkswood meadows are much better. It can't be easy to guide a horse over terrain like this when you've only got one hand because there's a great big goshawk on the other arm, flapping its wings as likely as not. They're heavy, goshawks are, specially the females. I wouldn't care for it myself . . . *Christ almighty!*'

It seemed to come from nowhere. There was a vicious *whoosh* as something skimmed the saddle pommel in front of Brockley and buried itself in the thistles and grass on the other side of the track. Brown Berry threw up his head and skittered in alarm.

'Crossbow bolt!' I shouted. It had come, I thought, from behind a big clump of gorse on our left. I had glimpsed a movement there. 'Brockley, *go!*' I screamed, and spurred Roundel forward.

Brockley at once leant forward to urge Brown Berry into a gallop, but as he did so, another bolt sang towards him. Again, it missed Brockley, but to my horror I saw it lodge in Berry's flank, just behind the saddle.

Whereupon, the cob bolted. Roundel tore after him, but Berry's speed was astounding. Normally, we took it for granted that Roundel, who had Barbary blood, was faster. Berry was a good steady saddle horse; Roundel was fleet. Not this time. This time, the fleeing Berry, keeping to the track out of habit, even though it curved, once round an abandoned cottage and then again round one of the few spinneys, produced a turn of speed that left Roundel, though she was doing her utmost, trailing behind.

Gasping encouragement to her, I was thankful for the cottage and the spinney, which between them must be putting barriers between us and the unknown crossbowman. I hoped to God that whoever it was didn't have a horse. And who *was* it? Those bolts had been aimed at Brockley, not at me.

Years ago, a man called John Wilton, a good servant of mine, had gone on an errand to Cecil and had not returned alive. I had not forgotten. I never would. Had I now brought catastrophe on Brockley, as well?

We careered onwards. The track streamed back beneath Roundel's hooves, seeming to flow like water. The wind of our passage buffeted my ears. On either side, the heath gave way to scattered trees and then to real, thick woodland, with trees and hazel bushes, all crowding closer to the track than they should have done. Landlords and local authorities were supposed to cut trees well back on either side of any main track, to make life more difficult for robbers. Whoever was responsible for this district was careless.

We had gone about a mile when, ahead of me, Brown Berry suddenly swerved, leaving the track after all and veering left on to the narrow belt of unkempt grass between path and woodland. He charged on, straight towards a hazel brake. I cried out, thinking he would crash headlong into it, but at the last moment he shied and reared, flinging Brockley to the ground. Then he collapsed into the grass.

I hauled on my reins and swung Roundel towards them. As I did so, Brown Berry, raising his head, let out a dreadful cry, a shrieking whinny, of pain and protest and desolation. His head dropped. I brought Roundel to a stop, scrambled down, flung her reins over her head and dragged her forward the last few steps. Brockley's cob lay quiet in the grass with hazel branches drooping over him and the crossbow bolt still sticking out of his flank. Blood oozed from the place, rolling across his hide, sluggishly now, for there was no heartbeat to drive it. Brown Berry was dead.

Brockley was on his feet, limping a little but otherwise uninjured. He came to my side and knelt, stroking Berry's neck. 'Poor old fellow. Poor Berry.' He looked up at me. 'I loved this horse! He was sweet-tempered, reliable. Used to turn his head and whicker when I came into the stable. Trotted up to me if he was out on the pasture. No trouble to catch, ever. The sort of horse you think of as a friend. If I ever lay hands on the bugger who did this to him, I'll screw his head clean off his shoulders!'

Brockley rarely swore, and certainly not in my presence. This was a sign of how angry he was. And not just angry. There were tears on his face as well. When he said he loved Brown Berry, he meant just that.

I touched his arm. 'I know. But, Brockley, we've got to get under cover. I think whoever did this was hiding behind a gorse clump, and I think I glimpsed a horse's tail. We may be pursued. Put your saddlebags over Roundel's saddle, and we'll get into the trees. Brockley, come *on*!'

'Let me alone!'

'*Brockley*!'

He got to his feet. I let go of his arm and grabbed at Berry's saddlebags, trying to haul them clear of the heavy, inert body. Brockley, still silently crying, stooped to help me. We flung them over Roundel's back and started for the woods. We had just reached their shelter when we heard the hoof beats. They were coming fast.

'Just in time,' Brockley said as we pulled Roundel deeper into the leafy shadows.

'If that's our man, we'd best get further from the track,' I said. If our bowman was pursuing us, we had only outdistanced him as much as we had because Brown Berry's dying panic had kept him going so fast for so long.

Brockley was coming back to himself. 'I want to see who it is.'

'We can't risk it. He . . . they . . .'

'Has gone straight past.' Brockley had started forward but too late. The hoof beats were fading in the distance already. 'Didn't see my Berry lying in the long grass so close under those hazels. Lucky the poor beast is brown and not piebald or grey. He's earth coloured. Can't be seen from the track, I fancy. If we stay under cover and watch the road, we may see whoever it was come back.'

'That crossbow bolt is sticking up. If he comes back more slowly, he might see that,' I said. 'Can you get it out?'

Brockley dragged it free. It was of a commonplace pattern,

which told us nothing. It was then that I felt thankful I hadn't let Hawthorn make a stag transfixed by a crossbow bolt for the centrepiece at Meg's feast. Brockley threw the thing out of sight among the hazels. Then we crouched behind the bushes.

We waited for more than two hours, judging by the sun, but no one came. This stretch of track was lonely. No wayfarer of any kind went by.

Eventually, we gave up. 'What now, madam?' Brockley asked.

'Try to find a farm or something, I suppose,' I said. 'We need another horse. You're limping.'

'I turned my ankle when I fell,' Brockley admitted.

I said: 'We'd better put Berry's saddle on to Roundel, and then you can ride and keep the weight off your ankle. She can take both lots of saddlebags, and we can fix my saddle behind you, though it'll be awkward for me to use it, so I'll walk and carry Berry's bridle.'

'But madam, it's not fitting for you to walk while I ride.'

'Nor is it fitting for you to walk on that ankle. Please, Brockley, do as I bid!'

TEN
Starting Hares

We didn't know the district and had no idea where the nearest habitations might be. But we did discover a path through the wood and followed that. Eventually, we reached some farmland and came to a small hamlet with a hostelry where there was a water trough and a manger for Roundel, ale and meat pies for us, and a chance of asking where we might hire another horse.

The place seemed mostly to serve the labourers from the farms roundabout, and several were there, taking a noon break. We presented ourselves fairly truthfully as having been attacked by highway robbers. Amid much head-shaking and tut-tutting from the landlord and his clientele, we said we had fled from them and escaped without being robbed but Brockley's horse had been wounded and fallen dead under him.

The landlord said there had been no word of such fellows thereabouts but you never knew; robbers could get driven out of one place and start up in another, yes, that's how it must have been.

A ploughman who claimed to feel for his own plough team much as Brockley felt for Berry, offered – for a consideration – to go out that evening with his friend who was a shepherd and find Berry and: 'Put 'un away proper. No need to leave 'un there for foxes and the like.'

We suspected that *put 'un away proper* probably meant feeding the carcase to the shepherd's sheepdogs, but somehow it felt better than the idea of foxes and crows. We didn't enquire. Instead, we asked about hiring a horse and were directed to a farmhouse about half a mile away. We thanked our well-wishers, finished our meal and set off.

The farmer, whose place was called Longfields, was helpful,

after some hesitation. Well, yes, there was a horse we could hire – given we brought it back inside of a week.

'Wouldn't do it for everyone, but granted, you don't look like horse thieves. Trouble on the roads – shocking thing, that is. Wouldn't want to turn anyone away that's had to cope with that.'

The horse had hairy fetlocks and a build which suggested that three of its grandparents had been plough horses, but it had four legs and seemed healthy. We offered to buy it outright, but the farmer said it was a good all-rounder and he'd rather have it back. 'We'll want it when harvesting starts in earnest.'

To show goodwill, we gave him more for its hire than he had actually asked, and since Berry's saddle didn't fit its broad back, we took the battered old saddle that was normally used when the animal was ridden. As further evidence of our honesty, we left Berry's saddle, which was a good one, with pommel and cantle dyed crimson, and a thick roll of leather in front of the rider's knees.

The farmer directed us to the nearest main track, and once on it, we encountered other riders, including a group of young men who were able to tell us that we were on the right road for Hampton Court. Getting there took a long time, however, because Brockley's left ankle needed gentle treatment and he couldn't press it into its stirrup with any kind of force. We arrived at nightfall, only to learn that the court, taking Cecil with it, had shifted to Whitehall. No one was left at Hampton Court except the permanent maintenance staff, who were now engaged in cleaning it, and the cesspit engineers. There was no accommodation for us.

'Well, there is this,' I said as we went in search of an inn for the night. 'If the court's at Whitehall, Cecil's most likely living in his house in the Strand. We'll probably find him there.'

We did find him there, though not until the following evening. We actually reached his house during the morning, having found a barge for hire that was equipped to carry horses. That way, we could travel to Cecil's private landing stage by river and save Brockley's aching ankle. We were welcomed pleasantly, by Cecil's dignified and learned wife Mildred, but Sir

William himself, she said, was with the queen at Whitehall
Palace, attending a meeting of the Royal Council and a banquet
for a visiting diplomat from Sweden and wouldn't be back
until late. Meanwhile, we could wash and rest, and perhaps,
said Mildred, I would join her for dinner.

Brockley was impatient at the delay, but the frightening day
just behind us had left its mark on me. I had slept badly in
the inn at Hampton. I was thankful for a good meal and a
chance to rest.

'So. What brings you to me that's so urgent?' Cecil asked,
when at last Brockley and I were summoned to him in his
study. He had come home so late that it was well after dark.
It was chilly, too, and a fire had been lit for us. We gathered
round a table with a triple candlestick on it, and by its light
I could see how haggard Cecil looked after his long day at
court, coping with his fellow councillors, emissaries from
Sweden, and my intelligent, subtle, moody and capricious
half-sister. The line between his eyes was a long, black trench
in his skin. I felt sorry to be there, sorry to be worrying him
when he must be longing to be left to spend what remained
of the evening in peace with his wife.

'It's this,' I said and handed him the letter that Hugh and
I had put together. 'It explains everything.' I was glad that we
had put it all in writing. Despite my hours of rest, I still felt
too jaded for complicated verbal explanations.

Cecil read the letter with his usual attention and then looked
up. 'My wife says you were attacked on the way here. I
understand that you have an injured ankle, Brockley.'

'It's only a wrench, sir,' Brockley said. 'We were ambushed
by a crossbowman. Close to where the Ferrises live.'

'You think that Walter Ferris inspired the attack?'

'We never saw who it was. It was someone skilled with a
crossbow, if not quite skilled enough. But he killed my horse.'
There was murder in Brockley's voice, and his face darkened
as he spoke.

Cecil looked down at the letter again. 'I am horrified to
know of these ugly threats from Anne Percy. It was remiss of
you to keep it from me, Ursula. I would have arranged protection for you. Lady Northumberland is a bad enemy.'

'I know,' I said, remembering how she had treated us when we were her captives. 'But we didn't think she could really do any harm,' I explained. 'Not while she's exiled away there in Bruges. And we were all taken up with getting Meg married.'

'No doubt. But you were still unwise. However, we must deal with things as they are. You want to know of any link between Walter Ferris and Anne Percy of Northumberland. That's the main point here.'

'Yes. Perhaps tomorrow one of your clerks could look up the family trees for her and her husband. I imagine that it's part of court records?'

'No need for clerks,' said Cecil. 'I can tell you the answer straightaway. Anne Percy was born into the Somerset family, who are Catholic. Walter Ferris, who is also a Catholic, is related to the Somersets by marriage. One of his father's cousins married into the family. It's hardly a close link, but Walter Ferris and Anne Percy have met. It wasn't long before the rising in the north. Ferris was visiting a kinsman near Corbridge in Northumberland, one of the Earl's houses. Thomas Percy and his family were there at the time and holding regular, illegal Catholic services. They would let anyone attend them – open house, as Queen Mary Tudor used to do. Ferris went to one of the services and made himself known to the family.'

'How do you know?' I asked, amazed.

Cecil smiled. 'I don't have a paid informant in your home, Ursula, though I have reports from Dr Fletcher, as you know. I do, however, have paid informants in a number of big houses, especially Catholic ones. I know who visits whom. Ferris was made welcome by the Northumberlands and was invited to dine. They apparently got on well. The link is there, slender though it is. I am sorry you had to ride so far – and run into danger – just to ask me such a simple question! Now, this other point – about the courier who brought the former Countess's threatening letter to you, Ursula. You say here that you want to trace him.'

He glanced at me questioningly, and I said: 'If Ferris really is her cat's paw, then she must have contacted him. It may not have been at the same time as her letter to me, and she could quite well have used a different courier. But it could be worth finding out. Hugh thinks it is. I can't suppose that she tried to make use of the Cobbolds, though. I can't understand what Jane Cobbold has done.'

'Perhaps we should go and ask her, madam, just as we've come here to ask Sir William for information,' said Brockley.

'I would discourage that,' said Cecil. 'Your best course, in my opinion, is silence. Don't shake the tree; you never know what might fall out on your head. Heron probably won't make a move without further encouragement, and the less stir you create, the better. Let Jane Cobbold alone and leave everything to me. I'll have this man Bartholomew Twelvetrees found. I agree with you there. But I don't want you, Ursula, starting any hares on your own account. Wait on events.'

'Can't Master Ferris be brought in and questioned?' Brockley wanted to know.

'I can't order that without bringing Mistress Stannard's name into it, and that's just what I don't wish to do,' Cecil said. 'Besides, on what grounds can he be questioned? Anne Percy's letter to you, Ursula, doesn't mention him. All we have, according to this –' he tapped the letter we had given him – 'is the so-called confession of a girl who is now dead and may have been merely delirious, and Ferris's admittedly disgraceful behaviour at your daughter's wedding. But from what Dr Fletcher told me, he ranted at you because his son had had a romantic tryst with a Cobbold girl on your premises! He could claim that his outburst was simply a fit of temper, and it would be hard to prove otherwise. People in a rage often do the most extraordinary things.'

'Could his house be searched for incriminating letters?' I asked. 'On the excuse of looking for signs of Popishness, perhaps?'

'No,' said Cecil firmly. 'It can't. That's about the only excuse that could justify a search, and just now it won't do. The queen doesn't want to be seen to encourage persecution of Catholics. That odious Papal Bull has made the whole religious question too delicate. If she starts hunting down people who are essentially loyal citizens but hear an occasional Mass in private, it will make her seem panic-stricken, and oh, how that would encourage the Pope and those of his English followers who really do want our queen deposed! Also, it could turn some of the loyal Catholics against her. I could not agree to anything of the sort. However, precautions for your safety would be wise. My wife says that after Brockley's horse was killed, you hired another from somewhere called Longfields Farm?'

'Yes, Sir William.' Brockley's face once more showed anger at the mention of Berry's death, but he spoke quietly enough. 'We promised to return it soon – and collect Berry's saddle. It didn't fit the animal we hired so we left it there. But I must get it back. It was expensive.'

'I'll send a couple of grooms to take the hireling back. They'll pick up your saddle and deliver it to Hawkswood. I'll lend you a horse from my own stable to get you home and send an escort with the two of you. Also, I have a physician here who will look at that ankle for you, Brockley. Take my advice, Ursula, please. Tread softly. All this may just melt away, and it's perfectly possible that Ferris has *not* been asked by Anne Percy to avenge her. He may really have burst into Meg's wedding feast because of a fit of temper about his son and the girl Christina.'

'Dorothy . . .' I began.

Cecil shook his head. 'Dying . . . half out of her mind . . . hardly able to speak . . . You could have misheard, or she could have been rambling. We can't place too much reliance on that. But Ferris getting into a fury over Christina Cobbold; yes, that's believable. If all I have heard about the Cobbold–Ferris feud is true, I fancy it goes deep,' said Cecil.

Brockley's ankle was easier the next day, and we made good time. However, four miles from home, we met Arthur Watts, who was riding out on Hugh's orders to see if he could learn any news of us along our route.

'Master Stannard was that worried, and so was Dale – Mistress Brockley – seeing that Hampton Court was only twelve miles away,' Arthur told us.

'We had to chase Sir William to Whitehall,' I said. 'My husband knew that something of that kind could happen, and so did Dale!'

'They got in a fuss, just the same,' said Arthur. 'Almost as if they'd sensed something wrong, especially Dale. And now here you are, with Master Brockley on that big black horse that ain't his, and with all these!'

All these were the well-armed, six-man escort Cecil had sent with us, as protection. 'We've a tale to tell,' I admitted to Arthur. 'But let all that wait till we're home. You can turn back with us now.'

When we clattered through the gatehouse arch at Hawkswood, Dale was there in the courtyard. She ran forward, crying out Brockley's name. He was out of his saddle at once, to embrace her and wipe away her tears of relief. She noticed at once that he was limping.

'You're hurt! Roger, you're hurt! What happened? I *knew* something had happened; I felt it! Mistress Jester kept saying oh, they've had to wait to see Sir William, he's always attending the queen, but I *knew*! And why are you riding that black horse? Where's Brown Berry?'

'Brown Berry,' said Brockley grimly, 'is dead. We have a report to make to Master Stannard. I have a twisted ankle and the ride has made it ache again, but it isn't serious.'

'I will talk to my husband first. You can join us later, Brockley,' I said. I had seen how hungrily Dale was watching him. 'Dale! Take Brockley to your room and look after him. A cold poultice might help that ankle. I will send dinner up to you. Brockley can see Master Stannard later.'

Hugh, arriving from the rose garden where he had once more been occupying himself during this time of anxiety, gave me an approving look and said: 'We will be in the small parlour after dinner. Brockley, you may come to us there.'

Dale took her husband away. Hugh and I set about making the escort welcome. When they and their horses had been handed over, respectively, to Adam Wilder and Arthur Watts, we went indoors. As we walked through the hall, Hugh said: 'What happened? Dale was obviously right when she said that she was convinced something had gone amiss. Cecil didn't send you back surrounded by six armed men for nothing.'

'We were attacked on the way, just the other side of Priors

Ford. A hidden crossbowman took a shot at Brockley and hit Berry. He bolted for nearly a mile and then dropped dead. Brockley is furious. And grieved. I never saw him cry before.'

'Good God!'

'There have been no reports of footpads or robbers hereabouts for at least a year,' I said. 'Or not that I've ever heard about.'

'*If* it was footpads or robbers,' said Hugh, understanding.

Brockley presented himself in the small parlour shortly after dinner. He had changed into fresh clothes and was wearing slippers instead of riding boots, so the binding round his left ankle was visible.

'Sit down, man,' Hugh said to him. 'You can't stand long on your left foot, anyway. That's obvious. Now, my wife has told me more or less everything, but I would also like to hear it from you.'

Brockley accepted the offer of a seat with obvious relief and embarked on a description of our adventures, an account which more or less repeated mine until he reached the death of Berry, when he burst out in renewed fury and savage threats against Berry's unknown slayer. Hugh took several minutes to calm him, before asking for the rest of the story.

'So,' my husband said when Brockley had finished. 'Now we know. The Ferrises really are connected to Anne Percy. And Cecil intends to have Master Twelvetrees found? He was definite about that?'

'I think so,' I said, and Brockley nodded agreement.

'I wonder,' Hugh said thoughtfully. 'Could you have been attacked to prevent you from taking that letter to Cecil?' But his voice faded at the end of the sentence, and he shook his head. 'No. That makes no sense. From what you say, only Brockley was the bowman's target. And how could Ferris know about the letter, anyway?'

'It was no secret in this house that we were writing to Cecil about something,' I said. 'But we didn't discuss its contents with all and sundry, and anyway, if one message failed to reach Sir William, we'd just send another, better protected. That can't have been the reason.'

'But our attacker was lying in wait for us,' Brockley said. 'As if he had been warned that we'd be riding that way.'

'That would mean that we have another Ferris spy here,' I said angrily. 'I hope that's not true! One was enough.'

'But it was no ordinary robber either. They don't work that way,' Brockley said. 'They stop you on the road and demand your goods. They sometimes kill, but it's nearly always at close quarters – because the traveller they've stopped won't take his rings off or shows fight. Master Stannard, I think this was an attempt to assassinate me, personally. It wouldn't necessarily mean that there's a spy in this house. Someone in Ferris pay could have been out and about, watching for an opportunity.'

We were all remembering the terms of Anne Percy's letter:

Soon, trouble and dread will overtake both you and your servant (or is he your lover?). And when they have wrung the last juices of hope and happiness from you, death and damnation will complete my vengeance.

ELEVEN
The Art of Picking Locks

'Let us leave it for a while,' Hugh said. 'I wish to think all this over, quietly.'

The sun was out, and as I had known he would, he returned to do his thinking in the company of his roses. I sent Brockley back to Dale and then went to find Sybil, to acquaint her with the latest news. I looked for her in the bigger parlour and then tried the hall but found only Gladys, mumbling over some sheet hems.

'Mistress Jester's gone to Woking, said she wanted to see the physician there,' Gladys informed me. 'Wouldn't say why. Didn't look sick to me. Rode off on one of the coach horses, on her own, and that's funny, look you, for she don't care for riding. And what's this tale that's going round that someone shot Master Brockley's horse? No one tells me anything these days. I get tired of that. Maybe I'll put a spell on you all, to loosen tongues!' She let out one of her dreadful cackles.

'Don't talk like that!' I said sharply. 'And no one keeps anything from you that you've a right to know, and you can't cast spells, you old fraud; you just pretend you can, and look where that sort of thing got you not so long ago!'

Gladys cringed at once. 'All right, I know; you got me out of that death cart . . .' She shuddered all over from head to foot at the memory and seemed to shrink inside her decent brown dress. 'And it's a-cause of all that, that you've been accused of witching; don't think I don't know it. I'm the excuse, and I'm sorry, and if you want me to go away . . .'

'No, Gladys, I don't want you to go away; we said we'd look after you, and as my husband told you not so long ago, we'll keep our word. Besides, you've been valuable to us at times, and we know it.'

That was true. Once, Gladys had helped us to the solution

of a most mysterious business. I was sorry I had frightened her. I sat down beside her and began to tell her about our expedition and Brown Berry's death, and what Cecil had told us. Just as I finished, there were quick footsteps outside, and Sybil came in, a little flushed from the open air.

'I'm not late for dinner, I hope, Mistress Stannard. I am so glad to know that you and Brockley are safe, and that you have news.'

'Yes, but Sybil, what took you to the physician in Woking? Gladys says that's where you went. To Dr Hibbert, was it? Are you ill?' I asked anxiously.

'No, I'm perfectly well.' Sybil sank down on to the nearest stool. 'I went to find out if something I've been considering could be true. Dr Hibbert thinks it can. He isn't sure, but he's very experienced, and he says yes, it's possible.'

'Sybil, what are you talking about?' I demanded.

'He thinks it's quite likely that clothes or sheets – things like that – that someone has used during an infectious illness, like leprosy or smallpox or plague – anything that's catching – can hold the contagion and pass it to anyone else who uses the things afterwards. After all, most people do boil sheets, or even burn clothes that have been used by someone with such illnesses. Mostly because the things are so stained, but I know I'd do it even if there weren't any stains – I'd feel they were unclean.'

'Course they are,' Gladys put in. 'Everyone knows that. Folk talk about witchcraft sometimes when all the while all they needed to do was boil a few sheets.'

This, coming from Gladys, who loathed washing even herself, almost made me laugh, except that I had guessed what Sybil meant, and if I had guessed right, then it was no laughing matter.

'What are you trying to say, Sybil?' I asked, quietly.

'That man Walter Ferris brought two used cloaks here to give to Mistress Meg and her husband. We all thought he did it just to be insulting. But what if there was more to it than that? Didn't you say to me once that Walter Ferris had a daughter who'd just died of smallpox?'

'Yes. That's true,' I said.

'Well, I've thought and thought. What if those cloaks that Master Ferris brought had belonged to his daughter? What if she was using them when the illness started? What if they were laid on her bed to keep her warm? What if he brought them here to give to Mistress Meg and Master George, on purpose?'

'The daft coot made a mistake if so,' said Gladys. 'Mistress Meg and Master George, they've both had the cowpox, ain't they? That's what Brockley said when he come back from there, the time you enquired after them. Folk get it from cows. Helped in the milking when they was young, I don't doubt. They won't get the smallpox now. Folk that've had the little one never get the big one. Milkmaids have the best complexions in the land. My mam always made sure we young 'uns milked cows regular, and that was why.'

'Yes, I know that theory,' I said. 'And now they're safe in Buckinghamshire, well away from Ferris and his schemes. Sybil, this idea of yours wants talking over. I'm going to fetch my husband. Will you find Brockley and Dale and bring them here as well? Gladys, stay here. I think we all need to put our heads together.'

It was instinctive for me to bring Brockley and Dale to our counsels. We had worked together so often. We were as much a team as a hound pack. Hugh and the Brockleys listened in astonishment to what Sybil and I had to tell them, while Gladys sat nodding her head in agreement at frequent intervals.

At the end of the recital, Hugh said: 'Let us get it all quite clear. Sybil thinks that Ferris actually tried to endanger Meg and George by giving them cloaks infected with smallpox? Perhaps to hurt Ursula?'

'It's possible, yes,' Sybil told him. 'And I've remembered something else. Christina Cobbold caught the disease, didn't she? Well, on the morning after the wedding, she borrowed one of those cloaks to wear while she went roaming round the garden.'

Brockley said: 'And if Ferris did bring the cloaks with that intent, then was he acting for the Countess Anne of Northumberland?'

'I can't see that he'd be acting for himself,' Hugh said. 'Why ever should he? But on behalf of Anne Percy . . . that's different. Cecil has confirmed that Ferris and the Countess are related and are acquainted with each other, if not closely. But if the lady is using Ferris as an instrument of revenge, how are we to prove it?'

'Search his house or haul him in for questioning and show him a rack!' said Brockley savagely. 'If he was responsible for Brown Berry . . .'

'Cecil won't,' I said. 'You know that, Brockley; you heard him say so. But if Cecil traces Bart Twelvetrees and he turns out to be the courier, that could give us the answer.'

'And if Twelvetrees says the only letter he ever carried that came from the Netherlands was the one he brought here?' asked Brockley.

'*If!*' I snorted, but then admitted defeat. 'Well, I see no other way of finding out. Ferris knows me, so I can't enter his service under false pretences and pry into his correspondence. If anything, that's a relief,' I added.

My work for the queen and Cecil had obliged me, at times, to do many strange and sometimes dangerous things, but of all the tasks that it had brought me, reading other people's letters was the one I most detested. It felt so intrusive, and I was always afraid of being caught, especially when I had to spend time on picking the locks of document boxes or desks or cupboards. This time, I couldn't possibly be tempted to undertake such a thing. I couldn't say I regretted it.

Then Sybil, quite calmly, said: 'Ferris doesn't know *me*. I wasn't in the hall when he burst in, and I've never been introduced to him.'

I gazed at her in astonishment. I was so used to Sybil as a companion. She had been a friend for me, a chaperone for Meg, a guardian for Gladys, even a surrogate mistress of the house when I was away. But never had I asked her to take part in any of my secret tasks for Cecil or the queen. She had known hard times before we met, which in my opinion was a good reason why she should never be required to endure any more of them.

Yet now, as though my venturesome nature were as

contagious as the smallpox, she seemed to think she was
expected to face danger on my behalf. But she'd had no practice at such things; I valued her too highly; and besides . . .

'You were with us when we dined at his home, that once,'
I said. 'I know it was a long time ago, but surely you were
there? I must have introduced you.'

'No, the invitation was only for you and your husband,'
said Sybil. 'You came back and said White Towers was like
a simple manor house trying to ape a palace, and that the
dishes were more elaborate than appetizing.'

'Her previous husband,' said Hugh, nodding towards me,
'nicknamed her Saltspoon because of her habit of saying
things like that. No, Sybil wasn't with us on that occasion.
But, Sybil . . .'

'Quite,' I said. 'Sybil, I don't want you to put yourself at
any kind of risk. If this man is acting for Anne Percy then
he's dangerous.'

'I should be very careful,' said Sybil. 'I've already thought
how to go about it. I don't think I need incur much risk. The
only thing is, Mistress Stannard, I think you should show me
how to pick a lock.'

'No,' I said. 'Once and for all, no. We can't let you do this.'

'Indeed we can't,' said Hugh. 'And – well, I should be loath
to deprive my wife of your company because I know how
much she values it. But if you persist in this, Sybil, remember
that I am the master of this house and I could send you away.
Take heed. You must not attempt this.'

'I should be sorry to leave Hawkswood,' said Sybil, with
an air of formidable determination that I had never seen in
her before. 'But I am not your employee, Master Stannard. I
am not paid for anything I do here. I have an adequate income
from leasing out the pie shop in Cambridge. On that I could
live quietly by myself, or else I could go to my married
daughter. She and her husband would willingly give me a
home. They have even suggested it. If you order me out, I
will do one of those two things. But I will go to White Towers
first. Please understand, I am not asking your permission for
this.'

'*Sybil!*' I protested.

'If you won't show me how to pick a lock, I'll have to rely on chance, or on stealthily borrowing whatever keys I need, or even having them copied. I owe you a great deal, Mistress Stannard, and here's a way of repaying it. I will do so even if you or your husband choose to dismiss me. If I succeed . . .' She gave us her sweetest smile, which was always beguiling. 'Well, perhaps you'll take me back.'

'If only,' I said, 'we could get White Towers officially searched, as Brockley recommends, or have Master Ferris questioned!'

'We can't,' said Hugh frankly. 'Cecil's made that clear. His hands are tied, by royal policy on one side – the queen is trying to draw the Pope's teeth by not persecuting Catholics – and by foresight on the other. If Ferris were to be questioned, he'd talk his way out of it. Cecil was right about that, I fancy. Ferris would say that a fit of temper over his son's love affair made him burst into our feast and shout at us. As for Dorothy's dying words – I expect he'd say you and Sybil made them up because you were angry about the way he burst into Meg's feast. I would, in his place.'

'There were the cloaks,' said Dale.

'Cloaks?' said Hugh. 'He'd say *don't talk nonsense.* Perfectly good cloaks, and he thought they'd be appreciated. He'd slide away from questioning like an oiled snake. But . . . dear God,' said Hugh, suddenly furious. 'If Ferris did plant infected cloaks on us, then Dorothy was probably one of his victims. He clearly doesn't worry too much about the safety of his own employees! Damn the man! And yet, *Ferris* isn't the one who has complained to the sheriff about you, Ursula. That was Jane Cobbold!'

'I know,' I said. 'And that's as extraordinary as the attack on you, Brockley. But we're getting off the point. Sybil mustn't be allowed—'

'You don't need to allow anything. I repeat, it's my choice,' said Sybil. 'I mean to get into that house.'

Dale said: 'If Mistress Jester is so determined, ma'am, might it not be better to show her how to pick locks, as she asks? Then she could open document boxes and things more quickly, and wouldn't that be safer?'

'Yes, it would,' said Sybil. 'I told you I'd been thinking things out. I could rent a cottage, at Priors Ford, perhaps. I've never been there, and I don't suppose anyone there would recognize me. Once I'm installed, I'll go to White Towers saying I'm a widow looking for work as a sempstress. I think Priors Ford belongs to the Ferrises, too – I would be their tenant. That might encourage them to employ me.'

'For the love of heaven!' said Hugh in despairing tones.

'If the Ferrises like to live in style, and you say they do, Mistress Stannard,' said Sybil, 'well, people like that are always wanting new clothes and curtains and cushion covers. I expect they miss Dorothy and are sorry they can't ever get her back. Once I get my foot over that threshold, I'll seize what opportunities I can. I'll use my maiden name and call myself Sybil Jackman, just in case the Ferrises have heard that there's a lady in your household whose name is Jester. Sybil is ordinary enough; I needn't change that. Surely you see that we need evidence, if we're to put a stop to all these mysterious happenings, and I'm the only one who may be able to get it.'

Hugh groaned. 'Is there anything in the world more maddening than an obstinate woman?'

I said: 'You can't take a cottage all alone and still seem respectable.' I was capitulating. I knew it. I looked at Hugh, and he rolled his eyes upwards in surrender. 'We'd better lend you a maidservant,' I told Sybil. 'Take little Tessie. I understand she is quite useful in the kitchen, and we can manage without her now that Netta's nearly well again.'

'Thank you,' said Sybil.

'Madness,' said Hugh. 'Utter madness. This is probably the only household in the land where the idea could even be considered!'

But, of course, we were such a household. I had a thoroughly unconventional past, perhaps because I had an unconventional nature. The queen and Cecil had used it; Hugh had accepted me as I was, and he accepted the situations that seemed to follow me as a tail follows a dog. He said no more about dismissing Sybil. The matter was apparently decided. Sybil had decided it.

Tessie raised no objection, though that wasn't surprising.

Our youngest maidservant was not only frightened of our rather aggressive black cockerel (which seemed to know it, and to enjoy flying at her and pecking her if possible), she also gave the impression of being frightened of almost everything. I knew that she had been orphaned young and reared by an aunt and uncle, just as I had, and suspected that her relatives had been harsh with her. She seemed anxious to please and was most unlikely to object to anything at all that we asked of her.

'Well,' Hugh said, 'since I see that the plan is going to go ahead whatever I may think, I had better offer some help. If Sybil is going to go off with your picklocks, Ursula, I think we should have them copied so that you can still have a set. I doubt if you'll feel properly equipped for life unless you do. The blacksmith in Hawkswood village has worked for me all his life and won't ask questions. Brockley, you will take the picklocks to him to copy – get two extra sets made while you're about it. Then Ursula can show Sybil how to use them.'

Tessie and Sybil went off the next Monday, riding pillion behind Arthur and Brockley on Roundel and one of the coach horses, with a set of picklocks in a pouch sewn inside Sybil's skirt. Both she and Brockley had learned to use them, because as Brockley said dryly (and in my hearing), given madam's temperament, one never knew when such a skill might prove handy. Sybil, though, had mastered them faster than he had.

A quarter of a mile short of Priors Ford, she and Tessie dismounted and went the rest of the way on foot, carrying their belongings on their backs. By arrangement, Tessie met Brockley outside the village that evening and said that they hadn't been able to find a vacant house, but had found lodgings. A widow with a large cottage was glad to let her upstairs rooms and was prepared to share her kitchen. Mistress Jester meant to go to White Towers in the morning to enquire for work.

After that, for over a week, we heard nothing.

Nothing alarming happened, either. We did not hear from Edward Heron, and there were no more mysterious attacks. Brockley's twisted ankle improved, and he ceased to limp. He and Arthur went to a market in Guildford to buy a replacement for Brown Berry and came back with a sturdy dark bay cob, a gelding, about eight years old, fifteen and a half hands, with an off-white nose, suggesting that a moorland pony featured somewhere in his ancestry. He was being sold only because his owner had died, leaving no heirs except an elderly aunt, and the establishment was being turned into money for her benefit. The cob's name, in honour of his pale muzzle, was Mealy.

Brockley had ridden to Guildford on Roundel but rode his new acquisition back, leading the mare. 'This lad's good-natured and sound,' Brockley said, slipping to the ground and stroking Mealy's nose. 'We'll be friends, I think. Poor Berry. I hope nothing like that happens to this fellow, anyway.'

Half the household was out in the courtyard, admiring the new purchase, when a young woman arrived, on foot, asking for me. She was a small, freckled girl, no older than twenty, with pale red hair and white eyelashes. Her best claim to beauty lay in her big grey-green eyes. She was well spoken, though, and well dressed, with a dark cloak over a tawny velvet gown with a green silk kirtle. She said her name was Margaret Emory.

The next part of this narrative belongs to Margaret. She was there; I wasn't. She shall tell it, in her own words, just as she told it to me.

TWELVE
Enter Margaret Emory

My name is Margaret Emory, as I've said. Until yesterday, I lived with my parents at Greenlease Farm, a mile or two the other side of White Towers, where the Ferrises live. Greenlease isn't as big a place as White Towers, but it's a fair size; we're not poor. We look on the Ferrises as friends and more or less as equals, and my parents have always thought that one day we might be more than that. All the same, it came as a surprise – well, a shock! – when, a few days ago, they told me to pick out whatever clothes and so on I wanted to take with me, because I was to leave home and go to White Towers. Where Thomas Ferris, my future husband, lived.

'You're to stay with his family until the wedding,' my father said. 'Master Walter Ferris wishes it. You won't feel too strange; after all, you've always known it's what we were planning for you, given that Thomas turned out well, and he has. He's a nice-looking, healthy lad. He'll make you a good husband. Our two families've been friends since Adam and Eve, I reckon.'

'It's what we want for you, sweeting,' my mother said. 'A future in a family with a house like White Towers, with a big hall and a topiary garden and all. We've worked and saved for this – we've been saving for your dowry ever since you were born, and it's as good a dowry as their girl Lucy had. In fact, it's a little better!'

'I won't say it's all gone as smooth as we hoped,' Father said grumblingly. My father isn't a light-hearted man. 'We've had an understanding with Walter Ferris for years, but when we wanted to come to the point, he started humming and hawing. Got it into his head that he could do better, I suppose. Can't think where, since there's not another Catholic family round here that I know of.'

'He's got connections elsewhere; I suppose he could ask them to find a bride for Thomas,' my mother said. 'It's worried us a lot.'

'They're only connections by marriage,' Father said grudgingly. 'His direct ancestry's nothing special! If we ain't got forebears who fought at Agincourt or went on crusade or came over with the Conqueror, neither has he. But some cousin of his dad's married into a family of that sort, and so Ferris thinks a lot of himself. I've had to work to get this match made final for you, my girl.'

Timidly, I said: 'I don't understand.'

'Your dowry ain't just money, girl. I had to do Walter a couple of favours – rather odd ones, but he said it was all in order and important, and he promised that, all going well, Thomas should be your husband and we'd clap hands on the deal. And so we did, in the end. I'm thankful. Your mother's right. This here's what we want for you.'

But – I was being sent away from home. It was all too sudden, and I felt frightened. My mother sensed it, I think. 'You'll not be getting wed straightaway,' she said. 'Seems the Ferrises want you to feel settled with them first, and they're saying next spring for the wedding. It's only October now. That will give you time, so they say, to fix Thomas's interest. They're expecting you in two days' time.'

I didn't argue; of course not. I'd been taught, ever since I was tiny, that a daughter should obey her parents, and although I had of course heard tales and legends of romantic lovers, like Sir Lancelot and Queen Guinevere, and I had heard songs about love, I had never thought of such things as real. I knew that my parents had had their marriage arranged for them by their own parents; I knew that for me they had their eyes on Thomas. It did not occur to me to raise objections.

Although, even then, in some corner of my mind, I kept thinking that it would be very odd, when the time came, to find myself alone with Thomas in a bedchamber, and expected to . . .

I know him well. We've visited the Ferrises and been visited by them, ever since I can remember. Religion's been a bond. My parents have often taken me to White Towers to share one of the private Masses they hold in their tiny private chapel. Peter Maine, the Ferrises' steward, is a Catholic priest.

In addition, when I was younger I used to go there three times a week to share Thomas's tutor. Thomas is two years older than me, but I could vie with him at lessons, and I learnt to speak as he does, without a country accent. He and I played ball games together when we were let out of the schoolroom, and we were sometimes partners in the little wickednesses of childhood: climbing trees to the peril of our clothing, taking apples from the orchard without permission. Later we danced together and rode side by side on hawking expeditions. Thomas always has well-bred horses while I use one of Father's hairy-heeled all-purpose horses, but as Thomas cheerfully says, if his mounts can gallop faster, mine are tireless. It was Thomas who taught me about hawking, and for my seventeenth birthday, Mistress Bridget Ferris sent me a merlin of my own.

All of which means that Thomas and I grew up together and see each other very much as brother and sister. I kept thinking that, for us, behaving as man and wife was going to feel extremely strange and not quite natural. And what was the meaning behind that odd remark about *fixing Thomas's interest*? Did he, too, feel that we were more like siblings than prospective marriage partners?

Besides, how does one fix a man's interest? I hadn't the faintest idea how to go about it. For the first time, it occurred to me to wonder whether, perhaps, he had his eye on somebody else. Some other young girl. Not me.

Both Mother and I cried at parting, though Father was annoyed about it, pointing out that I was only going a couple of miles away, to a place I already knew, and we'd see each other often enough in the future.

I made the journey on his pillion, with my belongings on a pack pony. He said the Ferrises had undertaken to provide me with a horse of my own. We were greeted by the steward-cum-priest, Peter Maine, who delivered us into the hands of Mistress Bridget Ferris. She was elegantly dressed, as she always is, and greeted us in her usual fashion, holding a little lapdog in her arms and seeing no reason to put it down while welcoming us. Mistress Ferris always keeps lapdogs – yappy little things, quite unlike our big sheepdogs at Greenlease – and she croons baby talk to them. Yet in other ways she's so cool and remote. Well, I suppose you must know her. She's tall, slender, with pale blonde hair that I've long envied, and she dresses beautifully and is always dignified.

So there I was at White Towers. Father exchanged a few civil words with Mistress Ferris, and then it was time for him to leave. He said goodbye, told me to be a good girl, promised to visit me soon, and then he was gone. Mistress Ferris put her little dog down, though it yelped in protest, and led me upstairs to my chamber with the dog scuttling at our heels.

I felt nervous. Mistress Ferris wasn't a stranger, and yet, now that I'd been placed in her care, she felt like one. The room she took me to was small but nicely furnished, with a tester bed, clothes press, washstand and a prie-dieu. My clothes had been unpacked and laid out on the bed. I looked at them doubtfully. It struck me that my plain shifts and my gowns and kirtles of wool and dyed linen weren't too impressive – not for someone who was going to live at White Towers.

My future mother-in-law stood me in the light and said: 'I know you're healthy. You had a bad rheum in the summer, I believe, but I understand that you recovered completely. That's a blessing. And there should be no trouble about children, with those wide hips of yours. Ginger hair is fashionable nowadays, of course, because the queen has the same colouring, but I'll have to show you how to darken your eyelashes. And we really must do something about your clothes.'

The little dog barked, another high-pitched yap, as if in agreement.

Tact isn't Mistress Ferris's foremost characteristic. I'd noticed that before. I found myself flushing under her scrutiny. Her eyes are grey, the dark kind of grey, beautifully set, but as she studied me, they held no warmth. In fact, she was surveying me from head to foot in a way that I resented. It wasn't as if she'd never seen me before! I began to stop being nervous and to start being indignant. In a moment, I thought, she'll feel my legs and want to look at my teeth, as though I'm a horse she's thinking of buying.

She noticed the flush. 'There's no need to be embarrassed,' she said. 'One must be realistic. Thomas's bride must be well dressed. Luckily, we have a professional needlewoman to hand. Our best sempstress left us not long ago, but this Mistress Jackman has just come to the district and is looking for work and seems skilled. She shall attend on you tomorrow and measure you for some new gowns. I have bought suitable materials. Peach colour, blues and greens and amethyst shades should suit you, and I have a length of strong brown cloth to make you a riding dress. We've found a nice little mare for you, by the way, a blue roan. We call her Blue.'

'Thank you,' I said.

'Well,' said Mistress Ferris, 'we must go downstairs, and you can sit and talk to Thomas. He's been helping his father with the estate accounts, but they should be finished by now. Oh, before we go down, I just want to make certain . . . I have always thought you had pretty teeth, but I have only ever seen the front ones. Can I just make sure that the back ones are also sound?'

'They are,' I said stiffly. 'But of course you may look.'

She didn't ask to feel my legs, and her tiresome little dog didn't widdle in my room. I supposed I should be grateful for these small mercies!

I met Mistress Sybil Jackman the next morning. She was quietly dressed in dark green with a dove-coloured kirtle and a small, old-fashioned ruff, and she was quietly spoken, too, but her face is unusual. I don't mean ugly – I thought her rather attractive. But it's as though her head has been compressed, just a little, between crown and chin so that her features are slightly splayed. She has some worn lines in her face, too, as though her life hasn't been easy. But her smile is sweet and her eyes friendly. She asked me to call her Sybil. I liked her at once.

She took my measurements, and then she and Mistress Ferris held up various materials against me to see how they looked. They were lovely fabrics, I must say. At Greenlease, Mother and I had one silk dress each, for best, and nothing in velvet. Here were silk and velvet in plenty. There was a brocade too, in shades of sea-green and peach, and a roll of white holland linen for ruffs.

It was decided that Sybil should make the clothes in the house rather than take the materials back to her lodgings. 'I know the cottage where you're staying. All the rooms are poky. Here you can have one with good space and light and a table big enough for the cutting out,' Mistress Ferris said, and Sybil agreed, obviously pleased.

Then I was sent out to make the acquaintance of Blue, the nice little mare, and told to go riding with Thomas.

We had spent quite a long time together the previous day, and we had talked of this and that much as we always had. I didn't mention marriage, and neither did he. It was as though we had made a silent pact to ignore the subject unless our elders raised it. For the first time, though, in his company, I felt self-conscious. I know I'm no beauty.

This morning, Mistress Ferris's maid spent half an hour dressing my hair in a complicated new way and putting it into a green silk caul, and then brushed my eyelashes with a darkening substance, but none of that made me feel more confident, only peculiar, as though I were not quite myself; as though the real me was being hidden behind a facade of hairstyle and paint. For the ride, Mistress Ferris lent me a smart hat, which hid my hair, but I was sure Thomas would ask me why my eyes looked funny.

He didn't comment, though. In fact, he didn't seem to notice anything different about me at all. We set off. It was nice weather for riding, cool and cloudy but not raining. We went out of the main gate and turned right, towards the common land where there are good places on the heath for a gallop. In the other direction, between White Towers and Hawkswood, it's mostly woodland. Thomas's chestnut started to pull and dance, and Thomas said: 'Shall we let them go? You'll want to see how fast Blue is, and Burnish is fretting to be given his head.'

That had a familiar, brotherly ring. More at ease, I said: 'Yes, let's,' and off we went.

Burnish took hold, and Thomas let him have his way. Blue has shorter legs and fell behind so I had plenty of time to slow down when Burnish suddenly threw up his head, pranced sideways and stopped. I caught up at a sedate trot.

Burnish had been startled by unexpectedly encountering a girl on foot as he and Thomas rounded a clump of bushes. As I came up, Thomas was apologizing in case he had alarmed her, while the girl stood staring at him, or rather, peering at him, because she had pulled her hat low over her forehead and drawn the edge of her cloak across her face. I wondered who she was. She was well dressed; no milkmaid would have a velvet cloak or such an elegant hat. But she was alone and must be some way from her home. The nearest house of any size was, I knew, Cobbold Hall, two miles away.

I was about to add my apologies to Thomas's, when suddenly, she uttered a sob, swung round with a swish of her cloak, which made Burnish shy once more, and dashed off along a rabbit track to our right, as though we were dangerous footpads bent on harming her.

'For the love of God!' said Thomas. He leant forward and went cantering after her. Puzzled, I followed and came up to Thomas for the second time just as he put Burnish across the girl's path to stop her and was swinging out of the saddle. She tried to turn away from him, but he looped his reins over his arm and caught her by the shoulders.

'Christina! *Christina*! Don't run away from me. Why are you running away? It's me, Thomas!'

The girl let out another sob. She tugged her hat down further than ever and went on clutching her cloak over her lower face. I sat still. I had halted close enough to hear as well as see, and I felt I was intruding.

'What's the matter?' Thomas was saying. 'Christina, what is it? Let me look at you.' He pushed her hat back and pulled at the cloak. 'Oh, *Christina*!'

I bit my lip. Oh, poor thing. In trying to evade Thomas, she had turned towards me, and as he took her hat and cloak away from her face, I recognized her as Christina Cobbold. Our parents are quite well acquainted, though I myself have only met her a few times. She's younger than I am. I know her elder sister Alice better. I was invited to Alice's wedding, though I was unwell and couldn't go. Christina isn't especially pretty, but she has nice beech-nut coloured hair and sparkling dark eyes. But now, below the cheekbones, her skin was heavily pitted with the marks of smallpox, and there was a scattering of reddened marks across her forehead.

'I didn't want you to see!' She shouted it at Thomas. 'I don't want anyone to see! That's why I come out and walk alone; so that I'm not with anyone, so that no one is looking at me. I hate anyone looking at me. I hate people feeling sorry for me. Go away, Thomas! Go away, Margaret! Go *away*! Even my own mother pities me . . . Let me go!'

'Don't be absurd!' Thomas actually shook her. 'So you've had the pox. So have thousands of girls, and no one thinks the worse of them. Do you think I'd abandon you for that? What do you take me for? It could have been me, except that I had it when I was very young, and then not badly. Would you have turned away from me for such a reason?'

'It's different for a man. I'm ugly now. No one will ever want me. I wouldn't expect you to . . .'

'You silly thing,' said Thomas, pulling her against him. 'You still have your bright eyes and your beautiful hair.' He pushed her hat right to the back of her head, and her beech-nut hair was as pretty as ever. He buried his face in it. Then he moved again, tilted her face upwards, and pressed his mouth to hers.

I sat very still indeed.

I knew what I was seeing. It was the thing that the love stories describe, and the love songs, the thing I hadn't believed could really exist. But when I looked at Thomas and Christina, I saw that it does. I recognized it. I was seeing people in love.

Those two, entwined together, blending their lips as though they were trying to melt into a single entity, were oblivious of me, oblivious of the whole world. Just now, they were each other's world.

I tried the signal that tells a well-trained horse to edge backwards, and Blue responded. I backed along the rabbit path, to give the pair more privacy, to get out of hearing.

After a time, they moved apart and stood talking quietly to each other. Then Christina turned and walked away, and

Thomas, after watching her go for a little while, remounted
Burnish and came back to me.

He looked at me sadly. 'So now you know,' he said.

I nodded.

'Margaret, I've known you since we were children, and I'm
as fond of you as any brother could be, but . . .'

'I know,' I said. I didn't know whether I was hurt or not. I
only knew the truth of what I had seen. 'I understand,' I said.

'I can't marry you,' Thomas said. 'But Christina is a
Cobbold. How she and I are to get past that, God knows. Only,
somehow, we must.'

I began: 'But . . .' and then stopped because I didn't know
what I wanted to say, and because he looked angry, which
frightened me. 'Thomas?' I said. 'I won't tell anyone, if that's
why you're cross. It's your business. I wouldn't interfere.'

'I'm not cross with you,' Thomas said. 'Only with myself.
I've got to tell my father, to make him understand, and I know
he never will, and I'm ashamed because I'm a big, strong
young man and I'm afraid of him. You don't know him. He
looks so harmless, but he isn't.'

I knew what he meant. Master Ferris is an ordinary, quiet-
spoken sort of man, and yet there is something about him, and
always has been, that makes me wary of him.

Thomas said: 'I'm sorry. Whatever happens, I'll have to
take the brunt. It isn't your fault.'

We rode slowly back to White Towers, and entered into the
midst of an uproar that for a short time actually drove our
private troubles out of our heads.

The uproar was in the hall, which at White Towers is large,
though not quite large enough for its furnishings. Do you know
it? I have always thought, secretly, that it's a pompous sort of
place. It has dark oak panelling that absorbs light, making the
room shadowy, and there's a great big stone fireplace with an
inglenook and cushioned seats, and there are two massive
sideboards with a lot of elaborate carving, and a long table
with carved, throne-like chairs at each end and wide oak
benches on each side, and it all takes up far too much space.
When people sit down to dine, those serving the meal have

to squeeze between the sideboards and the benches, there's so little room for them.

The Ferrises don't have rushes on the floor. That's made of highly polished planks and strewn with fur rugs: deerskin, bearskin, fleece, and a spotted leopardskin. I've often wondered where they got that one from.

When we went in, drawn by the sound of raised voices, Thomas's parents were standing by the inglenook, where I think they'd been sitting, since the fire was lit and one of the seat cushions was on the floor as though someone had got up in a hurry. Peter Maine was standing in front of them, and he was gripping Sybil by the arm and shaking it angrily. We just stopped and stared.

'—caught in the very act, Master Cobbold!' Maine was accusing Sybil of something. 'I couldn't believe my eyes,' he said. 'Standing there in your very study, sir, with your document box open in front of her! Aha, you thought we were all out of your way, didn't you, my fine lady? Saw the master and mistress sitting in the hall; saw me going out into the grounds! But I only went to speak to the gardeners for a few minutes, and as I came back, I saw you at your games through the master's study windows! Reading his letters! Wickedness! Dishonesty! Have you stolen as well as spied? Well? Have you?'

There was not only fury in Maine's voice, but also a kind of satisfaction, as though to catch someone out, to accuse them in public of wrongdoing, gave him pleasure.

Peter Maine is maybe forty, with a pale, plump face, a stomach a little too bulgy, and uncomfortable eyes, slate blue with a yellow ring in them. He is always dressed in black, including a black velvet cap which he keeps on indoors and out, and I know the reason because I once saw it blow off when he stepped outside on a windy day. He wears it to hide the fact that his greying hair is cut into a tonsure. I have never liked him much. Now I realize why. He has a cruel streak, and it was showing.

Sybil tried to speak, but Walter Ferris wasn't going to listen.

'Stop trying to explain yourself! There's nothing you can possibly explain! You have opened my document box – how, by the way? The keys are with me.'

'Picklocks!' said Maine. 'She had picklocks. These!' He put his spare hand into a pocket and brought out a set of thin metal rods with hooked ends. 'She's a professional thief, that's what she is. And what's more, I know *who* she is! From the moment she set foot in the house, I thought I'd seen her somewhere before, and when I caught her in your study, standing there with one of your letters in her hand, then it came to me. I've seen her in Woking, attending on that Mistress Stannard. The Stannards consort with witches, so why not with thieves? This woman was sent by the Stannards to spy on you, sir; I wouldn't be surprised!'

'Better put her in the cellar,' said Mistress Ferris. 'While we send for the sheriff.'

'Yes, indeed!' Master Ferris was bristling with wrath. 'Spying, thieving . . .'

'I haven't stolen anything!' Sybil shouted. 'And yes, I was sent by the Stannards, to try to find out why you've threatened them, Master Ferris! Didn't you burst into their daughter's wedding feast and fling accusations? And there have been other things, too. They want to know what you have against them!'

Sybil certainly had courage. In her place, I would never have dared to speak up like that. But it didn't help her.

'She's making excuses. Trying to say she wasn't committing a crime!' Maine shook his captive's arm again, and I could see that his pudgy fingers were clutching so tightly that he must have been hurting her a lot. And probably knew it.

I was upset, and bewildered too. I had taken to Sybil so strongly. I couldn't believe she was either a thief or a witch.

'She has certainly committed a crime!' Mistress Ferris spoke up. 'Breaking into a document box, reading other people's letters . . .'

'Quite. But the cellar's not the best place; I keep my good wine down there. She might break into that as well!' There was a mocking humour in Master Ferris's voice. 'Take her to one of the unused attic rooms and lock her in. There's an empty one next to the west tower; that'll do. Maine, see that someone reliable is on guard outside her door. And send for Sir Edward

Heron. Say the charges concern spying, forcing locks, possible intended theft, and association with witches.'

'I've stolen nothing, and I've never had to do with witches!' Sybil shouted. She was getting panicky. She cried out: 'Please, for the love of God, will someone let the Stannards know what's happened? I'm here on their behalf; please tell them!'

'You want to inform them because they have influence in high places!' Master Ferris thumped his fist on the inglenook wall. 'We all know they saved that witch Gladys Morgan from the rope! You expect them to mount a rescue for you! We will *not* send word to them. Take her away!'

No one seemed to have noticed us at all. Thomas pulled me backwards out of the door, and we took ourselves out of sight, into a parlour, while Sybil was being marched upstairs. The parlour was chilly, with no fire, and we didn't sit down but stood staring uncertainly at each other.

'What now?' I said. 'Thomas, you can't talk to your parents about . . . about . . . Well, not today, when they're already so angry.'

'No, I can't,' he agreed. 'I'll have to wait.'

'I think they were wrong not to let the Stannards know,' I said doubtfully. 'They'll find out in time, of course, but if Sybil is being employed by them, they do have a sort of right to be told about this.'

'Sybil?' Thomas frowned. 'Why are you worried about her? Or the Stannards?'

'I like her,' I told him. 'I don't think she's dishonest . . . or a witch, either. Thomas, couldn't *you* get word to Hawkswood?'

'No, I could not. Why should I?' said Thomas resentfully. 'Christina was at the Stannards' house, Hawkswood, when the daughter of the house was married, and I went there to meet her. Mistress Stannard caught us and hauled Christina away. She's against us, just like my parents. Why should I do anything to please the Stannards?'

'I suppose Mistress Stannard felt she was doing right,' I said timidly. 'If you weren't supposed to meet, and she knew that and then came on you, on Stannard land . . . She'd feel responsible.'

'And children must always obey their parents, no matter how unreasonable their parents may be, and good little girls like Margaret Emory always keep the rules.' His voice was mocking. He had never spoken to me like that before.

I didn't answer.

'If I'm forced into marrying you after all,' he said savagely, 'then will I spend my whole life hearing your prim little voice explaining the difference between right and wrong? Will I have to put up with you for ever as a living, breathing conscience, always at my side? What a bitter reminder that will be, of how I failed myself and Christina!'

And then I became angry, just as I started to do when his mother made remarks about my appearance and looked at my teeth. I felt my spine stiffen. My head went back. 'We're not married yet, and I don't have to do what you say,' I said to him. 'And I don't want to marry you any more than you want to marry me. I *like* Sybil. I think word *should* go to the Stannards.' I drew in a deep breath, and then, because he had been rude, had hurt and angered me, and because I truly thought he was wrong, and because, after all, no one had told me not to, I said: 'If you won't take the news to them, then *I will.*'

I turned from him and ran. I still marvel at myself. I've never done such an outrageous thing before, in all of my life. I've never acted on my own judgement without deferring to anyone else's, never shouldered responsibility alone, never defied any prohibition, even one that hasn't actually been spoken. No one had forbidden me to take Sybil's message, but only because no one had dreamed that I might want to. At heart, I knew that. But somehow this time was different; somehow, all of a sudden, *I'd* become different. *No one said I couldn't,* I told myself, and I clutched at the excuse, as though it were a coat of mail, and . . . *ran.*

I was still in my cloak and hat; I had no need to fetch any outdoor things. I didn't take Blue. A groom might have wanted to come with me, or asked if I had permission to go out alone. I couldn't be sure of anyone in this house. I didn't yet know what rules I would be expected to keep, and I didn't intend to ask. I did know that all of a sudden I hated White Towers, hated everyone who lived there. I had been looked over as though I were a horse for sale and was to be pushed into bed with a man who didn't want me there and had just made it clear in a cruelly unkind manner. I was going to *enjoy* defying them all.

So out I raced. I think most of the household was otherwise occupied by this time, aware of the drama and either chattering excitedly in the kitchen or upstairs helping to get Sybil locked up. No one saw me go except Thomas, and he didn't try to stop me. I went out by the front door but not by the main gate because I'd have had to pass the gatekeeper's lodge, and for all I knew he'd ask questions. I ran through the gardens and the patch of woodland that's inside the grounds, and got out through a little door in the boundary fence that I know about. It's always bolted, but on the inside. I could open it easily. Once outside, I made for Hawkswood, walking and running alternately. It was five miles, but I knew I'd get here in little more than an hour.

I was very afraid that Thomas would come after me to drag me back, or send someone else to do it. But he didn't. Thomas is good-hearted, really.

I think he was horrid to me only because he has done this strange thing called falling in love. But meanwhile, what I've come to say is: Sybil has been caught reading Master Ferris's private letters and is going to be charged with all sorts of awful things, and I thought you ought to know, and can you help her? I really did take to Sybil.

THIRTEEN
Wild Geese

We gave Margaret some wine, but she refused food and would barely stay long enough to drain her glass. 'I have to go back,' she kept saying. 'I don't want to; I detest the very thought of White Towers, but I have no choice. If I get back quickly, then perhaps they won't realize how long I've been gone. If only Thomas hasn't told them!'

Then she almost broke down. 'I don't know what to do about Thomas! I can't marry him! I've seen him with Christina, and I don't want to spend my life with a man who wants someone else. He'll hate me. But they'll make us marry; his parents will! What will that mean for me, in all the years to come? Oh, I'm sorry, I know you can't do anything about that. I know I have to go back, whatever happens, and I must go now!'

Brockley took her, not on a pillion but perched straddle behind him on Mealy, with her skirts bunched. That way, the horse could go faster. They went off at a canter. We had told Brockley to put her down in the woods before they were in sight of the house so that she could go in on foot and say that she had been walking in the fresh air because she was upset about Sybil. We could only share her hope that Thomas hadn't told on her.

'And take saddlebags,' Hugh said when instructing Brockley. 'Because, after you've put Margaret down, you'd better go to Priors Ford and collect that child Tessie.'

Brockley was back quite soon, with Tessie clinging on behind him and saddlebags bulging with the belongings she and Sybil had taken with them. I went out to meet them.

'I was that happy to see Master Brockley, come to bring me back,' said Tessie shyly. 'I wouldn't have known what to do, left all alone in them lodgings with no word from my mistress!'

'We will decide what to do; don't fret,' I said. 'You go and tidy yourself, and then I expect there'll be things to do in the kitchen.' She scurried away, and I thought that if we went on treating her well, she might one day become less nervous and might even become pretty and have a chance to make a decent marriage. I hoped so. I wanted to help her. I know what it's like to be brought up by people who don't want you.

Meanwhile, we had Sybil to worry about.

'What next?' I said to Hugh. 'What do we do? What *can* we do?'

'I think,' said Hugh grimly, 'that I must now pay that call on the Ferrises and hope I'll be let in. I won't involve Margaret, but I can reasonably say I want an explanation of Master Ferris's incredible behaviour at Meg's wedding and see if the fish rises. It ought to, seeing that they now know we sent Sybil there – or more or less. Short of locking her up ourselves, we couldn't have stopped her.'

'I doubt if they'll appreciate the difference,' I said gloomily.

'Maybe not, but they'll probably enjoy telling me that they have made Sybil a prisoner, and *then*, once I know officially – from them – that she's in their hands, I can try to get her out. I'll be there as an injured party, after all. I'll take my stand on that. I have a position in this county, and I don't think Ferris will risk laying hands on me. Ursula, I have to try. Besides, we want to know if Sybil found anything useful before she was caught. To do that, one of us needs to speak with her. I'll go at once.'

He was back before dinner. The day, which had started off cool and damp, had turned bitter, with a cutting east wind. Hugh had a fur-lined cloak and fur gloves, and had travelled in his coach, but when he returned his face was pinched with cold and his mouth was set.

'The fish rose, right enough,' he said. Once more, we had gathered our inner circle of the Brockleys and also Gladys. She was involved now and could not be left out. We were in the study, where I'd had a fire lit. Hugh sat down beside it, holding his hands to the warmth.

'I was let in,' he said. 'There was no trouble over that. But my welcome was chilly from the start, in every sense of the word. Raised eyebrows from that steward Peter Maine – some of this east wind would do that pale face of his good – and Mistress Bridget saying in oh such a cool, well-bred voice that she must ask her husband if he would receive me. I was left to wait for half an hour in a freezing cold parlour, and then in came Walter Ferris, looking as plain and ordinary as he always does but in a bad temper. He said he wondered I had the impertinence to enter his house.'

'Impertinence! He's a fine one to talk!' Gladys snorted.

'I agree,' Hugh said dryly. 'I said to him that it had been fairly impertinent of him to intrude on Meg's wedding feast. Then I started to ask him his reasons for what amounted to an attack on my family, but he cut me short and said that he was aware that I had introduced a spy into his house. He told me, triumphantly, that he had her under lock and key.'

'He meant Sybil?' I asked.

Dale, with a shudder, said: 'Poor Mistress Jester.'

'Yes, he meant Sybil,' Hugh said. 'Well, at least I didn't have to drag her into the conversation by a back door, as it were. I'd been wondering how to do that, if it came to it. I said yes, Sybil had gone to White Towers on our behalf, though not at our behest, in search of something that would explain his incomprehensible behaviour. She had done it out of loyalty to us, I said, and could I please speak to her. Ferris said no, I couldn't. I told him I was horrified to learn that she was locked up!'

He paused, his mouth set more grimly than ever. 'And then,' he said at length, 'he told me that a messenger had already gone to the sheriff, carrying an accusation against Sybil, of intended thievery and also of association with sorcery. Edward Heron has sent word back that he will come in person to White Towers tomorrow. No one mentioned Margaret, so I think Thomas has held his tongue.'

'That's a mercy, at any rate,' I said.

'I tried my hardest to get Sybil released.' Hugh passed a hand over his hair. When I had first met him, his brown hair had been turning grey; now it was all grey and becoming scanty. 'I told him,' he said, 'that she was an honest woman and certainly was neither a thief nor a witch. I said I had every right to know the reason behind his campaign against my household, that my family and his had been good neighbours for generations and I had found his behaviour unbelievable. I said we had worried about Sybil and that, yes, I had come partly in search of her. Do you know, I had the impression that he doesn't really believe in his own accusations against her? It's hard to say why – a tone of voice, an expression crossing his face; it was no more than that. But it was still an impression, and a strong one. Ursula, I'm sorry but . . . I think his real motive is that, for some reason, he simply wants to harm her.'

'But *why*? *Sybil* didn't help to defeat Mary Stuart's ambitions, or throw pepper at Anne Percy and arrange for her to lose her footing in her own kitchen and end up sitting on the floor with pottage all over her!' I said.

'No,' said Brockley. 'But she is your friend, isn't she, madam? To harm her is to hurt you. Just as you would have been hurt if Mistress Meg or her husband had caught smallpox.'

Hugh said tiredly: 'I am truly sorry, Ursula, but in the end, I had to leave, having had no success. I could feel Ferris's smile like a knife in my back as I drove away. Sybil is still there, God help her, and I never as much as glimpsed her.'

'But . . .' said Dale, and then stopped.

I turned to her. 'Go on.'

Dale was often a little diffident in Hugh's presence. But he looked at her encouragingly, and she said: 'I mean . . . she could still be charged, couldn't she? Wherever she was – there or here. Maybe it won't make much difference to her.'

'In this house, she wouldn't be locked up,' Hugh said. 'And if anyone came for her, we could make it clear that we were standing by her.'

Brockley said: 'I wonder if Master Ferris is any good with a crossbow?'

Hugh said: 'He does archery for sport, crossbow and longbow. He has a set of targets in his grounds. I could see them from the windows of that parlour.'

Brockley made a noise like a growl. 'And we *do* need to talk to her, to ask her if she found anything useful,' he said.

'But none of this,' I said, 'is the real point. The real point is that we can't leave Sybil in Ferris's hands. At least, I can't. I can't bear the thought of it. She put herself at risk for us, and I refuse to abandon her.'

'But *how* can we get to her?' said Dale.

Gladys emitted one of her dreadful cackles. 'Mistress Stannard's got it in mind to go adventuring again. I knows the signs!'

I said: 'I know the layout of White Towers. Bridget Ferris showed me round the place, the time we dined there. Margaret said they had put Sybil in an attic room just below the west tower. I think I know where she means. It's got a dormer window. Let me think. All the attic rooms looked the same way if I remember rightly. The other side of the attic floor is a passage. That has windows too, and I remember the midday sun pouring in. So the passage side looks south and the attic rooms must face north.'

'But how can you get into White Towers? They wouldn't let you in, surely? Or they might lock you up as well as Sybil and not let you *out*,' protested Dale.

'I wouldn't have to get into the house, exactly,' I said. 'I could go at night, and I think I could reach that attic window from outside. That floor isn't as wide as the rest of the house. It stands on a level roof, so to speak, and Bridget walked us all round it. The outer walls are low, with ornamental crenellations – like battlements, but not proper ones. The towers have doors opening on to it, though they wouldn't be any use to me, of course. I'd have to come in through those imitation battlements. I'd need a good long ladder. I'd have to break the window of the right attic and get Sybil out.'

'Getting over the boundary fence would need a ladder anyway,' said Brockley. 'I've seen the fence often enough from the outside. It's stout and high all the way round. But you can't go swarming over fences and battlements, madam, even fancy battlements. If anyone does such a crazy thing, it had better be me. If Ferris catches me, I would at least have the chance of a word with him about Brown Berry. Or maybe not just a word.'

'Brockley, it really won't help if you murder Ferris for

Berry's sake!' I protested. 'Or even if you just injure him! You'd end up arrested for assault as well as housebreaking. That wouldn't help Sybil. It's my task. If Heron is coming tomorrow, I'll have to go tonight.'

'You can't!' Brockley expostulated. 'Master Stannard, only you can forbid her! I beg of you, forbid her now!'

Just as ours was about the only household in the land that would have spawned Sybil's enterprising plan to get into White Towers, my husband was probably the only man in England who would *not* instantly have done what Brockley was asking. Hugh was silent.

It was a silence that went on and on, until Brockley said: 'Please, Master Stannard! Please!'

Even then, there was a further pause, until at last Hugh said: 'I could forbid her, Brockley, of course I could. And I know, Ursula, that from sheer loyalty to me, you might obey. I also know that if anything . . . happened to Sybil . . .'

'She could end up being hanged,' I said fiercely. 'You know what that means! We came near to seeing Gladys hang.' I saw Gladys shrink into herself. 'We did see the others die, who were in that death cart. If I thought that had happened to Sybil because I didn't even try to save her . . .'

'You'd blame yourself for ever,' said Hugh heavily. 'And if I had stopped you, you would blame me too. I would go myself, except that I can't climb ladders, not with my rheumatics, and in an emergency, I couldn't run away. As things are . . . Brockley, there was an occasion when I actually did command your mistress to undertake a certain task for the queen. It was against her will, but I insisted, and it led her into great danger. She has never once reproached me for it. But if I now hold her back against her will – either by claiming my right to forbid her or by using force – and Sybil comes to harm, I think that then she might well reproach me. Am I right, Ursula?'

I shook my head. 'No, Hugh. I wouldn't hold such a thing against you, of course I wouldn't. But I want to get Sybil out of that man's hands, and I believe I can. Let me go with your blessing.'

Exasperatedly, Brockley said: 'I know you, madam, the

same as Gladys does. Once again, you've heard the wild geese calling.'

I had first met Sybil some years ago, in Cambridge. As we rode through East Anglia on our way there, I had been interested by the skeins of wild geese that crossed the skies early each morning and again in the evening. They flew in V formations, honking in wild voices. I had been riding beside Rob Henderson, the friend who had for a while been Meg's foster father and who had come with his wife to see her married. Speaking of the geese, I had said to him: 'Their calls always seem to be full of salt winds and vast empty spaces.'

And he had said that this told him something about my nature. 'Will you ever settle for domestic peace?' he asked me. 'Or will the wild geese call to you for the rest of your life?'

Brockley had overheard. He had, since then, made it clear that he saw me in much the same way, and I knew that there was truth in it. I did want to be the one who climbed the ladder to rescue Sybil, not just because Brockley might indeed half-kill Walter Ferris if he got the chance, and not just because Walter Ferris would probably have Brockley taken up on a serious charge if *he* had the chance, but also because . . . I wanted to be the one to climb the ladder.

I had been glad, I thought, to leave adventuring behind and settle down to a peaceful home-loving life with Hugh. But now a new opportunity of adventure had come, and one so near my heart, in such a good cause!

Hugh had foreseen something of the kind. He had said so, when we were on our way home from Alice Cobbold's wedding. Brockley had recognized it now. The wild geese were calling once again, and yes, I wished to answer.

Dale was the one who said anxiously: 'What about dogs? Aren't there dogs? Could anyone get in, just like that, without guard dogs giving the alarm?'

'Oddly enough,' Hugh said, 'they probably can. There's no gatehouse at White Towers, just the lodge at the entrance to the grounds, a couple of hundred yards from the house. When I drove up, a pair of mastiffs rushed out on to the path, barking to tell the lodge keeper that someone had called. But I didn't see any dogs at the house, except for Mistress Bridget's lapdog. It yelped at me as if it wanted to bite me. Then, on my way out, while the lodge keeper was opening the gates wide enough for the coach, I put my head out of the window and chatted to him. I didn't want to behave as if I were leaving the place with my tail between my legs. The mastiffs were making a racket again. I admired them and said I might like to try Hero with one of them next time she's in season, and see what kind of puppies resulted, and I asked – just casually – if the dogs ran loose in the grounds at night as well.'

It occurred to me that Hugh had been ahead of me all the time.

'What did he say?' I asked.

'He said they were chained up at night. They used to run free, but there was some trouble over it. Once or twice, apparently, at night when no one was around to keep an eye on them, they went off on illicit hunting trips and got into the patch of woodland inside the grounds where Ferris rears pheasants and gobbled some of them up. Ferris was furious, and now the dogs are chained up at the lodge from dusk to dawn. And the lodge is on the south side of the grounds. The attics look north, you said, Ursula?'

'Yes, I think they must do.'

Hugh left his seat by the fire and went to his desk, where he pulled a sheet of paper out of a drawer and took up a quill. 'The one time that Ursula and I both dined at White Towers,' he said, 'Bridget Ferris showed Ursula round it, but the men stayed at the dinner table drinking strong liquors. I don't know the inside of the place at all well, because the present house is only a few years old. When Walter Ferris inherited after his father was murdered, the original house was still there – it was a small manor house, older than Hawkswood, and it was called The Oaks because the woodland roundabout is mostly oak. Walter had it pulled down and had the present place built instead. But if I hardly know the inside of White Towers, I do know the grounds and the surroundings. Ferris's father sometimes invited me to dine, and I've often walked in the gardens there. I don't suppose the grounds have changed much. They're like this. Look.'

As he spoke, he had been drawing a sketch. He held it up. 'See. Here's the house and the boundary fence that goes all the way round the grounds. Here are the woods that go round outside the fence except on the western side, and here – on the eastern side of the grounds – is the patch of wood where Ferris raises his pheasants. And here, to the north, are the gardens.'

'The attics overlook them,' I said. 'I remember that. So the attics do look north.'

'Round to the west there's a paddock and a bowling alley and the archery butts,' Hugh said. He gave Brockley a quick frown which kept my manservant quiet. 'The only entrances to the grounds are the lodge gates – here to the south – and the little side gate into the pheasants' wood, the one that Margaret Emory said she used when she ran out of the place to warn us about Sybil. She said it would be bolted on the inside so it isn't much use to us, and it's not in the right place, anyway. Now, here's the main track that leads through the woods to the lodge gate, and here, branching off before the lodge is in sight, is another track that would take you round to the north boundary. It's probably just wide enough for a cart, which is a good thing because you'll need a cart to carry the ladder. I'm not sure we have a ladder long enough, but there's a thatcher in Hawkswood, Harry Dodd, who has. It's one of those double affairs that extend. I'll borrow it from him.'

'It will be heavy. It will need two of us anyway,' said Brockley. 'Though, with or without the ladder, I'm going with her.'

'What about your ankle?' I said.

'It's as near completely better as makes no difference. I suggest, madam, that I should take Arthur with me, or young Joseph, while you stay here in safety.'

'No, Brockley! I agree that I'll need help with the ladder, so all right, you and I will go together. But no one else is to run into danger for me. See here, Brockley, I've rescued *you* from imprisonment in the past. I did that because I value you. I value Sybil in the same way.'

'Master Stannard!' Brockley once more turned to Hugh for support.

'I think,' said Hugh, 'that I have already agreed to let her go, and I won't renege on that. Ursula is experienced, after all.'

'Very well,' said Brockley, but angrily.

Dale's expression was bleak. She was biting her lip, hiding her feelings as, once again, Brockley and I laid plans to go adventuring together.

'Now,' said Hugh, pressing on. 'Details. The cart you use can't be big because the track you'll have to take isn't *that* wide. The smaller farm wagon could get along it, the one I designed myself with the hinged back that unbolts and drops down to make a tailboard. Even then, the ladder will stick out beyond it. But it will do.'

'That wagon only needs one horse,' said Brockley thoughtfully. 'We had best take one of the coach horses.'

'And wait until full dark before you start out,' Hugh added. 'I'll explain things to Wilder and send him to the village to talk to Harry Dodd.'

Dodd agreed to lend his ladder, though none too willingly. 'Had to know what we wanted it for,' Wilder told us. 'Or he wouldn't have let us have it. He's got others, but not so long as this one, and he said he never knew when he'd need his special, as he calls it. I had to make it clear it was life or death for Mistress Jester.'

Dodd and his son brought it to us just after dinner, trundling it on the home-made handcart they used for carrying it about. When night had fallen and Brockley and I were ready to leave, we met in the hall, with Hugh and Dale and Gladys to see us off. From Brockley, I had borrowed breeches, a linen shirt and a buff coat, all of them a trifle loose on me but suitable for scrambling over fences and up a ladder. I had a set of picklocks in one of the coat pockets. Just as we assembled, Joan Flood appeared, unbidden, with cinnamon cakes and marchpane fancies and mulled wine especially for me and Brockley. My unusual attire clearly didn't surprise her at all.

'We all know where you're bound, madam, Master Brockley,' she said. 'So I thought I'd bring something to warm you before you start off for that White Towers place. Sky's cleared, but it's still proper parky out there. I know! I been to the village after dinner, knocked up that woman as sells spices and bought some fresh cinnamon sticks.'

'How did you know where we're going?' Brockley demanded. 'Does the whole house know?'

'Probably,' said Hugh. 'Wilder had to explain things to Dodd, and you know how talkative the Dodds are. Didn't they have something to eat in the kitchen here before they went home? Having their mouths full wouldn't stop them talking. What of it? The whole business will be over before the news can spread beyond this house.'

'Dodd's a blabbermouth,' said Brockley bluntly. 'And so's his son. But I won't say no to a warm drink and a cinnamon cake, all the same.'

I was glad of them too and thanked Joan for thinking of it. And then it was really time to go. At the last minute, Hugh brought me a small dagger to hang from my belt. 'A means of defence is always useful, and I see that Brockley has a dagger too. But, Brockley, you are *not* to attack Ferris, even if you get the chance. I mean it!'

We went outside. Hero and Hector, who, unlike the White Towers mastiffs, were never chained up at night, frisked excitedly round us as we put the ladder on the cart, evidently hoping to be taken too, and Arthur Watts came out to see us off. He asked to be in the party, but I shook my head at him, and Hugh said: 'The fewer people on this expedition, the better!'

At the last minute, John Hawthorn appeared, along with the Floods, Netta and Tessie. The news certainly had permeated right through the house. They all said things like *good luck* and *Godspeed*, and they all kept their voices low, as though they feared that an enemy might overhear them.

Brockley climbed into the cart. Just as I was about to follow, Hugh took my arm and drew me aside. Very quietly, he said: 'If I were younger and fitter, you wouldn't be doing this, Ursula. I *would* do it for you; you know I would. You didn't marry me for love, but believe me, I love you.'

'I know, and Hugh, I *do* love you, only I can't desert Sybil . . .'

'No, you are loyal. To her and to me. Though I sometimes

wonder what would happen if Matthew de la Roche were suddenly to appear, in person, at Hawkswood.'

'*Hugh!*' I was shaken. This was entirely the wrong moment to discuss such a matter, and I didn't want to discuss it anyway, under any circumstances. The truth was that I had sometimes wondered the same thing. I had never known any tranquillity with Matthew, yet he was the most beautiful man I ever saw, and the memory of his love-making would melt my very bones for the rest of my life. If it ever came to such a direct and immediate point, which man would prevail? I hoped I would never know the answer.

'It's all right,' Hugh said. 'I just wanted you to know how much you matter to me. I shall worry through all the hours until you return. I beg you to take care.' He glanced up at Brockley and called to him: 'Look after her, Roger. I am entrusting her to you. And look after yourself too.'

'I'll do that, sir, never fear.'

Hugh stepped back, and I joined Brockley on the cart. I took the reins and chirruped to the horse. As we finally went out through the gatehouse, Brockley said: 'I wish to heaven you weren't here, madam. You shouldn't be here. Master Stannard should have stopped you. I would, in his place. Will you never learn?'

'When I'm too old to leave the fireside, perhaps,' I said, trying to make him smile. I failed.

'By this time next year,' he said, 'you'll probably be a grandmother.'

I couldn't think of an answer.

FOURTEEN
Mission by Night

We went on for a long time without speaking. The sky was perfectly clear now but it was indeed very cold, and though the moon was up, it was still young and cast little light, while the track was overhung by trees. In the darkness, we missed the fork to the track leading to the north side of White Towers, only realizing our mistake when we saw the roof and chimneys of the lodge outlined against the stars.

'We've got to turn round,' I said.

It was difficult, because the trees and bushes were so close on either side and the ladder stuck out so much. We had to lift it off and lay it on the ground, turn the cart round and then put it back as soon as we were facing away from the lodge. At least we hadn't gone close enough to rouse the dogs. We drove slowly back, found the turn we should have taken, and steered our load into it.

This path was barely wide enough for the cart, and it was not merely overhung but roofed by branches. Tree roots jutted into the track. There was a sharp tang of autumn in the air and the smell of leaves and leaf mould. Twigs brushed the sides of the cart, and the wagon wheels bumped over the roots, but the damp earth deadened the horse's hoofs so our progress was fairly quiet. Once or twice we heard faint rustlings in the woods, but whatever creatures had made them never appeared. I felt no fear of them, however. It was not like the night when I followed Christina through the gardens of Hawkswood. Now, I was on a mission to outwit people who might well be dangerous, but were entirely human.

However, when an owl hooted, always a spine-tingling sound in the dead of night, I was moved to break our renewed silence by remarking: 'I've been accused of witchcraft, Brockley. Do you believe in witches?'

'No,' said Brockley uncompromisingly.

'What would you do if a coven of cackling hags on broomsticks suddenly swooped down on us?'

'Shout *boo* very loudly, madam, and they'd all fall off their brooms. It always works.'

I chuckled, and so did he. It was one of the absurd, companionable jokes that we often shared. We couldn't get out of the habit. Hugh, wise Hugh, was tolerant, but it would have wounded Dale to hear us.

'There's the boundary fence,' said Brockley.

The track had brought us to the locked gate into the private wood, but it continued on, following the curve of the fence. We made our way along it, and I was relieved to find that, from now on, there were places where the trees thinned out and we could see some of the stars. We couldn't find the Pole Star, but glimpses of the Plough told us where it must be. Without that, we would have found it hard to be sure when we'd reached the northern edge of the grounds.

Finally, Brockley said: 'I think we're on the north side now. Stop.' We halted and secured the horse to a tree, using a knot that could be freed with a single tug. Then we carried the heavy double ladder to the fence.

The fencing was solid, providing no footholds, but nevertheless, this part of the adventure was not too challenging. The ground was level, and we could base the ladder safely. It jutted well above the fence, but Brockley, going up first, swung himself easily off the rungs to sit sideways on the top. I climbed up after him. I was more awkward about getting off the ladder, but Brockley gave me a helpful shove so that I too could perch myself on the fence, with the ladder between us.

We did have some difficulty with dragging it up from below and tilting it to drop on the other side, and we couldn't help making a little noise, but we were a long way from the house as yet. I was thankful for the freedom of movement that my breeches gave me. 'All right,' Brockley whispered at last, after shaking the ladder to make sure it was firm in its new position. 'Follow me down.'

He descended quickly, and I followed. Getting back on was easier than getting off. I stepped off at the foot, and there we were, inside the boundary of White Towers. There were trees all round us, but just here the wood had narrowed and we had only fifty yards to go before we emerged into the garden, which we must cross to reach the house itself.

We advanced with caution along a path between vegetable beds, carrying the ladder between us. It was an awkward burden, and we went slowly. We came to a yew hedge and passed through an archway into a topiary garden. Now we could see the house ahead of us, quite clearly, for its white walls showed even in this faint moonlight, and its chimneys were as visible against the sky as those of the lodge had been.

'Here we go,' Brockley said. He glanced back. 'I like the way the wood grows right up to the fence. We can use it if we have to run for it without the ladder. I dare say you can climb a tree if you have to, madam.'

'I hope so,' I said. Out of memory, I dredged a telling phrase. 'It would be a matter of using what's there, as Carew Trelawny used to say.'

'Yes. My old friend,' Brockley said soberly, and for a moment I know we were both remembering Trelawny. He had been a short, dark, tough Cornishman with a small pointed beard. He had been so resourceful, so brave and so full of laughter that other people could catch fire from him. Just to be with him put heart into one.

'You must miss him,' I said. I was missing him myself. Now that we were here, I was cold with dread and could have done with Trelawny's heartening company.

'Always,' said Brockley. 'But we must just manage. And I wish it wasn't a matter of *we*. You shouldn't be here. Getting into other people's houses at night, creeping about, rescuing prisoners, it's no work for a lady.'

'May I once more remind you how, long ago, I rescued you from imprisonment? In a cellar, if I remember rightly. You didn't mind me getting into someone else's house that night.'

Brockley, in answer, merely snorted.

We went on. It seemed a lengthy plod through the topiary garden. The tall yew trees were carved at the top into spheres and cones and cylinders, and the main path through them curved annoyingly. The ladder kept hitting them. Brockley muttered under his breath and steered us to the right, where there was another, straighter path, close to a low hedge, box this time. Glancing over it, I could make out a paddock, and quite nearby I could see the archery targets that Hugh had mentioned. The moon wasn't big enough to show details, but the white circles in the target picked up what light there was. Brockley noticed too.

'Someone here certainly likes shooting,' he muttered.

We left the topiary and plodded on through a knot garden. Then we found ourselves on a wide gravel path encircling the house. Brockley halted us. 'That'll be the west tower, to the right. That window beside it will be the attic you think Sybil's in?'

'Yes. Will the ladder reach it?'

'Just, I reckon, if we extend it as far as it'll go.'

We worked quickly, drawing it out to its greatest length, fixing the hooks and bolts that held its two sections together, and then put it against the wall, once more making sure it was securely placed. 'We don't want accidents,' said Brockley grimly. 'It only just goes high enough. It'll mean climbing up all of it.'

I went to take hold and start the climb. And then he put a hand on my forearm and said: 'No.'

'What do you mean?' I muttered at him.

His fingers tightened. 'Master Stannard asked me to look after you, and I intend to. I am going up. You are not.'

'Of course I am! It was agreed. It—'

'You are not. You are precious to Master Stannard, more than you know. Letting you do things like this! I can't understand it. He's either a saint or a fool, I don't know which, but I'll guard his back if he won't guard it for himself. I'll look after both of you.'

'Brockley, you're supposed to be my manservant. It's your duty to take my orders.'

'Not this time, madam. Now, you hold this damned ladder while I go up and get Sybil. And don't argue. We can't have raised voices now!'

That was true enough. Seething, I gave in. I stood holding the ladder firm while Brockley disappeared up it.

And then I heard the baying of the dogs.

The mastiffs were not chained up at the lodge tonight. By the sound of them, they were round the corner, on the west side of the house, but drawing nearer. I let go of the ladder and ran towards the sound, hoping to heaven that they had handlers with them who would restrain them from actually sinking their teeth into me but wanting to stop the said handlers from catching sight of Brockley.

I was used to dogs and knew that quite fierce ones could sometimes be disconcerted by a quarry that rushed at them instead of running away. When you train guard dogs, you use their hunting instincts, the ancient urges that make them want to chase their dinner. Dinner that marches towards them, shouting, '*Down, sir!*' stands a chance of confusing them.

So: 'Down, sir!' I bawled as I rounded the corner of the house and found myself, as I expected, confronting the dogs. I drew my dagger, in case they attacked, and hoped that Brockley had heard them, was hearing me, and would make his escape quickly enough.

The dogs continued to bay, but yes, they were on leashes. They were straining towards me but were being held back. I made out the shadowy figures of the men behind them. I stopped.

Someone snapped an order to the dogs, and they subsided. The reception party came up to me.

'Well, well,' said Walter Ferris. 'If it isn't Mistress Stannard in person. Come to rescue your friend Sybil Jester, I take it! Where's your man Brockley? He's with you, don't lie!'

'No, he's not!' I retorted. 'I wouldn't let him. I forbade it. I'd put Sybil in danger; I wasn't going to do that to anybody else!'

'Bah! Your husband never let you come alone; don't expect me to believe that.'

'No, he didn't. I slipped out without him knowing. We don't share a room,' I said mendaciously. 'I've left a note where he'll find it in the morning.'

The dogs scented me, but they can't tell their handlers if

they've scented Brockley as well. Escape, Brockley! Get down
that ladder and get away and warn Hugh!

'By God, I'm glad you're not my wife!' Ferris sounded
disgusted. 'I'd kill my wife if she ever behaved as you do – as
you have a reputation for doing! Look at you!' He glowered
at what he could see of me by starlight and a quarter of a
moon. 'Wearing breeches like a man! And carrying a dagger!
Give that here!' He snatched it from me. 'You're a disgrace!'

'Mary of Scotland has been known to wear breeches,' I
said. 'When escaping from places, or hunting, or riding to
war.'

'Queens can do as they please. Other women cannot. You
can rest assured that your friend Sybil is quite safe. You shall
join her!' He turned to the dog-handlers. 'Get on round the
house and see if you can find anyone else. I don't trust the lady
an inch.'

After which, he turned without warning from bully to perfect
gentleman and presented a crooked elbow for my convenience.
'Perhaps you would take my arm, my lady.'

FIFTEEN
Useless Proof

H e had six men with him. Two of them went off with the dogs, but the other four surrounded us as I was taken indoors, as though even now Ferris feared I might break free. We went in by what proved to be the kitchen door. A single flambeau at the far end cast a wavering light over pinewood tables and a wide fireplace with a banked fire, and caught metallic gleams from cooking pots and utensils. No one was there, however. In many houses, kitchen servants bed down in front of the hearth, but here, as at Hawkswood, it seemed that the servants had proper sleeping quarters.

I had taken Ferris's arm as requested, or ordered. It felt iron-hard, the kind of arm that would be reassuring if it belonged to a friend but was frightening when it was attached to an enemy.

I was walked across the room and then through a low door on the right, which opened on to stone steps going downwards. One of the men took the flambeau from its bracket to light our way. Ferris detached himself from me and pushed me down the steps ahead of him.

Brockley, did you escape? Was there time? You won't have the ladder; you can't run carrying that. You'll have to climb a tree to get over the fence. Have you managed it? Get away, Brockley; tell Hugh what's happened. You must have heard the dogs and me shouting at them and being taken. You had a chance. Pray God you took it!

'We're going to keep you close,' Ferris told me. 'But you won't be alone. We moved Mistress Jackman down here just before nightfall. After your husband's visit, I did wonder if there would be an attempt to rescue her, and so, on second thoughts, the cellar seemed a wiser choice. You will find bedding there. Myself, I wouldn't have troubled to set out mattresses for intruders, even female ones, but my good wife suggested that if you and Mistress Jackman appeared before the sheriff looking too scruffy, it might not reflect well on this house. You and we are all gentlefolk of standing, and there are proprieties to observe. My wife is a fool, as most women are, but once in a while she says something sensible, and clearly she had my welfare – my good name in this case – at heart. The sheriff will be here tomorrow. How you'll be treated once you're in his hands, of course I can't say. He may be less good-hearted than I am. Watch your footing. Not that these steps are unduly steep. Wine barrels have to be carried up them, after all. Here we are.'

And here, indeed, we were, at the foot of the stairs, facing a cellar door. By the light of the flambeau, I recognized Peter Maine as he moved ahead of us, produced a bunch of keys, and unlocked the door.

'One moment,' said Ferris. 'We took some lockpicking implements away from the Jackman woman. Mistress Stannard, you do have something of a reputation. Did you bring some along as well, in case they would be useful in releasing your friend? If so, hand them over to me. Unless you want us to search you for them.'

Sullenly, I felt in the pocket of my buff jacket and brought out the picklocks I had been carrying there.

'Thank you,' said Ferris, taking them from me. He nodded to Maine, who swung the door open. 'It isn't the first time you've been a prisoner in a wine cellar, I think,' he said as he propelled me through. 'Don't get drunk, will you?' The door shut behind me, and I heard Maine's keys jangle as he locked it.

Before the door closed, the flambeau had given me a glimpse of what was in the cellar. I had seen a lot of barrels, set in rows, on one side of the room, and on the other side some rough-looking mattresses on the floor. On one of them, sitting up and blinking, clutching a blanket to her, white-faced and wide-eyed, was Sybil. As the door shut, the torchlight vanished, but after a moment I realized that there was a fair-sized grating high up on one wall, letting in a glint of moonlight. I could see enough to make my way to her.

'It's me,' I said. 'Ursula. Sybil, are you all right?'

'Only frightened. Oh, Ursula!' Her voice shook and then broke, and I threw myself down beside her and put my arms round her.

'I'm here now. You're not alone any more. Hugh will do something to help us, I know he will. Hush, now. Hush.'

'I'm not as brave as I thought I was!' Sybil tried to speak calmly. 'I'm so glad to see you, but oh dear, I didn't want you to be caught too! Did you come for me? I know that Margaret Emory reached you – she crept down here last evening and whispered through the door that she'd managed to get word to Hawkswood. She's a nice girl. She's the one Thomas Ferris is supposed to be going to marry. We made friends before I was taken, and I can't understand why Thomas prefers Christina Cobbold to her! I gather that he does. She told me that when we talked through the door. There's no accounting for love; it's just not reasonable.'

'No, it's not,' I agreed. My earlier marriages had taught me that. The mattress crackled under me, and I felt it with my palm. 'Straw,' I said with distaste. I felt about for the blanket. It had an unpleasant texture and it smelt, but I was cold. I pulled it over me and settled myself against Sybil, to share her warmth.

'They don't mean us to freeze,' said Sybil. 'Even if this sort of bedding is horrible, it's better than lying on a stone floor. Oh, Ursula, I'm so sorry I let myself be caught. I must have been careless. But that pale, soft-footed creature Peter Maine wears silent shoes and slinks about like a cat!' I had rarely heard the well-mannered Sybil sound so scathing. 'He came into Ferris's study while I was there, looking in the document box. I never heard him coming! Only, he said he'd already seen me through a window, so I suppose it wouldn't have been any use thrusting the box back on to the shelf where I found it and saying I'd missed my way in an unfamiliar house. As it was, he caught me red-handed anyway.'

'Brockley came with me,' I said, 'but with luck, he's got away. Sybil, did you hear that remark about this wasn't the first time I'd been a prisoner in a wine cellar? That's evidence enough for me that Ferris has been in touch with Anne Percy, or she with him. A wine cellar is where she had me and Brockley locked up last winter.'

'Oh, as to that . . .' Sybil tried to laugh but it turned into a sob. 'I found the proof you wanted. Useless, now that we're both trapped in here, but before I was caught, I'd seen it. There *was* a letter to Ferris from Anne Percy in the Netherlands. Oh, Ursula!' At home, among other people, she usually called me Mistress Stannard, but here in this underground prison, sharing fear and peril, the intimacy of Christian names seemed natural. 'I had time to read most of it. It was *horrible.*'

'What did it say? You'd better tell me.'

'It was much as we'd thought – she was telling him to . . . to harm you and Brockley. That's what we expected – but to see such things written down . . . such hatred. Such spite! It – she – tells Ferris . . . I think I can recall the words . . . for the love that kinsmen should have for each other, and for the child who has never seen her father, and for the glory of the Catholic church and the hopes of Mary Stuart of Scotland, and to avenge the indignity you put upon her – the Countess, I mean – he should find a way to destroy you. And also, before you are destroyed, to cause you to suffer in any way he can find. And Brockley too, because he helped you to defeat the rising and make a fool of her.'

'She's a proud lady,' I said. 'The trap Brockley and I laid for her in that kitchen probably made her as furious as our interference in matters of state! Hence the crossbow ambush, I think. It was nothing to do with the letter to Cecil. Brockley was right. He was the target. He was probably right about that business with the pearl necklace, too. Someone was trying to get him arrested for theft.'

'In the letter, she calls him . . . calls him . . . Oh, Ursula!'

'Tell me!' I said. 'I'd rather know.'

'Your . . . lapdog,' said Sybil, speaking very low. 'And your . . . your . . . well, you told me that in her letter to you she suggested that he was . . . was . . .'

'My lover? She's wrong,' I said, privately thanking heaven that I spoke the truth, near thing though it had once been.

'I know,' said Sybil. She added, in a more practical fashion: 'The letter doesn't actually give instructions about how Ferris should go about things, but she says she knows she can rely on his cunning, and there was one helpful suggestion.' Sybil said the word *helpful* as though it tasted nasty. 'She obviously knows all about Gladys. She knows that Gladys was once convicted of witchcraft and that you appealed to the queen to save her. I should think Ferris told her. The letter somehow read as though the Countess had been in regular touch with him. I suppose he'd know about Gladys. The whole locality does. Well, she says you've protected an evil witch and suggests that Ferris might be able to use that, somehow.'

'And his reward?' I asked. 'If he succeeds? Surely that was mentioned?'

'Yes,' said Sybil, with distaste. 'She says King Philip of Spain would pay. He's giving her a pension, and she says he has consented to pay a bounty of five hundred pounds for the two of you. Three hundred for destroying you alone, and two hundred for Brockley.'

Three hundred pounds would keep a yeoman farmer and his family for a year; two hundred would at least keep the farmer. But to the Countess of Northumberland, to the King of Spain, it ought to be small change. Though Philip of Spain had a reputation for being careful even with that.

'In my opinion,' I said, trying to speak lightly, 'I think that both Brockley and I are worth a lot more than the lady's estimate, but perhaps she couldn't risk asking too much of King Philip! *What's that noise?*'

The grating above our heads allowed sound to reach us from the world outside. Somewhere, not far away, the mastiffs were baying again, and there were men's voices, shouting. We sat straining our ears. The sounds were moving away. After a moment or two, they had faded into the distance.

'Were they after Brockley?' Sybil said, whispering, as though she feared she might be overheard.

'Perhaps. But if so, that means they haven't caught him yet. With luck, he's well away by now. He should have had time.'

During the pause while we were listening, I had done some thinking. 'I'm trying to follow in my mind what Ferris has been doing,' I said. 'He sent Dorothy Beale to spy on me, and then, I suppose, just took his chances. First he tried to get

Brockley arrested. Then he came to the wedding feast to frighten me with a threat about being accused of witchcraft; then he attacked Brockley again and tried to murder him. And I think you're right – those cloaks he presented to Meg and George were infected, and he hoped they would give smallpox to someone – me or people I cared about.'

'And he then saw how that could be linked to the accusation of witchcraft, to make it stronger than all that nonsense about love potions?' Sybil said.

'Yes, or . . . No, that can't be right. Jane Cobbold was the one who reported me for spreading sickness by magic. I can't make that add up to anything sensible.'

Wearily, Sybil said: 'I can tell you about that as well. 'That man Maine did some boasting after I was taken. He oversaw the men who brought these horrid prickly mattresses in here. Walter Ferris was behind what Mistress Cobbold did, only he had to go about it sideways and get someone else to drop the idea into her ear, because Cobbolds and Ferrises don't speak. Ferris knows Sir Edward Heron even better than the Cobbolds do. He and his wife dine at Heron's house sometimes. I expect,' said Sybil thoughtfully, 'that he realized Heron might hesitate to pursue a charge of witchcraft against you because you're related to the queen and Sir William Cecil is your friend. At any rate, according to Maine, he decided to get the accusation backed up by somebody other than him, and he settled on a Cobbold. No one would suspect collusion between Cobbolds and Ferrises.'

'Maine told you that?'

'Yes. It was this way. When he'd seen the mattresses brought in, he lingered to tell me that I needn't think I'd escape. I'd not only been caught peering into a private document box, with picklocks in one hand and one of Master Ferris's letters in the other; I'd also been sent to the house by a woman who was going to be charged with causing death by witchcraft. I said it was nonsense, that I knew what Jane Cobbold had done and I could only think that she was so upset by her daughter's illness that she was half out of her mind and doing things she'd presently be sorry about. But he laughed and said it wasn't like that at all. Margaret Emory's father knows the

Cobbolds, he said, and when Master Ferris heard that Christina had smallpox and was going to be scarred, he got *Emory* to encourage her to report you for witchcraft to the sheriff. I think Maine is proud of his employer's cleverness. He wanted to boast about it.'

'And Jane was upset enough over the damage to Christina's face to swallow it and lay the complaint? I wonder if Anthony Cobbold went along with it? That puzzles me. From what I've seen of him, I wouldn't think it likely. I'm surprised he let her.'

'Maybe she didn't talk to him about it – but just went and did it,' said Sybil. 'According to Maine, Ferris told Emory that if Jane Cobbold wouldn't take the hint, he was to go to Heron direct, but that Jane would be the best person because she could claim that you'd injured her family. He said that if Emory would do as he asked, then Thomas could marry Margaret.'

'But Thomas and Margaret don't want to marry,' I said.

'No, quite. But Margaret's parents are very anxious that they should. When she came to whisper to me through the attic door, she told me that her father did some favours for Ferris, in exchange for getting Ferris's final consent to the match. Making a tool of Jane Cobbold was one of the favours, presumably. It was quite clever of Ferris, in a way,' said Sybil angrily. 'Jane Cobbold is the silliest woman I have ever met. You only have to put an idea into her head, and it takes root like a dandelion in a vegetable patch.'

'Do you really dislike Jane so much? I've never heard you sound so salty before about other people!'

'You can be salty, too,' said Sybil. 'You've set me an example. I've detested Mistress Cobbold from the day I first met her, but it wasn't my place to say so. *Then.*'

'Maine must be a fool,' I said. 'You could repeat what he told you in court, if it came to that. It would be evidence against Ferris.'

'I said as much to Maine, and he just laughed. "Who'd listen to you?" he said. "You'd be there as a prisoner accused of attempted theft and consorting with witches. They'd expect you to make up stories, and who's going to believe such a taradiddle? Who else is here to listen to what I've told you? It would be your word against mine and Master Ferris's, and Emory wants to marry his daughter to Thomas so much, he won't spill any beans, believe me." Maine was almost swaggering.'

'Oh, Sybil!'

'I'm trying to be brave, but I don't feel it.' Sybil's voice was breaking, on the edge of tears once more. 'Oh, Ursula, what *are* we going to do? I wasn't asleep when you were brought down here – I can't sleep. I'm too frightened. But I heard what was said just outside this door. They took my picklocks away when Maine caught me, and now they've taken yours. We've no hope of getting out.'

'Oh, haven't we?' I said. 'Don't you remember? My husband had two extra sets of picklocks made before you came here. I brought them both with me. I had one set in my jacket pocket, and I handed that to Walter Ferris. But the other . . .' I fished under Brockley's loose-fitting shirt, found the cord that lay beneath it, and pulled. 'Here's the third set. I've had it slung round my neck. I think, if we let a little time go past so that Ferris and his minions have a chance to get to sleep, we might escape after all. Though you'd better be prepared. When it comes to getting over the boundary fence, you may have to climb a tree.'

We waited for quite a long time. There were no more sounds from above. 'Time to go,' I said at last.

I had no difficulty in letting us out of the cellar. The lock was one of the easiest I had ever had to force. The difficult part came next. Would there be anyone on guard in the kitchen, with or without the dogs? We could only hope for the best. As noiselessly as possible, we crept up the stone steps. I led the way and pushed open the door to the kitchen.

The dogs were not there. Nor were any human guards. All was dark and quiet. The flambeau hadn't been replaced. We groped our way to the outer door, and I discovered by feel that it had bolts on the inside. They had been shot. 'I hope everyone is indoors by now,' I whispered. 'Except for Brockley. I hope *he* isn't. Come along.'

In the darkness I fumbled with the bolts but got them open in the end. We crept warily out and stood for a moment, listening, but no dogs gave tongue, no voices shouted. With luck, the hunt was over – *may it have failed; Brockley, please be safe!* – and the mastiffs had been chained up again, I hoped, in their usual place at the lodge. 'This is the west side of the house,' I muttered. 'We have to get to the north side. Follow me.'

We kept close to the wall, in shadow, and edged along the wall and round the corner. We would have to leave it to cross the grounds to the fence, but at first, I led us on by the wall for some way, because there was something I wanted to know. I stopped.

'What is it?' Sybil breathed shakily in my ear.

'I want to see if the ladder is still there.'

'Ladder?'

'We thought you were still in the attic. We had a long ladder so as to reach high enough, and for getting over the fence. No, it's gone. Well, Ferris's men were bound to find it, and then he'd know that someone was with me. He'll know I couldn't handle such a big ladder alone.'

'Was it taken away or just left on the ground? If it's there, can't we use it? There are two of us, after all.'

I considered that. The ladder would slow us down, but I was not at all sure how good we would be at climbing trees. I was fairly active and might be able to do it, but Sybil was older than me, had led a more sedentary life, and was encumbered with skirts. 'Let's see,' I murmured.

We found it, laid on the ground against the wall. Someone had closed it up again, which would make it easier to handle.

'We can carry it between us,' I whispered. 'But we shan't be able to go fast. Well, all right. This way. We have to go through the knot garden and the topiary and then the kitchen garden.'

The moon had set. In the starlight, the knot garden lay as still as though it were under an enchantment, though I had no superstitious frisson now. If a witch or a ghost had suddenly appeared, I would have followed Brockley's recommendation and said, 'Boo!' When one is listening for mastiffs, the supernatural seems toothless. I almost regretted that. A phantom or two might frighten the mastiffs.

We reached the topiary without mishap and paused to listen, but were reassured by the silence. Cautiously, we moved on, into the kitchen garden and through it, and at last into the wood. Here beneath the trees, the darkness was intense. It was hard to manoeuvre our burden between the trunks, and twigs kept snatching at our hair and clothes. The fifty yards of woodland between the garden and the outer fence seemed to take forever to cross. There was a very bad moment when we knocked the end of the ladder against a tree. The thud sounded to us like a clap of thunder.

As far as I could make out by peering intently at the trees, none of them had low boughs. I couldn't imagine how either Sybil or I could ever have climbed any of them.

We were halfway through when we heard it.

'Oh no!' Sybil gasped.

It was in the distance, but there was no mistaking it. The mastiffs were baying. And the sound was coming nearer. There was little doubt that they were on our scent.

Hound voices are exciting when you are following the pack but not when you're the quarry. Then, your guts churn and your heart pounds as though it wants to burst out of your chest. I had experienced it before and had hoped never to do so again. 'Run!' I said.

We ran, not worrying now if we bumped the ladder against trees in our haste, only concerned not to collide with them ourselves or to trip over roots or the snares of trailing ivy. We never reached the fence. The mastiffs were on us just as it came in sight, and this time they were not on leashes.

They had been well trained. They didn't attack, but sprang in front of us and stood there barring our way and snarling. I shouted at them, as masterfully as possible, but they went on snarling, and I knew that they wouldn't let us pass. Sybil was whimpering with fright.

And then Walter Ferris and Peter Maine, both wearing cloaks over their nightshirts, came through the trees behind us, carrying lanterns.

'Did you think we were fools?' Ferris sounded odiously

pleased with himself. 'You'd never have handled that great double ladder by yourself. Whoever came with you, Mistress Stannard, got away, but in case he came back with reinforcements I had the dogs left loose. They must have been on the wrong side of the house when you got out, but they got your scent in the end and we heard them, so here we are.'

I said nothing. I could hardly bear it. We had so nearly escaped; so very nearly. The fence was only a few feet away. If only we could have had a little bit of luck, a few more minutes. If only. *If only!*

'I can't think how you got through that locked cellar door,' Ferris was saying thoughtfully. 'That really does look like supernatural powers. More evidence of witchcraft, wouldn't you say, Mistress Stannard?'

I then made a foolish mistake. I was tired, frightened, bitterly disappointed at this last-minute failure and exasperated with this reiterated accusation of witchcraft. I wanted to refute it. I wanted to be done with it. I wanted to prove it was a lie and throw the lie in this man's stupid face.

I pulled out my spare set of picklocks and brandished them at him.

'There's your witchcraft!' I shouted.

Just as he had snatched my dagger, he now snatched my spare picklocks. Of course.

SIXTEEN

Inverting the Truth

Back in the wine cellar, we were left to get what rest we could during the little that remained of the night. 'But Brockley must have got away,' I said to Sybil as soon as our captors' footsteps had retreated. 'And in any case, unless we both get home safely, Hugh will come. He'll know what to do. And there is that letter that you saw. It's good evidence against Ferris; in fact, it ought to exonerate us. Take heart, Sybil.'

Sybil said fearfully: 'If only Ferris doesn't go and destroy it! Where would we be then? What Maine told me won't be any use – he was right, it would just be my word against his. Ursula, I've never met or even seen this man Edward Heron, but I have heard things about him. When it comes to cases of witchcraft, he's always hot against the prisoner. And he has more than one judge in his pocket.'

We tried to rest, and I think I did doze, towards daybreak. The body looks after itself in the end. But in the morning we were still both exhausted and very grubby. I have never longed so much for warm water and a comb.

Eventually, Peter Maine, dressed formally in full-length black velvet and accompanied by two men, presumably as bodyguards, came with breakfast – of a sort. It consisted of a jug of small ale, two glass tumblers, some yesterday's bread, and a lump of cheese.

We ate and drank and of necessity made use of a bucket which had been left for us in a corner. Maine's two henchmen came again after a while to take away our tray and the bucket, replacing the latter with an empty one. I won't say a clean one, because it wasn't. It looked as though it had been used for mixing paint. They didn't speak to us. After that we were left to ourselves. The morning wore on.

Cool air came through the grating, and from what we could see, the day was bright: good October weather. I reckoned that it was about ten of the clock when we heard a timid tapping at the door and a little voice whispered: 'Mistress Jackman! Mistress Stannard!'

Sybil sprang up and went to the door. 'Margaret! What are you doing here? Won't you get into trouble?'

'No. I asked Mistress Ferris if I could bring you a comb. She said yes, it would be a Christian gesture and I could probably push it under the door. She couldn't give me the key, because Master Ferris has it, she said, and we'd better not ask him in case he was angry and forbade me to bring the comb. Here it is.'

Something scraped at the bottom of the door and a comb slid under it. 'They're all in the great hall waiting for the sheriff to arrive,' Margaret said. 'No one knows I went to Hawkswood. They thought I'd run home! When I came back, I said I'd just been walking because I was upset. Thomas didn't tell. But something dreadful happened yesterday. Master Ferris looks so ordinary, but now that I'm living here, he's begun to scare me. His wife, and Thomas, both seem nervous of him. When he's there, they seem to be careful of what they say. And yesterday . . .'

To our distress, Margaret began to sob. 'Yesterday evening, Thomas tried to tell his father that he couldn't marry me, that he still meant to marry Christina, and Master Ferris beat him! He made Maine and another man hold him down! I wasn't there, of course, but . . . I heard things . . . noises. Mistress Bridget did too, and she went and shut herself away. This morning, Thomas looked wretched – awful – and I had to ask him why. I told him what I'd overheard. Because we quarrelled yesterday, I was afraid he would say it was none of my business, but after all, we'd been friends for so long, it was natural for him to talk to me, so he did. Poor Thomas!'

'Don't cry!' whispered Sybil. 'Don't, dear. It's over now.'

'The quarrel's forgotten,' Margaret said. 'And I've promised him that I'll beg my father to break the betrothal and take me away. Thomas loves Christina Cobbold. I've seen them together.'

'Take care, my dear,' said Sybil. 'Don't let Master Ferris know about that promise.'

'No, I won't.' Margaret checked her tears. 'I wish I could bring you washing water and fresh clothes, but I can't. You must need them.'

She was right about that, but the comb at least was a help. We thanked her earnestly. When she had gone, we set about tidying ourselves. We both had our hair bundled into woollen nets, but restless nights and the twigs in the wood had turned our heads to birds' nests. 'Except,' said Sybil, trying hard to be brave, 'that any self-respecting birds would be ashamed to make such messy nests!'

With the comb, we smoothed out the tangles and repacked each other's hair in a more orderly fashion. We could do little about our clothes, however. Everything we had on was horribly creased, and Sybil's little ruff, which should have been sparkling white, looked as though it had been roughly created from a used dishcloth. We were still a sadly dishevelled pair when Peter Maine, once more accompanied by two other men ('How dangerous they must think we are!' Sybil whispered to me), fetched us to confront the sheriff in the great hall.

It had been rearranged. The table and benches had been pushed to one side, and Edward Heron, dressed like Maine in a formal black gown, was seated in one of the throne-like chairs, which had been placed in a commanding position. Walter Ferris was occupying the other, not quite beside Heron, but a couple of paces back, giving Heron the advantage. Also set a little back was a small table and chair, and on the table was paper and writing materials. Standing next to Heron, on the other side from Ferris, stood another dark-gowned man, holding a parchment scroll. I wondered if this was Heron's chaplain, the one who so earnestly agreed with his master on the subject of witchcraft and had been known to preach on the unwisdom of allowing witches to survive. He had a face full of vertical lines and eyebrows rounded like Norman arches. I disliked him on sight.

Bridget, Thomas, and Margaret were present but were seated in the inglenook, observers but not participants. Bridget was as cool and dignified as ever, her hair immaculately coiled under an embroidered hood, the skirts of her brown velvet gown carefully disposed, her ruff fashionably large, and a heavy pearl and silver pendant round her neck. Her hands were quiet in her lap, and her little dog was sitting at her feet. Thomas was white-faced and very still, and for all his size and strength he looked curiously young. He was sitting upright, not letting his shoulders touch the seat-back behind him. At his side, Margaret, unobtrusively dressed in dove-colour, sat as quietly as Bridget, and she too had clasped her hands in her lap, but her light eyes seemed enormous and were watching us anxiously.

The men with Peter Maine had withdrawn, but Maine, it seemed, was to stay. He, Heron and the chaplain together were a trio to make one shudder. They looked like three black crows, waiting to peck us to death.

'Here are the prisoners, Sir Edward, Master Ferris.' Maine was presenting us, smoothly obsequious. 'Mistress Ursula Stannard—'

He pushed me forward, and I attempted a correct curtsy but knew very well that my breeches made it look ridiculous.

'—and Mistress Sybil Jackman.'

Sybil, when thrust forward, made a more successful obeisance.

'What a pair,' said Sir Edward disapprovingly. Chilly grey eyes scanned us both from head to foot. 'One seems to be wearing clothes made out of unwashed remnants, and the other, shamefully, is dressed as a man. Let them hear of what they are accused.'

Gladys had been through this, I thought, and under worse circumstances, since she had been in a court, not in a private house, and was alone. At least Sybil and I had each other. I also knew that this hearing, this confrontation, this interrogation – whatever one might call it – was taking place here in the Ferris hall and not in a cell or a courtroom because I was who I was: sister to the queen and wife of Hugh Stannard, who was a respected figure in Surrey.

But the fear was the same. Heron would not have agreed to conduct this enquiry unless he had decided to take it seriously. If he were once convinced that I had indulged in sorcery with lethal intent, then my connections would not help either me or Sybil. We must refute whatever evidence there was against us or we might end where Gladys had so nearly ended, in the death cart, pinioned, ropes round our necks. Gladys had been saved barely one minute before the cart was drawn away from beneath her. We might not be so fortunate.

'This is not a court of law,' Heron said, echoing my thoughts. 'It is at this stage a preliminary investigation into the accusations against these women. The Reverend Giles Parkes will read them out.' I had identified the chaplain correctly.

Parkes unrolled his scroll. 'I will deal first with the woman Sybil Jackman,' he announced. He had a creaky voice, like a door hinge in need of oiling.

The woman known as Sybil Jackman, he said, had at first been accused of entering the Ferris household for the purpose of prying into the personal correspondence of Mr Walter Ferris. Picklocks had been found in her possession, and it was possible that she had also intended to commit theft. Sybil and I exchanged startled glances, wondering what *at first* could possibly mean. But we were not left wondering for long.

'It was discovered, however,' said the chaplain, 'that the reverse was very likely the case. She was caught in the act of putting a letter *into* the document box, and Mr Ferris has testified that he has never seen the letter before. It contains matter that reflects upon Mr Ferris himself, and it seems that the woman Jackman in fact came to plant a forgery. Mr Ferris says he will produce it if required.'

Sybil gasped. I felt as though I had been kicked in the stomach by a mule. I had clung to the thought of that letter and had been alarmed by Sybil's suggestion that Ferris would destroy it. That he would have the audacity to admit to it, and invert its meaning and turn it into evidence *against* us, had never entered my head.

'Finally,' said the chaplain, 'the woman Jackman comes from a household that harbours at least one known witch. I will now proceed to the allegations against Mrs Ursula Stannard.'

The woman Ursula Stannard, read the chaplain, was a known defender, protector and associate of a convicted witch by the name of Gladys Morgan. Ursula Stannard was suspected of supplying a love potion to bewilder the wits of Christina Cobbold, a potion for which Thomas Ferris, son of the said Walter Ferris, had paid.

'And Thomas will testify to this under oath!' announced Ferris. 'Will you not, Thomas? Speak up!'

Oh no, I said inside my head. *I don't believe it. I CAN'T believe it! First Anne Percy's letter to Ferris is turned from a help to a disaster, and now this! It can't be happening!*

But it was happening. Once more, I recalled the dreadful closing words of Countess Anne's letter to me:

Trouble and dread will overtake both you and your servant . . . and when they have wrung the last juices of hope and happiness from you, death and damnation will complete my vengeance.

I did not want to believe that curses could have power, but once more I remembered that night in the garden at Hawkswood when I had known the fear of evil. It seemed to me that I could feel Anne Percy's ill will grasping at me from across the sea like a pair of cold hands, their nails grown into curving claws. Those claws were sinking deep into me now, as if I were a mouse in the power of a cat.

All eyes had turned towards the inglenook and Thomas. 'Well?' said Ferris to his son. 'What have you to say?'

'Yes, it is true.' Thomas's voice shook, and he did not look at me. 'I feared that Christina was growing cold towards me. I wanted a potion to . . . to change that, and I thought of Mistress Stannard, since the witch Gladys lives in her house. People say that Gladys is careful these days, and so I thought she might refuse me, but Mistress Stannard could have . . . have . . . learned from her, and if I offered gold . . .'

'How much?' said his father remorselessly. 'Say it. How much gold did you give?'

Thomas said nothing. His pallor changed to a flush.

His father repeated the question, more loudly. 'How much? Out with it, boy!'

'Twenty pounds,' said Thomas miserably. 'In gold angels.'

'Enough to pay my chaplain's annual stipend,' said Walter venomously. 'And it's my money, as it happens, money I give you to play with, spoilt, undutiful brat that you are.'

Sybil choked in shock. Bridget half-rose, as if jerked into it, but caught Ferris's eye, bit her lip, and sank back into her seat again. Panicking, I shouted: 'It's all lies!' but Heron ordered me to silence, threatening to have me removed if I would not wait until I was asked to speak.

I subsided, shaking. All the same, I had noticed something. In that moment, that brief moment when Thomas had not answered the question about how much gold he had paid me, I had seen Ferris's face show fury, but not just that. I thought I had seen astonishment too. Margaret said he had beaten Thomas yesterday, and he had probably believed that the boy was completely under his control. He had not expected even that momentary resistance. But I recalled how, when I came on Thomas with Christina under the bay tree, I had noticed how mature he had become.

It was likely that Walter had been bullying his son for years. But yesterday, he had needed the help of two other men. He could no longer master Thomas on his own. Just now, Thomas looked dreadful, as though he might be sick at any moment. He was still in fear of his father. But soon, I thought, the time would come when Walter wouldn't be able to control him any more. Though whether it would come soon enough for me or Sybil was another matter.

'Please continue,' said Heron to the chaplain.

'The next accusation against Mrs Stannard,' read Parkes, 'is that of casting spells to create a epidemic of smallpox to bedevil and endanger the members of her household, and others besides, and also of unlawfully entering the Ferris premises at night, to take away the woman Sybil Jackman and thus obstruct the processes of the law.'

It went on and on. Picklocks had been found in my possession as well as in Sybil's. These had been removed, but I had still passed through a locked door, taking the Jackman woman with me. The final count against me was that I had used sorcery to undo the lock.

At that point, with my knees threatening to give way, I fairly gaped at Walter Ferris and Peter Maine, but neither reacted, even by a twitch of an eyebrow.

'There is also evidence,' creaked the chaplain, whose sermons must have been quite painful to listen to, 'that when the woman Ursula Stannard came to the house last night, she had a companion, who has escaped. We shall ask the name of this person, and Mrs Stannard would be well advised to answer truthfully.' He let the scroll roll up.

Sir Edward said: 'That completes the details of the accusations. They are not charges as yet. I will proceed with this enquiry by first asking Ursula Stannard what she has to say in answer to them. The accusations against her are more serious than those against Mrs Jackman. Parkes, you will take notes of her testimony.'

The chaplain moved to the little writing table, selected a quill and opened the ink pot in readiness.

Sir Edward said: 'Well, Mrs Stannard?'

I had taken a hold on myself now. I had grasped Ferris's strategy. He wanted me convicted of witchcraft, and he had been manufacturing evidence, which had finally taken the shape of a pitchfork. One prong was the lie that I had sold love potions to Thomas, who had been forced to confirm it. Yesterday's beating had probably not been all on account of Thomas's illicit love affair. Ferris had planned ahead and paid Dorothy to try and arrange for me to make a medicine – any medicine – for Christina. The other prong was the smallpox-laden cloaks, which he had hoped would start an epidemic. As they had.

Where, oh where, was Hugh? Why hadn't he come to help me?

Well, as yet he hadn't. Somehow or other I mastered my failing knees. I cleared my throat. 'It's a long story,' I said, looking at Heron as steadily as I could. 'It begins when I received a letter from the Netherlands, from Anne Percy, the exiled Countess of Northumberland.' I couldn't see Edward Heron as likely to sympathize with her. He was no Catholic supporter. 'The letter in question contained threats against me, threats of trouble and dread, death and damnation . . .'

'Ah! A letter from Countess Anne. Like the forgery placed in my document box?' said Ferris. 'Can you produce it, madam? Have you perhaps prepared another forgery?'

Unexpectedly, Heron now revealed the side of him that Jane Cobbold had once described as *a man of integrity and a great upholder of the law.* He frowned at Ferris and said: 'Please allow Mrs Stannard to speak.'

A little encouraged, I did so, explaining that during the recent Catholic rebellion in the north, Countess Anne had been involved and I had helped to defeat her part in the business.

'Also,' I said, 'she made prisoners of me and my servant Roger Brockley, but we escaped. We were chased as we left the house where she was keeping us, by her and others. We threw pepper in their faces and spilt oil on a floor, which caused them to lose their footing. I think the Countess felt I had made her look absurd.'

That pleased Heron, as I had hoped. I saw a glint, just a glint, of amusement, in both his eyes and those of Parkes. I went on, gaining confidence.

There had been the threatening letter from Anne Percy, and then things had begun to happen. My manservant Roger Brockley was nearly accused of theft. Master Ferris, with whom my family had no quarrel, had burst into my daughter's marriage feast and flung accusations of witchcraft at me. The potion he spoke of was nothing but a harmless medicine I gave Christina Cobbold to calm her when she was upset over her hopeless love affair. My own servants would confirm this, as they had seen me make it. It certainly wasn't a love potion, and I had never been approached by Thomas Ferris to supply such a thing.

'And whatever Master Ferris may say, I don't believe that if it comes to it, if Thomas finds himself in a real court of law, giving testimony on oath, that he will swear to buying any kind of potion from me.' I felt was on firm ground here. 'If he does, he will be committing perjury!'

In the inglenook, Thomas moved uneasily. His father glanced at him, and he was still once more.

'I think not,' said Ferris, though whether he was denying that such testimony would be perjury, or denying that Thomas would withdraw it, wasn't clear.

'*And*,' I said, 'Master Ferris brought what he called wedding gifts for my daughter and her bridegroom. They were cloaks. *Used* cloaks. A studied insult – or so we all thought at the time. Later, we – my husband and myself – came to suspect something worse. The smallpox broke out after the wedding. There had been smallpox in the Ferris family, just before. And a Woking physician has confirmed that the clothing of a sufferer can carry the sickness with it.'

'But where does the Countess of Northumberland come in?' Heron asked.

'I'm coming to that,' I said hurriedly, nervous again, afraid I would be halted before I had finished. I described Dorothy Beale's deathbed confession, our bewilderment at finding that Ferris had been spying on us, and how we had begun to wonder if he was Anne Percy's instrument. I had set out with my manservant to find out from Cecil if they were related, and Brockley had been attacked on the way. However, we had reached Cecil eventually, and he had confirmed the existence of a relationship.

'And after all,' I said, 'Ferris is a Catholic.'

Whereupon, Ferris interrupted me yet again. 'My relationship with Anne Percy's family is remote, and as for my religious views: I keep the laws of England as regards attendance at my parish church, and my private opinions are my own affair. Sir Edward respects them, though it may be with regret.'

'It is with regret,' said Heron. 'But it is true that you conform to the law, at least in public, and it is also true that on other matters, we are at one. That counts for much, in my eyes. However, Mrs Stannard may continue.'

'The attack on my manservant was made with a crossbow,' I said. 'I believe you are skilled with the crossbow, Master Ferris?'

It was a direct question, and with a nod, Heron indicated that Ferris should answer it.

'Many men practise archery, with longbow and crossbow. Many are skilled,' he snapped. 'As far as I'm aware, it is not an offence.'

It was best not to reply to that. 'That's nearly all,' I said, sensing that Heron was growing impatient again. I went on to say that Sybil – 'her real name is Sybil Jester; Jackman was her maiden name' – had set out to discover whether Walter Ferris had had instructions from Anne Percy. 'She tells me that she found a letter containing such instructions. The one that Master Ferris claims is a forgery.'

'Hm,' said Heron, non-committally.

I couldn't tell what sort of impression I was making. Heron was being fair to me, making sure I had a hearing, but how far was I being believed? If only Hugh would come!

Heron had turned to Ferris, eyebrows questioningly raised.

'The letter is quite definitely a forgery,' said Ferris. 'There is no doubt of it, sir. When I came upon the woman that we now know is called Sybil Jester, she had the letter in question in her hand, folded, and was in the act of laying it into my document box, which she had unlawfully opened.'

'I was putting it *back*!' Sybil protested.

'I see.' Heron looked at me sharply. There was no trace of amusement now. He addressed me as though he and Ferris were two divisions of an army, attacking in a pincer move-ment. 'There are still points you have not covered, Mrs Stannard. Please tell us how you escaped from a locked cellar when your picklocks had been taken from you?'

'I had a second set, as Master Ferris knows very well! When we were caught at the boundary fence, he accused me escaping from the wine cellar by using witchcraft and I brandished them at him. He took them from me! He has both my sets of picklocks. If he is ready to speak the truth, he will bear me out.'

'Of course I am ready to speak the truth. Mistress Stannard is the liar,' said Ferris, with raised eyebrows and a glint of triumph in his round pebble eyes. 'She did not have a second set of picklocks. You were there, Maine, when we caught up with her last night. Did you see her flourish any picklocks at me?'

Maine, sleek and pale in his long black gown, gave me a self-satisfied glance and said: 'No, sir. I did not.'

'There you are, then. She got herself and her confederate out of that cellar by sorcery, Sir Edward. I demand that she be charged with it and Sybil Jack— *Jester* with her . . . Maine, I

can hear a disturbance of some kind out in the entrance vestibule.
I thought you left your escort outside, Sir Edward. Why didn't
they stop uninvited callers?'

'They had no instructions to do so, Mr Ferris. This is not
my house; I wouldn't dream of taking such a thing upon
myself.'

'Maine,' said Ferris, 'go and find out what that noise is.'

I looked towards the door. There was indeed a disturbance.
And then, out in the entrance vestibule, I heard a familiar
voice. It was that of Roger Brockley, ringingly raised in a
demand to see Mistress Stannard.

SEVENTEEN
Stark Unreason

I was thankful to hear him, but also concerned. Last night, Ferris had suspected that Brockley had accompanied me. I didn't want Roger Brockley seized on suspicion. I stared at the hall door, praying that Hugh had come with him. Hugh had a standing that Heron might respect.

But when Maine led the new arrivals in, Hugh was not there. Instead, Brockley was with tall, grey-haired Adam Wilder, who was for some reason carrying a hamper. They saw me and Sybil at once, and Brockley made unceremoniously towards us. I noticed he was implying peaceful intentions, since he wore no dagger, but there was aggression in his step. There was also a limp. His ankle must be giving trouble again. His attention, however, was all for me and Sybil, and if his manner was aggressive, it sprang from his concern for us.

'Madam . . . Mistress Jester . . . are you unharmed? When young Jacky came back last night and said he'd had to leave you here, I was most alarmed.'

'Who is Jacky?' Ferris demanded.

Good, clever Brockley. Like a skilled chess player, he had moved himself out of danger and put a useless pawn into it instead. An invented pawn. We had no manservant, young or otherwise, by the name of Jacky.

'He is a lad in our employment, and he accompanied me last night,' I said shortly. 'Though you could hardly expect me to tell you so, Master Ferris. I am glad that he returned safely to Hawkswood. But Brockley, where is Master Stannard?'

'He couldn't manage the journey here, madam. He can only travel by coach, as you know. Jacky got the wagon home, but the horse can't be used today after being out all night. Master Stannard has sent Arthur Watts off on the other coach horse, to find Sir William Cecil and tell him what's afoot.'

This was absurd. It would have been perfectly possible to hitch the plough horses to the coach. Hugh was ill, I thought, feeling panic rise again. He must be ill or he would be here.

Brockley dropped his voice so that only Sybil and I could hear. 'Wilder and I rode over on Roundel and Mealy. We'll have to ride double to take you two home, madam.'

I opened my mouth to ask about Hugh, but Brockley had been surveying the dishevelled state of myself and Sybil with obvious disapproval, and he now swung round to address Ferris.

'These are gently reared ladies, and they look as though they have been treated very ill. Why?'

'Who is this man?' Edward Heron's voice rang out. 'And what is he doing, interrupting the interrogation of a witch and her associate?'

'Quite,' said Ferris. 'What, sir, do you imagine you are about, marching uninvited into this hall?'

'Your steward brought us in,' said Wilder with dignity. 'This is Roger Brockley, Mistress Stannard's personal manservant. I am Adam Wilder, steward to Master Stannard.'

'And,' said Brockley, 'you, Master Ferris, are in no position to complain about people marching uninvited into *your* hall. I'm sorry to intrude on an interrogation, but it was necessary. I'm here on behalf of Master Hugh Stannard, to ask why his wife and her gentlewoman are being kept here, and, by the look of them, not in the most hospitable of conditions.'

'You can ask that?' barked Ferris. 'When one of them has opened my document box with picklocks, read my private correspondence and was caught depositing a forgery into the midst of it, while the other was found preparing to break into the house at night, also with the aid of picklocks?'

'And the evidence of witchcraft,' said Sir Edward, 'is distressingly convincing. I have listened to Mrs Stannard's defence with due attention, but there is too much against her. There is a young man who admits to buying a love potion from her; there are two men who testify that she got herself and Mrs Jester through a locked door and must have done so by magic. There are the deaths among those who have lately visited her home. Alas, there is so much hidden sorcery in the world; so many people, often women, who have dealings with demons and secretly seek to harm their fellow creatures. It is an offence to God and all righteousness . . .'

His voice had risen. I had heard that same rising tone in the voice of the vicar who preceded Dr Fletcher at Hawkswood.

I raised my own voice and cut across Heron's. 'They took away one set of my picklocks, but I was carrying two! I used the other to set Sybil and myself free last night. But we were caught again, and I was foolish enough, Brockley, to show my second set to Master Ferris when he tried to pretend we'd escaped from the cellar by casting a spell! Now he's still pretending it, and so is Maine, who was with him.' I pointed at Maine. 'They are claiming that the second set didn't exist.'

'It seems,' remarked Ferris to the air, 'that everyone in the world is lying except you, Mistress Stannard.'

'Those picklocks did exist!' said Brockley said, addressing Heron, Ferris and Maine impartially. 'I know that. Witchcraft indeed! And there's something else – I have another purpose here, if Sir Edward will permit.'

'What would that be?' enquired Heron.

'Wilder,' said Brockley, 'you've got something to show.'

Wilder went to the table, set down the hamper and undid the hasps. 'Your ankle,' I muttered to Brockley. 'It's paining you again. What happened?'

'I did it making my escape last night,' Brockley whispered. 'But it doesn't amount to much. Shh.'

He nodded towards Wilder, who was pulling something out of the hamper. One in each hand, he held up two velvet cloaks, one green, one golden-brown.

'What is this?' Heron demanded.

'Those are the cloaks I mentioned!' I said. 'The ones Master Ferris brought as wedding gifts for my daughter and her bridegroom. The *used* cloaks!'

'Yes,' Wilder said. 'They were handed to us by Master Stannard, as evidence in his wife's favour, if needed, and judging by what's going on here, needed they certainly are. Walter Ferris presented them, as Mistress Stannard says, to her daughter and son-in-law, and they certainly are well worn. Hardly the sort of things one would expect a man such as

Master Ferris, who owns a house like White Towers, to offer as wedding presents. Can anyone say who originally owned them?'

Bridget Ferris made a sharp movement, and her little dog yelped as one of her feet caught it. Walter glanced at her, and like Thomas earlier, she was still. There was a silence. If Bridget knew the answer to Wilder's question, then she was not going to say so. She would not disobey Walter. Probably, she dared not. I found myself wondering about their marriage. Walter, no doubt, had insisted on her compliance in everything. She had kept her dignity by holding herself aloof from the world, never complaining and never crossing him. She had made herself into a figure of cool elegance and turned for love to her little dogs. I looked appealingly at her, but she avoided my eyes. There was no hope to be had from her.

And then Margaret, who had been gazing at the cloaks with a frown on her small freckled face, suddenly got up and went to look more closely at them. Wilder was still holding them up. She handled them both, examining their linings and then looked at Heron.

'This green cloak used to belong to Lucy,' she said. 'Thomas's sister. It's certainly hers. Hers was worn at the neck . . . just like this . . .' She pointed to the scuffed place where the nap had worn away. 'And here, the lining has been mended. I did that myself! It was before Lucy was married. She lived here then, and we knew each other. I was better at needlework than she. She liked this cloak,' Margaret said. 'Even though it was old. She said it was warm, and she liked the colour.'

She looked at Thomas questioningly, a mute request for support, but he stiffened, noticeably still holding his back away from the bench behind him. 'Well, I'm sure this was Lucy's!' she said. Thomas still kept silent, and looking deflated, she went back to her seat.

I seized my chance. 'Lucy, Thomas's sister, is the one who lately died of smallpox. It was just before my daughter's wedding. Thomas said as much, when I . . . met him at that time.'

'No doubt,' said Heron. 'But as to whether the green cloak was really hers . . . Margaret Emory is a sweet young girl, but for that very reason, I can't give too much weight to what she says. A few marks of wear on a cloak are not enough to prove its provenance.'

'There is something I wish to say,' Sybil announced.

Ferris glared at her, but Heron nodded.

'When I looked in Master Ferris's document box, in his study,' said Sybil clearly, 'I found – *found* – the letter from Anne Percy, the one Master Ferris has said is a forgery. It isn't. It was there in the box. Wasn't it said, earlier, that Master Ferris has offered to produce it? I ask that this should be done. I also ask that Anne Percy's original letter to Mistress Stannard should be brought here so that the handwriting can be compared. I have seen both letters, and I can say that they will match.'

'As it happens,' said Brockley, 'I have that letter with me. Your husband gave that to us as well, madam, along with the cloaks. He said he wanted to arm us with anything we might need to prove that there is a campaign against you, possibly – even probably – on behalf of Anne Percy.'

I drew a long, thankful breath, thanking heaven that I had stopped Hugh from burning that letter. But Heron looked annoyed. Indeed, he resembled a heron who has aimed a stab at a fish, only to see the fish flick away just in time. His nose was not only long and slightly curved, I could swear that it was also, slightly, tinged with yellow, the finishing touch for his remarkable resemblance to the bird whose name he bore. I wondered if the name were really a coincidence, or if the long legs and long neck and yellow tinged aquiline nose were inherited characteristics that went back for generations and had won the family the name of Heron, in some previous century.

But Wilder and Brockley had brought something forceful into the room with them. Sybil and I were no longer two defenceless women; we had champions. Also, Sybil's request was reasonable, especially as the letter she wished to have displayed was actually to hand. A responsible sheriff could scarcely refuse her. Jane Cobbold had said that Heron had integrity, and I had seen already that this was true. Bigoted though he was, he would not have been appointed sheriff unless he possessed a sense of responsibility. I held my breath, hoping that it would prevail.

It did, though I think only just. There was a pause, and then: 'Very well,' he said. Grudgingly, but he said it.

'I will accompany Master Ferris to fetch his letter,' said Brockley, meaningly. 'Just in case something should happen to it on the way.'

'I am perfectly willing to produce it,' said Ferris coldly.

The two of them went off. While they were gone, Wilder busied himself in laying the cloaks out on the table, evidently hoping that someone else besides Margaret would inspect and identify them. Brockley and Ferris reappeared, Ferris holding a sheet of paper. 'Here it is,' Ferris said.

Sir Edward took it from him. Brockley pulled a small scroll from under his doublet and handed him that as well. 'This is the letter that was sent to Mistress Stannard.'

I knew Anne Percy's words to me by heart, and Sybil had told me what was in her message to Walter. Sir Edward was a Protestant. He must surely be repelled by such documents, full as they were of hatred not only for me, but also for the religion that both he and I followed.

Heron read both letters and then sat with one in each hand, glancing from one to the other. 'I agree,' he said, 'that the writing on these two seems to be identical.'

The admission came easily, freely. I exchanged a glance of sheer relief with Sybil.

And then stark unreason filled the room.

'I said before,' said Ferris, 'that the letter Mistress Stannard claims was sent to her could be a forgery as much as the one that was put in my document box. These people are clever. They are quite capable of inventing clues to clear themselves and point fingers at me.'

'Yes. I am not satisfied,' said Sir Edward Heron. He handed the letters to Parkes, who tossed them casually on to the table. 'I am very far from satisfied,' Heron repeated. 'I will deal with the letters first. That the letters were written by the same hand proves nothing. Mr Ferris has a point there. Both could indeed be forgeries, prepared as a means of defence against the charge of witchcraft – by incriminating him instead. One could well have been planted in this house by the woman Jester and the other made ready to support it.

'Now, the matter of the love potion. Thomas Ferris is clearly willing to testify under oath that he purchased such a potion from Mrs Stannard. She claims that her servants would say otherwise, but the testimony of loyal servants can only be suspect. If she did make such a philtre, it was not illegal, but would indicate that she is acquainted with the dark arts. I have to say that the way in which she attempted to escape last night seems to bear this out. Mr Brockley says there was a further set of picklocks, but he is clearly one of her loyal servants and his evidence is doubtful on that account. As for the two well-worn cloaks; I repeat, I cannot trust the word of a young wench like Margaret here. Many old cloaks look alike.'

'I know the green one was Lucy's cloak!' Margaret spoke up valiantly. 'I recognized where it was mended; I mended it myself! And she had a brown one, as well, just like the other cloak!' She pointed.

'Young Mistress Emory no doubt believes what she says,' said Heron, not speaking to Margaret but to the whole room. 'But I repeat, many cloaks look alike, and many may have mended linings.'

'I know my own needlework!'

'Be quiet!' ordered Ferris. 'The sheriff is speaking. You are not to interrupt. Where are your manners, girl?'

'It may be that Mistress Emory wishes to defend people she has come to like,' said Heron, while Margaret went crimson and her eyes filled with tears of chagrin and helpless rage. 'Either way, her testimony is as doubtful as that of Mr Brockley.' Brockley swore aloud at this point, and I saw that on his high forehead, there were specks that were not freckles but sweat. Heron paid him no heed. 'On the other hand,' Heron said, 'I have known Mr Ferris for many years. Despite our philosophical differences, I find it hard to believe that he is the villain that Mrs Stannard pretends.'

Sybil exclaimed: 'But . . .' and was silenced by Peter Maine, who stepped forward and put a hand over her mouth.

'And there is one more thing,' said Heron. 'There is a further piece of evidence against Mrs Stannard – and therefore against her creature, Mrs Jester – which I have not as yet mentioned.'

He sounded triumphant, like an assassin who has just whisked out a hidden dagger. Or a heron who has impaled an elusive fish at last.

'I suspect,' he said, 'that Mrs Stannard, and therefore, most probably, her woman servant, are coven members, since they are associates not only of the witch Gladys Morgan, who has so far escaped justice, but also – and this is certainly true of Mrs Stannard – of the condemned witches Jennet Ward, Margery Seldon and their servant, the whore Elizabeth Hayes, more commonly called Bessie. I dismiss the so-called evidence in their favour as worthless. They are now under arrest.'

EIGHTEEN
Unspoken Bargain

Brockley said: '*What?*'

And Sybil cried: 'Oh, no!'

I was momentarily speechless. This was another thunderbolt from a blue sky, even more shocking than Thomas's lying testimony, far more shocking than having Anne Percy's letters dismissed as forgeries.

Then I found myself babbling incoherently: 'But this is nonsense; Jennet and Margery, they're two ordinary, decent women; and little Bessie's no whore, she's just a young girl who made a mistake, but Jennet and Margery are going to look after her and her child—'

Heron raised a silencing hand, and my wild outburst died away.

'I have had suspicions for a long time concerning the two women Jennet Ward and Margery Seldon,' said Heron. 'Mrs Seldon has a reputation for brewing herbal remedies, to the point where some of her neighbours regard her as their local wise woman, and the gap between witch and wise woman is notoriously narrow. In addition, she and Mrs Ward have for years lived unnatural lives. Until lately, Mr Ferris was an occasional visitor to their home, taking an interest because one of them was the widow of a former employee of his. He has reported that even in warm summer weather, the two of them shared a bed.'

He was using the past tense. I began to tremble.

Heron pressed on. 'They were often heard to address each other by endearments, and they divided the business of living in the way that husband and wife would do. Mrs Seldon worked with Elizabeth Hayes, cooking and cleaning the house – and also growing herbs and brewing potions – while Mrs Ward looked after the money.'

'Mrs Ward does beautiful embroidery,' I said, defiantly using the present tense, but I knew as I spoke that my protest was trite, feeble.

'And,' said Heron, unmoved, 'their willingness to shelter a wanton like the girl Bessie Hayes is a further proof of their low morality. That you, who shelter Gladys Morgan, have also sought their company makes them still more questionable – even if there were not more serious evidence against them, and there is. When we met at a wedding, some time ago now, Mrs Stannard, did I not mention that a certain type of book had been found in a number of houses? I decided, recently, to have their home raided. Such a book was discovered there, hidden in a pile of music. That was when I ordered their arrest.'

I stared at him, dumbfounded.

'The book was a collection of recipes for magical potions,' Heron said. 'It was the work of a printer who was executed in the days of King Henry for producing seditious literature. The women denied knowing that the book was there, of course, but to me, it was the evidence that proved their guilt. All three were executed yesterday, in Guildford. I was present, as was my duty. That was why I could not come here until today.'

'I did not witness the hangings myself,' Ferris remarked. 'But I understand that they all died hard.'

There was a whimper from Margaret, who had hidden her face in her hands. Nausea clenched at my guts. Ferris's face was smug; the expression of one who has brought a difficult mission to a satisfactory conclusion.

My mind worked feverishly. The full nature of the campaign against me was now clear. It had three prongs, not two. It was a trident instead of a pitchfork. The weakest prong was the nonsense about the love potion. The other two were the infected cloaks and the incriminating books. The books had been put into a household which was already under suspicion, and the ladies there had been persuaded to further their acquaintance with us, to cast the shadow of that suspicion over us – or me – as well. Hadn't they said that Ferris himself had suggested that they should invite Hugh and myself to dine? From the start, Ferris had known that Heron would not be anxious to

accuse me officially. He had done all he could to load the dice
against me.

He had multiplied his chances by planting not one book on
poor Jennet and Margery but two. Hugh had burned the other
one. I recalled our moment of doubt when Hugh found it. If
even the sceptical Stannards could wonder (for Hugh had
shared my uncertainty), then Sir Edward would have been all
too easy to convince. I was ashamed now of those doubts. It
was plain enough to me that Jennet and Margery and their
hapless maidservant were also Ferris's victims, tools in his
campaign to harm me, used and then abandoned to their fate.
He had built on the friendship that was already growing
between us. Dear God, we had almost signed their death
warrants by inviting them to Meg's wedding.

But I still couldn't take it in. I could see, in my mind, their
pleasant thatched house, the polished furniture, the musical
instruments that occupied every corner; I could hear Margery
and Bessie laughing in the kitchen, hear Margery warning
Bessie against reaching to a high shelf or lifting a heavy
saucepan . . .

They couldn't be dead. They couldn't have died like *that*!
What had it been like for them when they were seized and
taken from their charming home, their happy, harmless occu-
pations, to be shut in some horrible cell in Guildford amid
dirt and foul company and then dragged before a judge who
probably shared Heron's bigotry? They can hardly have
believed what was happening. In Gladys I had witnessed the
terror they must have felt. Jennet. Margery. *Bessie!*

'Bessie was with child!' I said desperately. 'She can't have
been hanged! It isn't right! It would have killed the child as
well! It—'

'A child of the devil, no doubt,' said Heron coolly.
'Engendered, most likely, in the course of their unholy rites.'

In his creaky voice, Giles Parkes said: 'Thou shalt not suffer
a witch to live. Nor a witch's spawn. Perhaps you were present
when the spawning took place?'

The very air around me seemed to be growing dark. I looked
frantically round, and it was Brockley, understanding, who
took my arm and steadied me on to a bench before my legs

gave way completely. 'Take deep breaths,' he said. 'Lean forward, put your head between your knees.'

I did as he said, and the darkness receded. I sat up again, slowly. I had not fainted. I was still conscious and able to look about me. I looked at the faces of my enemies: Heron, whose chilly eyes were like spears; the chaplain, self-satisfied and vengeful both at once. Peter Maine and Walter Ferris, both smiling contentedly. The three black crows.

Strange alliances here: Catholic and Protestant united to destroy me, though not for the same reasons.

My spinning brain clutched at reality, as someone falling downstairs might grab at a banister to stop themselves from toppling further. Walter Ferris had guided poor Jennet, and Margaret, and Bessie, into close contact with me. I was sure he had planted those books on them. Had he also planted some at Hawkswood? Through Dorothy, perhaps. We might not have found them. Somehow, I must get a warning to Hugh! And there was something else. According to the boastful Maine, it had been Walter who, by using a third party, had made Jane Cobbold—

My backbone stiffened. I hoped that Cecil would help if need be; it was also true that the queen might step in. *Might.* She'd done that for Gladys, but it had set a dubious precedent. I dared not hope too much. I must break free without her help, if I could. And I thought I could see a way. I rose from the bench and went to stand in front of Heron.

'Sir Edward! I have something of importance to say.'

Heron surveyed me in no friendly fashion, but said: 'By all means, Mrs Stannard. Is it a confession?'

'No, it is not. Sir Edward, you are the sheriff of this county and in charge of seeing that when charges are brought, all the facts that have a bearing on those charges are known and can be presented to the judges. Do I – and Mistress Jester – not have the right to produce witnesses who will speak for us? For we can produce them – other witnesses, I mean, besides those present.' I glanced at Brockley and Wilder. 'And,' I said, 'would it not be best to hear them before we are brought before a judge? So that if they can refute the charges against us, then those charges can be dropped, and no judges will have their time wasted.'

'Who may these witnesses be?'

'Mistress Jane Cobbold,' I said, 'and Master Paul Emory.'

There was a stir all around me, of murmurs and whispers and the rustle of clothes as people turned to look at each other. The chaplain's rounded eyebrows rose.

Walter went rigid. 'That is unthinkable. No Cobbold has set foot in this house for over a hundred years, and no Cobbold ever will again.'

Did I detect fear as well as anger in his voice? Ignoring him, I said: 'Brockley can fetch them. Can you not, Brockley? It surely won't take too long.'

'I know this district well. It would be a round journey of only seven miles or so,' Brockley said. 'No, it shouldn't take me long, given that they're at home.'

'I will not have a Cobbold in my house!' Ferris shouted.

There was silence from Thomas and the two women, but I saw all three of them looking intently at Heron. Ferris, sensing, I suppose, that the Cobbold–Ferris feud was not of interest to most of us, changed his tone. 'This is all folly. What can Mistress Cobbold and Master Emory have to tell us that has any bearing on this?'

'If they are asked, we may find out,' I said. I kept my eyes on Heron. Behind me, I heard Sybil whisper: 'Good, good.'

'It was Mrs Cobbold who first complained to me that she believed that Mrs Stannard had been indulging in the black arts,' Heron said. 'Yet you wish to call her as a witness on your behalf, Mrs Stannard. That seems strange.'

I said: 'It would be best, I think, to let Mistress Cobbold and Master Emory speak for themselves.'

I had been right. Heron, however bigoted, however fanatical in his beliefs about witchcraft, was not corrupt. He wished to be a conscientious sheriff. Once more I waited, as the two sides of him struggled with each other. Hoping desperately that the right one would prevail.

Finally, he said: 'Very well. Return the accused to their cellar meanwhile. I will send two of my own men to fetch the individuals in question. Mr Brockley is too much of an interested party. We don't want our witnesses tampered with. Mr Brockley, you will instruct my messengers as to the likely

whereabouts of this Jane Cobbold, and of Mr Emory, but you
will remain here, as will your companion.'

'I can't admit a Cobbold here, and this is *my* house!' Ferris
spluttered.

'But I am conducting this enquiry, Mr Ferris. The witnesses
will be fetched,' said Heron. 'That is all.'

Sybil and I were brought back from the wine cellar three hours
later. We had been given water to drink and some more bread
and cheese in the interim, a replacement for dinner. I gathered
that the delay was because Paul Emory had been out in his
fields and it took time to find him. We were escorted back to
the hall, once more by Peter Maine and his two henchmen.
We had found out by then (because Sybil asked) that one was
a kitchen hand and the other, a very brawny man, was a groom.
As we came into the hall, I saw Brockley glance sharply at
the groom, but he did not speak.

Little had changed in the hall. Everyone who had been there
before was there still, and they had been joined by Jane Cobbold
and Paul Emory, who were standing side by side, looking
bewildered. When we came in, Jane was staring about her and
declaring that she couldn't think what her husband would say
about her being brought here. He was on an errand to Woking,
and she hadn't been able to ask him if she ought to come, and
she had agreed only because it was by order of the sheriff
himself, and what in the world was happening?

Since she was the first Cobbold to set foot in the house for
at least a century, her agitation was understandable. Ferris was
glowering at her and standing well away from her, as though
she might contaminate him.

She must have been working in her kitchen when the sheriff's
men arrived, since her open collar and her creased brown dress
were both dusted with flour. Emory, fresh from his fields, was
clad in workmanlike breeches, with a sleeveless leather jerkin
over an old shirt and earth clinging to his boots. He looked angry.

There were used plates and glasses on the table and some
wine flasks. Refreshment had evidently been served. I could
have done with some wine myself, and no doubt so could Sybil,
but no one offered us any.

'Well,' said Heron, opening the proceedings. 'Here are your witnesses, Mrs Stannard. What do you imagine they can tell us? You have my permission to question them.'

The interval had let me gather my thoughts. I turned to Jane. 'Mistress Cobbold, you have laid an accusation of witchcraft against me. It was based on the idea that I might have created the recent smallpox outbreak by casting a spell, and thereby put your daughter Christina's life at risk, and in the end, permanently damaged her complexion. In fact, the outbreak was probably started by the old cloaks that Master Ferris brought to my daughter's wedding. Christina borrowed one of them – when she went for a walk in our garden, before you all left for home. That cloak has been identified as formerly belonging to his married daughter Lucy, who lately died of smallpox.'

'There is no proof that either of the cloaks were Lucy's,' Ferris broke in.

Margaret said: 'The green one *was*!' and was rewarded by a sharp nudge from Bridget Ferris's elbow.

I kept my eyes on Jane. 'Did anyone suggest to you that I might be responsible for the smallpox? Or was it all your own idea?'

'It's not the sort of thing I'd be likely to think of,' said Jane in a flurried fashion. She eyed me, though, with blatant dislike. 'But there it is, you have kept that witch woman Gladys Morgan in your house and . . . and you're unwomanly!'

Jane, alarmed at having been brought to the Ferris house in such a hasty and unceremonious fashion, and now confronted by me, the person she had officially accused, blurted out her opinion of me, more candidly than ever before. 'You've travelled about and got yourself caught up in high matters and enterprises that aren't the proper sphere for ladies. I've worried, thinking: what sort of example are you setting to Christina? I couldn't say much because Anthony and your husband are such friends, but girls are so easily led astray; she seemed to admire what she'd heard of you, and I didn't like that. And then she got the pox and her face is all spoilt, and soon after that, Master Emory came to see us and said to me, isn't it queer, a trouble like smallpox breaking out in the Stannard

household, all of a sudden, and spreading beyond, and did I
know the bride's uncle died of an apoplexy just after he got
back home, too? And there's a known witch at Hawkswood,
he said. He thought I ought to report it, seeing that Christina
was an injured party.'

Brockley had moved to my side. 'So that's how she got to
know about Ambrose Blanchard dying,' he muttered. 'But how
did Emory know?'

'From Ferris, I expect,' I muttered back. 'And he'd have
got it from gossip, I dare say. Or maybe we were right when
we wondered if Dorothy was the only spy in our house.'

Emory was talking now, partly to me. 'Hawkswood's got a
funny reputation, ever since that woman Gladys Morgan was
brought back from London and you Stannards gave her a
home. She should have been hanged, but you Stannards got
her off. You choose strange company, Mistress Stannard. And
it's sad to see a lass like Christina with her looks so damaged.'

'Yes, it broke my heart, seeing her like that and hearing her
weep over it and thinking that no one would ever want to
marry her now!' Jane cried. 'It was a wicked thing to happen
to a girl, and it all started up after the wedding at your house,
Ursula Stannard, and everyone knows it's the sort of thing
witches like to do, making misery that goes on for years and
years, through lifetimes, and—'

'Yes, and so I told Mistress Cobbold!' Emory declared. 'I
thought, since she knew Sir Edward here, she could go to him
about it. I wouldn't have liked to go to such a great man
myself.' He gave a sketchy bow towards Heron. 'Seems she
acted on what I said,' he added.

'You're quite mistaken in me,' I said to Jane. 'I'm just . . .
not the same sort of woman that you are. We're not all alike.'
I turned to Emory. 'I believe, sir, that you have lately done a
favour or two for Master Ferris. Were those the favours? Telling
Mistress Cobbold about Master Blanchard's death from
apoplexy – and urging her to accuse me?'

'No,' said Ferris sharply.

'But he has done favours for you?' I asked him.

Margaret stared at her father, biting her lip.

'Oh, I've done him a good turn now then,' said Emory

easily. He gave another polite little bow, towards Ferris this time. 'I'm glad enough to be of service to a good neighbour. I once got some value knocked off someone else's young bull, too, so as he could get it cheap. That kind of thing.'

'Gossiped about murrain on the farm the bull was bred on, did you?' enquired Brockley in an interested voice.

Beside me, Sybil had raised her chin. 'Maine!'

'Madam?' said Peter Maine.

'You told me that Master Ferris asked Emory to suggest the witchcraft charge to Mistress Cobbold. He knew a Cobbold wouldn't accept the idea from him. You told me that Master Emory obliged, in return for the match being settled between his daughter and Thomas. You said he agreed that if Mistress Cobbold didn't take up his suggestion, then he'd go to Sir Edward himself.'

'Nonsense!' said Ferris.

'I certainly don't recall saying such a thing,' said Maine, smiling slightly but fixing her with eyes in which there was no smile at all. 'Tell me, Mistress Jester, was anyone else there at the time?'

Sybil stared back at him and did not reply.

'Come. Answer,' he said.

'No,' said Sybil unwillingly.

'I thought not. You mustn't make up tales, you know, even to protect your friend.'

'I'm not making it up!'

'She certainly is,' said Paul Emory and Walter Ferris simultaneously.

There was a silence, in which terror ran through my veins like ice water. Every piece of evidence I and my friends had produced had been brushed aside or dismissed as lies. Ferris and Maine – and, under compulsion, Thomas – had been the liars, but I couldn't prove it. The letters – oh, mere forgeries. Margaret was a silly girl who could not possibly know for sure that an old cloak had once belonged to any particular person. No one could prove that Ferris had used Emory to drop a poisonous idea into Jane Cobbold's receptive ears and unintelligent brain. No one could prove that the mysterious favours had nothing to do with buying stock cheap. I would

waste my breath if I said that Ferris himself had fostered the
link between my household and that of Jennet and Margery.
He would just deny it – another lie – and they were not alive
to testify. I thought once more of how their deaths must have
been for them, and the nausea rose.

And then Paul Emory startled everyone. Clearing his throat,
he announced: 'I have something to say.'

Heron inclined a polite head (*or stooped a long yellow beak*,
I thought distractedly) and said: 'We will hear you, Mr Emory.'

'I don't quite understand what all this is about, but it sounds
as if this Stannard woman wants to blacken the name of Master
Ferris, and I'm sorry about that. He's a friend of mine, and
it's true enough that I want his son as a husband for my girl
Margaret, there. That'll settle her in life, with a good home
and a fine healthy young man. And here we all are, in this
hall, with witnesses aplenty and two men of the cloth here. I
don't doubt Sir Edward needs a bit of time to think over what
he's heard. Why can't we pass that time by tying the knot,
here and now, between Thomas Ferris and my Margaret?' He
fixed his eyes on Walter Ferris. 'What do you say about it,
my friend?'

Everyone looked at him in astonishment.

'You want,' said Heron, as though he wasn't sure he had
heard correctly, 'to interrupt a . . . an investigation into a crime,
by holding a marriage ceremony?'

'A bit unusual, I grant you,' said Emory. His gaze was still
on Ferris. 'But it need only take a few minutes. Then it's done
and Margaret's safely wed to a good husband. Ferris ain't
against it, I think? Once more, what do you say, Walter?'

Something was passing between those two: unspoken, but
it was there. Emory's attitude to Ferris had changed. Earlier,
he had had a respectful air, but the respect had vanished now.
He was addressing Ferris as an equal or even an inferior. As
though he had power over him.

Heron had noticed it too. 'I have a feeling,' he said, 'that
something is going on here to which I am not privy. What is
it?'

'It's just my wish to see my daughter settled and to take
the opportunity, while she's here and young Thomas is here

and we have a chaplain on hand,' said Emory stolidly. 'Been trying to bring this match about for a long time, I have.'

'Indeed?' Heron's voice was anything but encouraging.

Emory, however, was unmoved. 'Well, why not?' he said. 'Given Master Ferris here agrees.'

'This is hardly the time or the place,' Ferris said. 'Certainly, I am in favour of the marriage, but here and now . . . No, this is no way to go about it. It should take place in a church or in our own small chapel, with guests and a feast . . .'

'Oh, come. I'm not asking for the moon, you know. Just a neighbourly favour, like I did for you over the young bull,' said Emory.

Ferris was silent. He was going to give in. Obliquely, Paul Emory was telling him he must. I was watching them, and I could see it. Emory had a hold over Ferris all right. Well, of course. He had assuredly been Ferris's mouthpiece in persuading Jane to accuse me, and I would have sworn on oath that Ferris had told him of Uncle Ambrose's death and bidden him to pass that piece of news on, as well. And now Emory was tacitly threatening to say so, if Ferris didn't consent to the marriage.

I opened my mouth to shout it all out, before it was too late, but Thomas got in first.

'No one,' he said, 'has asked me, or asked Margaret, whether we are willing. And I for one am not.'

His father rounded on him. 'You will do as you are bid. Before God, you will. You know what will happen if you don't. I expect obedience from my son. Remember this, if nothing else moves you: I can always will my property to someone else.'

Thomas, who had half risen, sank back into his seat. So that was the final lever, I thought. When violence could no longer control him, the fear of losing his inheritance might.

'And Margaret,' said Paul Emory, 'will also do as she is bid. Margaret is a good obedient daughter, and I have no doubt of that.'

Margaret said nothing. She looked as though she were shrinking inside her clothes. Bridget said nothing, either.

'Very well,' said Ferris. 'Sir Edward, I know it seems strange, but this is after all my house, and surely there is no harm in pausing for a pleasant few moments, before you proceed with the arrest of these women.'

'If I do so proceed,' said Heron. 'The two witnesses Mrs Cobbold and Mr Emory have certainly interested me. This is an odd situation. I find virtually all the evidence in Mrs Stannard's favour to be unconvincing, but I begin to think that after all there is a formidable amount of it. Small bits and pieces and all dubious . . . but a lot of them.'

So he wasn't as sure as he had seemed to be. I had achieved that much. I had damaged his certainty.

'I do indeed need time to consider,' Heron was saying. 'Mr Ferris, if you want to fill the gap with a wedding ceremony which in no way affects my deliberations, you may do so.'

Jane Cobbold, not looking at me, said: 'Thomas, you may as well. Believe me, you will never marry Christina. My husband will only agree to that when it starts to snow in hell. Cobbolds can't marry Ferrises, and that's that, as he's said to me and to Christina, many a time, and—'

'Enough,' said Heron. He turned to Giles Parkes. 'You are willing to perform this ceremony?'

'We would prefer my steward, Peter Maine, to do so,' said Ferris. 'Since this is a Catholic household. He is a priest as well as a steward, and we do have a private chapel. It is small, but it is consecrated.'

'I have heard about it,' Heron said sharply. 'A Popish place, polluted by incense and Papistical rites. I have not hitherto interfered in your private devotions, Mr Ferris, but I cannot allow Popish rites to take place in my presence. The ceremony will be conducted here in the hall, in decent Protestant fashion. Mr Parkes!'

'By all means,' said the chaplain. 'We can use my writing table to represent a homely altar, and perhaps a ring could be found . . .'

NINETEEN
Fox in the Hen-Run

I t seemed strange to me, and somehow inappropriate, that the terrifying events in which I was trapped seemed to be inextricably tangled up with weddings. Weddings, after all, are supposed to be joyous. But there it was. First there had been Alice Cobbold's marriage, and then came Meg's, and now it was the wedding of Margaret Emory and Thomas Ferris. Alice's was the only one that followed the conventional pattern. Meg's was outrageously interrupted by Thomas's father, and as for that of Thomas and Margaret . . .

To begin with, although the Reverend Giles Parkes, Sir Edward Heron's creaky-voiced chaplain, was a genuinely ordained vicar, the ceremony wasn't taking place in any kind of chapel or church, but in front of a makeshift altar in the great hall of White Towers. There were no bridesmaids, no flower garlands, no wedding breakfast. In addition, both of the parties looked as unhappy as though they were there to be executed rather than united in marriage.

There had been some attempt to create a proper wedding atmosphere. Bridget, coming suddenly to life, had rushed Margaret upstairs and changed her dove-grey dress for a silk gown in lightning-blue, over a bright pink and silver kirtle. She had put a blue hood on the girl's head and provided an open ruff.

I thought Bridget must have lent the clothes. Margaret probably had nothing suitable. Not that the borrowed finery was suitable either. It was much too garish for Margaret and didn't fit properly. The wide ruff was too old for such a young girl, and the elegant hood and the gown were both too big. Margaret kept on nervously pushing the hood straight, and the shoulders of the gown kept slipping down on to her upper arms, while her body rose from an oversized farthingale like a small pin from a very large pincushion. The ensemble was completed by a rope of rose quartz beads which hung too far past Margaret's waist, and a pair of matching earrings.

Bridget hadn't changed, but she had put on dangling pearl and silver earrings to go with her pendant. Before taking Margaret upstairs, she had whispered something to Thomas, who had shaken an impatient head. I fancied that she had suggested that he too change into something more suitable for a bridegroom than the plain buff doublet and hose he was wearing, and he had refused.

So there we were, a highly unorthodox wedding party. Sybil and myself, prisoners under a cloud of terrifying accusations. Sir Edward Heron, who was supposed to be here to hale Sybil and myself off to prison. Brockley and Wilder, our would-be rescuers, looking bemused. Peter Maine, steward and priest, sullenly standing aside because he wasn't conducting the cere-mony himself. Jane Cobbold, who loathed me and whose presence in this house was such an affront to Walter Ferris that he scowled every time he looked at her. Walter Ferris himself, forced to see his son married in this fudged-up and extraordinary fashion and visibly detesting it.

And there was Master Emory, who had intimidated Ferris into agreeing to it – Emory, who was now cast as the father of the bride, with the duty of leading her to the makeshift altar. There was Bridget Ferris, attempting to look as though she were a perfectly ordinary mother of the groom, and trying to pretend that the hall was a church. And there were the unhappy couple, neither of them appropriately dressed: Thomas, with a face as mournful as a funeral, and a tight-lipped Margaret who had said nothing while her future life was arranged for her and had let herself be adorned for the occasion as though she were a doll.

Parkes had provided a prayer book, and Bridget had produced a ring, a little gold hoop with a pearl in it. 'I think it will fit,' she said.

The prayer book now lay open on the table with the ring on top of it. Bridget had asked if there could be some lighted candles, but Parkes had sharply refused. Thomas, prodded by his father, took his place in front of the table. Paul Emory, looking pleased with himself, took Margaret's arm and led her to Thomas's side.

The ceremony began.

It started with an interminable prayer, unmelodiously intoned by the Reverend Giles Parkes, who was, I thought, enjoying himself. It gave him pleasure to be introducing Protestant customs forcibly into this Catholic household.

But the kernel of the matter was reached at last. Emory placed Margaret's hand in that of Thomas and stepped back. Parkes began to administer the vows. Thomas, asked if he took Margaret Eleanor Emory to be his lawful wedded wife, and was willing to love and cherish her, muttered 'I will,' and was made to repeat it, louder.

Parkes turned to Margaret. 'And do you, Margaret Eleanor Emory, take Thomas Henry Ferris as your lawful wedded husband? Will you love, honour and obey him, and will you be bonny and buxom at bed and at board . . .?'

Paul Emory's normally dour face broke into a smile as he waited for her reply. Even Ferris, on the other side of Thomas, smiled a little.

'Margaret?' said Parkes, since she hadn't spoken.

'No,' said Margaret.

Her voice, though not loud, was clear and icy. The word fell through the air like a single and obtrusive hailstone. Thomas turned and looked at her in amazement. Emory and Ferris stared at her, two comical faces, mouth and eyes stretched open.

Peter Maine said audibly: 'Scandalous!'

Bridget gasped: '*Margaret!*'

Sybil simply gasped. Wilder looked embarrassed. Heron didn't visibly react at all.

Brockley murmured: 'Well, that's put a fox into the hen-run and no mistake. What now, I wonder?'

The calmest persons present seemed to be Margaret herself and the Reverend Giles Parkes. 'I repeat,' said Parkes, 'will you, Margaret Eleanor Emory . . .'

Margaret waited until he had got to the end of the promises she was supposed to ratify and then said: 'No, I said no. I meant no. I don't want to marry Thomas, and he doesn't want to marry me, and aren't we supposed to be willing? Isn't that why we're asked to say *I will*? Well, I *won't*. I can't take vows I know I shan't keep. Thomas shouldn't have to, either!'

She spun away from them all, from Thomas and the altar and her father. Emory clutched at her, but she evaded him and ran for the door. It was Bridget who caught her and pulled her back. 'What is the meaning of this? How dare you so insult my son – and embarrass us all! You were brought into this house to marry him; you've known it from the start. I am ashamed of you . . .!'

'Let me go!'

'I will *not* let you go. Come back to the altar and take your vows as you should, as you have known for years that you would one day have to do. Do as I bid!'

'No!' screamed Margaret.

Bridget slapped her, and Margaret, no longer calm, but losing her head entirely, kicked Bridget's shins. Bridget slapped her again, very hard indeed, and Margaret shrieked and burst into tears, causing Brockley's Sir Galahad streak to appear.

'Here!' he said indignantly, striding over to them and pulling Margaret away. 'Easy, now. Who wants to marry a bride who's all over bruises?'

'Bring her back here!' Emory rushed at them. 'Give her to me. What are you about, you silly girl? Straighten your hood; what do you think you look like, with it over one ear? Come back to the altar and—'

'One moment!' Heron had risen sharply to his feet. 'I will not have this! I will not allow anyone to take marriage vows under duress, not in my presence. It is against the laws of the church, and it invalidates the vows.'

Yes, Heron, for all his obsession with witches, was fundamentally honest. He had stepped between the Emorys and the altar. 'Let go of your daughter, Mr Emory. Let go, I say! Margaret, will you explain yourself, please? You need not fear me. Are you resolved against this marriage, or just overcome by its suddenness, and frightened, as a young girl might well be, confronted by such a solemn undertaking, without time to prepare or ask your mother the questions that you might naturally wish to ask? Have you, because you were frightened, said things you will later realize you didn't mean? Speak freely.'

Margaret, dishevelled, crying, pressing a hand to her reddened face where Bridget had hit her, merely whimpered, but Emory released her, and as he did so, Brockley guided her over to me. I put an arm round her. With Brockley on her other side, she was protected from Emory and Bridget alike. She was becoming quieter. Heron repeated his questions.

Margaret gulped, but answered him. 'I can't marry Thomas. I can't. He wants to marry someone else, and I . . . have no wish to take her place. Besides, I think of Thomas as a brother. It isn't right for us to marry. I am not frightened of marriage. I just can't agree to this one.'

'Good. That is enough. There will be no marriage. Parkes, give the ring back to Mrs Ferris. We will resume our earlier business. Find a maidservant to take care of Margaret. Wash her face and get her out of that hideous rainbow of a gown and into something modest and decent. We will then—'

A sudden hammering on the front door, sounding clearly across the entrance vestibule that lay between it and hall, interrupted him. He stopped short. We all looked at each other with eyes that said: *what now?*

'Answer it,' said Heron.

Ferris nodded at Maine, who disappeared into the vestibule. A moment later, he reappeared, accompanied by two men. One was our gnome-like Arthur Watts, looking tired, with the dust of travel in the lines on his seamed brown face. The other, large and sun-reddened, a glowing East Anglian beacon of rectitude, was Bartholomew Twelvetrees, courier, of Norwich.

TWENTY

So Faint a Stain

'Sir William Cecil found him,' said Watts, addressing me and Brockley mainly, but with an uncertain nod towards Heron, who had resumed his seat, which was obviously a place of honour. 'His men, they'd just brought him to Hampton Court when I got there. This here's Bartholomew Twelvetrees, and he's a courier by trade. Master Stannard and Mistress Stannard, they wanted him found.'

'I come back with Master Watts,' Twelvetrees agreed, in his slow Norfolk voice. He pulled off his hat and bowed politely. 'Seems these folk, the Stannards, think there's questions I can answer.' His voice was slow and accented but perfectly self-possessed. 'Well, here I am. Ask anything you want.'

Any resemblance the gathering had ever had to a marriage party had leached away. No one had had time to take Margaret out of the room and she was still with us, sheltering between me and Brockley, but with her face reddened from Bridget's blows, and her oversized farthingale sagging badly, she hardly looked like a bride. The Ferrises and Paul Emory were standing about, apparently beyond speech but flushed with outrage. Jane Cobbold had retired to the inglenook, looking as though the whole situation was beyond her. Master Twelvetrees was the centre of attention.

'Who is this?' Heron demanded. 'A courier, he says? What has that to do with anything?'

'He brought the letter that Anne Percy of Northumberland sent to me,' I said. 'Master Ferris insists it was a forgery, but that wasn't so.'

'What is all this?' Ferris shouted. But there was fear in his eyes.

'Is that what you want to ask about?' asked Twelvetrees. 'That letter?'

'Is it?' Heron said to me.

'Yes,' I said. 'Master Twelvetrees, this is Sir Edward Heron, sheriff of the county. Please will you tell him – tell us all – did you, in August, bring a letter to me, handed to you in Norwich by a man who had arrived from the Low Countries? And on what date did you get it to me?'

'Ah. I'm none so good at dates,' said Bartholomew, 'but it wor August right enough. I brought that there letter to your house, Hawkswood, sometime in the first half of that month. There was two letters, matter of fact. One for this house, and one addressed for a Master Ferris that wor here at this place. Said they was both urgent, he did, the fellow that hired me, that come off the ship in Norwich. I called here first, if I remember right.'

Brockley and I looked at each other, drawing simultaneous breaths of relief. The essential questions had been answered, before they had even been asked.

Ferris, however, was fighting back. 'Oh yes, you came here,' he said. 'Of course you did, but what of it? You brought a letter on a business matter.' He was trying to sound offhand. 'Nothing to do with any Countesses of Northumberland. That letter this prying Mistress Jester was caught with, that's still lying there on the table, it's just a forgery that she put among my papers to make a criminal of me!'

Heron looked uncertain, and silently, I cursed.

What is the matter with the man? Isn't it obvious that Ferris is lying to save his skin? Any fool ought to be able to see it! Will this man dismiss every piece of evidence in my favour or Sybil's? Why? But I knew the answers. Heron wasn't corrupt, but he wanted, so much, to catch some more witches.

'Just a minute,' said Brockley. 'I was there when you brought the Hawkswood letter, Master Twelvetrees. There's something I remember about it. It was in the form of a scroll, but there was no outer covering, was there? Wasn't it just a single sheet of paper, rolled up and sealed?'

'Aye, well, that's how it looked,' confirmed Twelvetrees.

I said: 'I wondered if maybe the lady was short of both parchment and paper.'

'Oh, must we listen to this?' Ferris enquired of the room in general.

Heron turned to him. 'I think we must.' Once more, I saw the honest sheriff in conflict with the witch-hunter, and once more, the sheriff gained the upper hand. 'If it is relevant, that is. Is it, Mrs Stannard?'

'Very much so, Sir Edward!' I had begun to hope again. 'I think I know what Brockley has remembered. Master Twelvetrees apologized as he handed me the letter, because it had a dirty mark on it. During the journey, it was accidentally dropped. It didn't matter. It wasn't much of a mark, and it was on the outside. It didn't spoil any of the writing – not the superscription or the letter itself. If anything could spoil such an ugly message,' I added bitterly.

'Exactly. And I saw the grubby mark on the back of the sheet when I came into the room when Master Stannard was reading the letter aloud,' Brockley declared.

'You mean that if the letter on the table has that mark, then it is genuine?' Heron asked. He looked at Twelvetrees.

'Aye, just so,' said Twelvetrees.

'Perhaps you would look for yourself.' Heron pointed to where the two letters lay.

Twelvetrees went to the table. 'These them?' He picked the two letters up, turned them both over and then held one up. 'This here's the one I brought to Hawkswood, to Mistress Stannard. That's your name on the back, mistress, and there's the dirty little stain where it got dropped out of my saddlebag in a muddy inn-yard, and I'm still sorry over that.'

'I'm not,' I said. 'Show the mark to Sir Edward Heron, please.'

Twelvetrees did as I asked. Heron stared at it. 'So faint a stain,' he said. 'With so much to say. Fellow, how did it come about that Sir William Cecil sent to find you?'

'Master Stannard and I asked him to do so,' I said. 'We thought, if Master Twelvetrees could be traced, we might learn something of any messages that Anne Percy had sent to White Towers.'

'Sir William's men asked after me in hostelries in Norwich,' said Bartholomew. 'They found someone as knew I'd gone to Thetford. They got on the road to Thetford and met me on my way back. Brought me straight to Hampton Court, they did. Said I'd nothing to fear, but afeard I was, a great man like that wanting me found!'

Heron was still gazing at the trace of dirt on the back of the letter. 'Let me see the other one again,' he said. Parkes brought it to him, and as Heron studied them, a frown creased his forehead. He turned once more to Parkes. 'Where are the notes you took, Parkes?'

'Here, Sir Edward.' The small writing table had a drawer beneath it, and Parkes had slipped his notes into it. He brought them out.

'Thank you.'

There was a pause while Heron read the notes through. Finally, he set them down and once more compared the two letters.

'I see,' he said at length. 'Yes, I see a good deal. The two letters are in the same hand. Of that, there is no doubt. This alters things considerably. It appears to me that the letter to Mrs Stannard must be genuine, since its courier vouches for it. In that case, the other letter, the one to Mr Ferris, must be genuine too. Yes, that changes the situation altogether.'

'Couriers can be bribed!' Ferris burst out.

'I ain't been bribed. That's a bloody insult, that is!' Twelvetrees snapped.

'I think not,' Heron said, addressing Ferris. 'I can hardly suppose that either Mr Twelvetrees or his companion really knew, before they got here, just what questions were going to be asked, or why. I admit I had no wish to find these letters genuine. Even now I find it difficult to believe what this evidence appears to say. I have known you, Mr Ferris, for most of my life, and much as I deplore your religious views, I have always respected you. But it seems that, after all, you did receive instructions from Anne Percy of Northumberland to destroy Mrs Stannard and her manservant Roger Brockley. I cannot now avoid that conclusion. And from the time that you received this letter, the attempts to harm Mrs Stannard and Mr Brockley began. I can see the trail now, in Mr Parkes' notes, like a line of footprints, leading on from that faint, grubby stain.'

He picked up the letter to me once more and stared again at the dirty mark. 'So very faint . . . and so telling.' He was musing aloud.

'This is all complete nonsense,' Ferris shouted. 'You can't make so much out of a little smear of grime on a piece of paper!'

'Here!' said Twelvetrees indignantly. 'Are you saying I can't remember if I dropped a rolled-up letter in an inn yard or not, and what the smear looked like? I surely can. It's the sort of thing I don't like to happen, and if that if it does, it'll stick in my mind. I tell you *that's* the letter and *that's* the smear.'

'You would go into court and swear to that on the Bible?' Heron asked him.

'Yes,' said Twelvetrees belligerently. 'I would. And there's plenty of folk in Norwich would give me a character and swear I'm no liar.'

Brockley said: 'I wish to make a request.'

Heron turned to him. 'Indeed? And what might that be?'

'When Mistress Stannard and Mistress Jester were brought back here after the witnesses Mistress Cobbold and Master Emory were fetched,' said Brockley, 'they were escorted in by Maine here, and two other men. Those two aren't here now. I'd like to see them again.'

'You have a reason for asking this?'

'Yes, Sir Edward. A very good reason.'

'Fetch them, Maine.'

Ferris bristled on hearing his steward ordered about by Heron, but he said nothing. Maine went out and came back in a very short time, with the two men in question. Brockley then asked the name of the brawny groom.

'John Hunter,' said the groom.

'I've seen you before,' said Brockley. 'And I know your voice. You were bellowing loud enough when you came marching into the Lion Inn in Woking, shouting that something valuable had been stolen from your saddlebag! If I hadn't just that moment handed the landlord a precious necklace that turned up in my saddlebag when it shouldn't have, where would I have been?'

'In trouble,' said Hunter frankly. 'But it was all just a

mistake. There were several saddlebags hanging up in that stable. I fancy I put the pouch with the necklace in the wrong one. My apologies.'

'Or had you been ordered to put it in the wrong one?' Brockley wanted to know. 'Just a bit of a coincidence, wasn't it? You making a mistake like that just after your master had had orders to ruin me and Mistress Stannard?'

Hunter was silent, looking disconcerted.

Heron enquired: 'Will you, Roger Brockley, also repeat what you have just said when you are on oath?'

'I most certainly will.'

'And I will repeat my own testimony on oath,' I said. 'Because every word of it, every single word, is the truth.'

Ferris audibly ground his teeth.

'Sir Edward,' I said, 'who was it suggested to you that evidence of witchcraft might be found in the home of Mrs Ward and Mrs Seldon?' It was hard to say their names calmly. Just thinking about them made me want to cry. But the question needed to be asked.

'It was Mr Ferris,' said Sir Edward. 'But that time, he was proved to be right.'

'A piece of jewellery planted in Brockley's saddlebag,' I said. 'Incriminating literature planted in the house where Mrs Ward and Mrs Seldon lived. Two similar tricks. Two *dirty* tricks!' I stared at him in anguish, pleading with my eyes. And then said it. 'They were innocent. *Innocent*! And Ferris here as good as murdered them!'

'That is merely a theory.' Parkes's chin had risen, and so had the round arches of his eyebrows. 'It is your opinion only and not proven fact. Indeed, the idea is absurd. How could Mr Ferris obtain the incriminating literature which has been mentioned? Such books are not easy to find, the Lord be praised.'

Heron, however, was frowning. 'As I think many people know, I confiscate such books when they are discovered and destroy most of them, but some I keep for purposes of training my staff – so that they know what to look for when they raid a property. I keep the books at home, on a shelf in a cupboard which is normally locked, but now and then I let friends see them – just briefly. In August, Mr Ferris, you and your wife visited me at home, and I showed them to you then. And the next time I opened that cupboard, which was some time in September, I noticed that the books were not packed as closely on that shelf as they should have been. When I looked more carefully, I found that four were missing. The only keys never leave my key ring. But it is true that when I was showing them to you, I left you alone with them for a short time, because my wife called me for something or other.'

He stared fixedly at Ferris and then at Bridget, who paled.

Heron tapped his fingers on the arm of his chair, thinking aloud. 'The book found in the house where Mrs Ward and Mrs Seldon lived was the same as one of the books stolen from me. But other copies of that book exist and have turned up on occasion, during various house searches. The women swore they had never seen it before – but they *would* say that anyway, whether they were guilty or not.'

'Quite!' Parkes declared, apparently unimpressed by the news of stolen books. 'It is necessary to take a stringent view of such things. Witchcraft is an abomination. It may even be worthwhile taking a few innocent lives, as long as the guilty are not allowed to escape. It is like the casualties in a just war.'

'Yes. And there could have been other occasions when the books could have been stolen. I have many visitors, some of whom know of that cupboard, and I have been known to leave my key ring lying about.' He shook his head. 'I have no certainty. The women Seldon and Ward may well have been guilty. Mr Ferris may have been in the right.'

I hated him. Three harmless women and an unborn child had come to a dreadful death because Ferris had tricked him, but he wasn't going to admit it, and Parkes would support him. Parkes's conscience (even if he had one) wouldn't be disturbed. Heron did seem to possess a conscience, but he clearly didn't mean to let it be aroused this time. He was unstable, two men in one skin, sheriff and witch-hunter locked in everlasting conflict. To hurl furious accusations at him might jeopardize my own safety and Sybil's, and it wouldn't give back life to his victims.

And then, at my side, Margaret Emory suddenly cried: '*Thomas*! Take off your doublet and shirt! Show them what your father did to you last night! You said to me that he did it because you told him you couldn't marry me – that you wouldn't give Christina up. Was it? Or was it to make you say what he wanted you to say about that silly potion? I don't believe a word of that love philtre story! You wouldn't need a love potion for Christina! I've seen you together! So why would you tell such a tale if you hadn't been made to? If I'm right, then show them!'

Everyone, including Thomas, gaped at her. Ferris spluttered: 'Christina? He *knows* he can't marry a Cobbold! He'd *never* have dared come to me and—' He stopped, looking huntedly around him, realizing his mistake.

Margaret stamped her foot. 'If I'm right, Thomas, *do it*!'

Thomas's hands went to his doublet buttons and then stopped. With an exasperated cry, Margaret broke away from me, ran to him and began to pluck at the buttons herself.

'All right,' he said. 'All *right*!' He started to help her. The doublet came off and then his shirt, and we saw what was beneath: the purple welts that criss-crossed his back, and here and there the dark-red blots of dried blood. All the time that he was sitting in the inglenook, he must have been in considerable pain.

'To make you say that you had bought a love potion from Mrs Stannard?' Heron asked.

'Yes,' said Thomas. He looked at Margaret. 'I couldn't tell you. I was ashamed of what I was being made to do. So I pretended to you that I'd told him I wanted to marry Christina.'

'So *that* was why . . .!' Bridget's voice was outraged. She backed away from Ferris, staring at him as though he were a repulsive stranger.

'I *see*,' said Heron.

The proofs against Ferris were piling up, item by item, and Heron was listening and coming at last, even against his will, to an unavoidable conclusion. Ferris knew it. Now, with all eyes on the proof of how he had enforced his son's obedience, I saw the knowledge dawn in his.

He crumbled. It happened all in a moment, taking every

one of us by surprise. It was physical; his knees gave way, and his face folded like that of a child about to burst into tears.

'All right. All right! I was afraid from the start that I couldn't do it! It was a compliment to be asked; I wanted to serve the lady of Northumberland; I *tried*! But nothing went right. It was too difficult!'

Incredibly, it sounded like an appeal for understanding. I thought of what he had done to Jennet and Margery and Bessie, and I shuddered away from him. He looked such a commonplace little man, crouching there on the floor. Had he perhaps resented being commonplace? So much that he had tried to overcome it and in the end let the struggle turn to evil?

He had bullied his son and probably his wife; he had been flattered to be chosen by Anne Percy as her instrument. Had she picked him because, during their one meeting, she had sensed in him the useful, usable presence of wickedness? But the task had been too big for him. He'd made his schemes up as he went along, but they were too unwieldy and he hadn't been cunning or far-seeing enough to carry them through.

No one responded to his air of pathos. He went on talking, wildly. 'I did my best. I had to use what was there.' He could never have met Carew Trelawny, but those were Trelawny's words, just the same. There was a flash of indignation in Brockley's eyes. Ferris gabbled on. 'If only I'd had clear instructions. I tried this, and then that . . . I tried to do my duty . . .'

Bridget was standing with her hands pressed to her mouth and her eyes stretched wide. Ferris gazed at an unmoving and unmoved Heron. 'I tried so hard, so very hard, to do right by my God and my queen, the noble Queen Mary, and by my kinswoman of Northumberland, but it wouldn't go the way I meant it to, it *wouldn't*.'

He might have been complaining that a felled tree had fallen in the wrong direction or a flock of wayward sheep had dodged the pen. 'I wanted to get that man Brockley first,' he said, 'before I trapped Ursula Stannard, because the Countess said she cared for him and my orders said: *make her suffer*. But he escaped every snare I laid!'

'You sound,' said Brockley, 'as though, as an honest citizen, it was my moral duty to cooperate with you!'

'That Stannard woman,' said Ferris, unheeding, 'outwitted and made a fool of my kinswoman, and now she's made a fool of me. My orders said try to make her look like a witch. So I got a girl into her house with orders to tell me things, and I told her: "Get Mistress Stannard to give that Christina Cobbold a potion of some sort – any sort." I reckoned I could make Thomas say whatever I wanted him to say . . .' He darted a venomous glance at his son. 'When I was packing up my poor daughter's things, I saw those cloaks, and then I saw what I could do with them. It was all clear in my head. Make it look as though the Stannard woman was selling magic potions. Make it look as if she'd raised the sickness and spread it around her. I knew clothes could carry contagion. It ought to have worked . . .'

'Did you steal those books from me?' Heron interrupted. 'I seem to recall that you said you had heard of them and would like to see them. I showed them to you at your request.'

'I . . .' It seemed as though Ferris, having crumbled and begun to blurt out the truth, was now realizing his peril and wanting to retreat. 'I . . . I . . .' He was stammering. Then he stopped.

'Sir Edward, he can't have walked away from your cupboard with stolen books under his arm.' Parkes chimed in on the wrong side, as might have been expected. 'Someone would have noticed!'

'One moment,' said Heron. 'Mrs Ferris, you look distressed. Is there something you wish to tell us?'

Bridget's hands dropped from her mouth. 'Yes, there is!'

'Hold your tongue, Bridget!' Ferris screeched. 'Don't interfere! A wife can't bear witness against her husband!'

'But whatever your lady seems about to tell us, you were, I trust, going to reveal anyway,' said Heron. 'Weren't you confessing? And this is not a court of law. Mrs Ferris may say what she wishes.'

'I want to speak!' said Bridget, making up her mind. She straightened her back and raised her chin, visibly gathering that cool dignity of hers round her like a mantle. 'It's time I spoke! I've been silent too long. I've endured his contempt too long!' The words were tumbling out of her as though they

had been pent up and were now breaking free of their own
accord. The little dog at her feet whimpered and cowered,
frightened. 'I want to tell the truth!' said Bridget fiercely. 'I
want to tell it for the sheer pleasure of hammering a few nails
into his coffin!'

'*Bridget*!' Ferris shouted.

Everyone else gasped. This was something that none of us
had expected.

'If, after all this, Sir Edward is still not convinced,' Bridget
declared, 'then I dare say my husband will kill me, even if he
did intend to confess everything himself. He does not like me
to utter a word without his permission, even to think a thought
for myself. I hate him for that, and for what he has done to
Thomas, not just yesterday, but many times before, though
yesterday his reasons were so shameful I can hardly bear to
think of them! And I hate him for doing the same to me, on
occasion, and to my dear daughter Lucy, though a more trac-
table girl never lived. She was terrified of him, all through her
girlhood. And now I hate him for what he has tried to do to
Mrs Stannard. I read that letter from Anne Percy, though I
never thought he would try to carry out such monstrous plans!
Well, if I do die at his hands in the end, my life is not so
happy that I am much troubled to defend it and—'

'Bitch! Be silent! Wives don't speak against their husbands!
What I say or don't say is my business. It's not for you to
intrude! You'll pay for this, you'll pay . . .!' Ferris's voice
rose to a shriek.

'Certainly, he stole those books,' said Bridget. 'He ordered
me to help him. He gave me a bag to hang under my skirts.
He took four books, but not large ones, and I had such a
wide farthingale, such big skirts! He put them in the bag.
They were well hidden. I'm sorry for what I did, Sir Edward.
But he is my husband and I was in his power. I couldn't
refuse.'

'You mean,' said Wilder with interest, 'that four books were
bumping under your skirts all the rest of the day? How
uncomfortable!'

'Yes, it was,' said Bridget. There was poison in the way
Ferris was glowering at her, but she was speaking to Heron

now and would not look at her husband. 'As soon as I could, I went upstairs. I said I wanted a shawl. We were staying overnight so we had clothes and such things with us, and my husband had brought his saddlebags to our chamber. My maid was there, pressing something that had got crumpled on the journey, but I managed to unfasten the bag of books and put it in one of the saddlebags without her seeing.' Bridget was still dignified but as white as a ghost.

'Ferris?' said Heron. 'What did you do with the books you purloined? Tell us!'

'Very well! Very *well*!' Beleaguered, Ferris was crumbling again. 'Yes, I hid two of them in that house, where those women lived. Didn't you find the other one? And yes, I tried my best to get *her* –' he stopped glowering at Bridget and pointed at me instead – 'tangled up with them . . .'

'We found the second one when we dined with Margery and Jennet,' I said. 'And burnt it. But if you stole four, what did you do with the other two? Were they planted at Hawkswood, by any chance?'

'Maybe,' said Ferris. It was a sneer.

'So that when Sir Edward was eventually persuaded to raid Hawkswood, they'd be found,' I said with fury. 'But you feared that he wouldn't be easily persuaded, so you created evidence against two defenceless ladies and their maidservant. I was to be steered into friendship with them, to smear my reputation. How despicable.'

Theory had unquestionably been turned to proof. The odious Parkes was shrugging his shoulders, defeated but unconcerned. Heron, however, had turned the colour of whey.

Thank you, Ferris. You have made him see it. Sir Edward Heron, may Jennet and Margery and Bessie and the ghost of the child that was never born haunt your dreams for the rest of your life.

'I did it all for the Countess!' Ferris shouted. 'It was a nightmare, trying to work through other people, never feeling I was in control!' He clenched his fists as though this maddened him above all things. 'Emory, Mistress Cobbold – it was so bloody difficult! I even used my son's hand in marriage as a bribe! What do you think that felt like?'

'My girl not good enough for you otherwise, then?' Emory shouted.

'*I was only trying to do my duty! No one can condemn me for that!*'

Now, although he kept glaring at me, Thomas and Bridget in turn, he had also started to snivel. I felt ill with loathing. And Brockley was furious.

'So you admit it!' Brockley shouted at him. 'You get three poor women hanged, you try to get my mistress hanged as well, and you tried to kill me with a crossbow. *Was* that you? You lay in wait for me yourself?'

'Yes. I'm a good shot.' There was hurt pride there. 'But you got away,' said Ferris, whining now, resentful. '*You* didn't come to any harm! Everything I tried, you escaped from . . .'

'Didn't come to any harm?' Brockley bellowed. 'You missed me by inches, and you killed the best horse I've ever ridden! I loved Brown Berry!'

He was unbuttoning his jacket. He tore it off, threw it aside, and sprang. His onslaught roused Ferris from his abject crouch. A second later, they were fighting.

It didn't last long, but it was spectacular enough. Brockley was furious, raging, punching with both fists, calling Ferris all manner of names at the same time. Ferris was saving his breath for the fight, but he was returning punch for punch, his vigour renewed. The two of them swayed this way and that. A chair went flying, the dining table shook as they crashed into it, and the deerskin rug skidded under their feet, all but bringing Brockley down. All the women, me included, huddled into the inglenook out of harm's way. Maine tried to intervene and was swept aside as though he were a cobweb. Most of the men were shouting, some encouraging one or other of the opponents, some wanting them to stop. Brockley and Ferris behaved as though they couldn't hear.

Then Ferris, throwing himself backwards to get momentarily out of Brockley's reach, thrust a hand under his doublet and pulled out a dagger.

It is not usual for a gentleman in his own house to wear a dagger, least of all when he is entertaining (if that is the right word) the sheriff of the county. Ferris must, I think, secretly have feared the outcome of this enquiry and come armed in case he had to fight his way out. The blade flashed as he drew it, and there were angry shouts from the watching men. It is disgraceful to draw a weapon on an unarmed opponent, and Brockley had left his own dagger at home. Brockley, too, was outraged. He emitted a shocking, animal snarl, lunged forward to grab Ferris's right wrist and tried to wrestle the dagger out of Ferris's grasp.

They lurched back and forth and trod on another rug, the leopardskin this time. Like the deerskin, it slid, as the floor of the hall was so thoroughly polished. Once more, Brockley was caught off balance. He jumped sideways, trying to save himself, and came down on his weak ankle. I saw it give way. He crashed to the floor, taking Ferris with him. They rolled, with the dagger between them, and then Brockley had torn himself loose, and the front of his shirt was splashed with blood but it wasn't his. The blade had gone into Ferris's chest, and he was sprawled on his back, uttering horrible noises, halfway between coughs and screams, clawing at the hilt, and blood was coming up past the blade and oozing from his mouth.

Brockley got to his feet. He panted for a moment, doubled over, and then found breath enough to speak to Heron.

'He as good as murdered Mistress Jennet and Mistress Margery and their girl Bessie, and he caused all those deaths from smallpox, as well as killing my beautiful horse,' he said. 'But I didn't mean to kill him! I just wanted to get the dagger away from him. It went into him by accident. But God's defended the right. And done your hangman out of a fair bit of pay.'

'He drew a dagger on a man who had no weapon,' said Heron. 'We all saw. We were all witnesses. There will be no need for an inquest.'

TWENTY-ONE
A Time to Heal

Ferris did not die instantly, not until his desperate dragging at the dagger hilt finally freed the blade. Then blood spurted from the last frantic pulse of his heart, and he lay twitching and choking for what I suppose were about thirty seconds, though they felt to me like thirty years, before he fell silent and still and his eyes went blank. The blood was all over his doublet and his right hand, which still gripped the dagger hilt. The floorboards beneath him were splashed with it.

Then Bridget, completely overset, broke down. Her cool dignity abandoned her. She burst into tears, wailing pitifully. Her little dog began to howl. And then confusion took over. Just what happened during the next two hours, I don't know, because Heron said: 'You ladies, get Mrs Ferris away. I do not intend to proceed against her for conniving with her husband. She was clearly in fear of him. See to her.'

So the four of us, Sybil, myself, Margaret Emory and Jane Cobbold, picked up the dog and helped a half-fainting Bridget out of the hall and up to her chamber, where her maid greeted us with wide-eyed horror. We gathered that the servants had been ordered to keep away from the hall unless they were sent for.

In the circumstances, Jane Cobbold and I worked together. In time to come, it was likely that if we met in Woking's main street, one of us would cross it to avoid the other. For the time being, however, we were concerned only with settling Bridget on her bed, taking off her embroidered hood and loosening her stays while Sybil freed her from ruff and farthingale. There was a ewer of water, a basin and facecloths in the room, and Margaret, displaying much common sense and an unexpected air of command, sponged Bridget's brow, while simultaneously ordering the maid to the kitchen for wine to revive her and for a bowl of water for the dog.

Presently, Bridget quietened and her tears ceased. 'I'm glad he's dead,' she said. 'I'm safe from him now. Free. He always had to be in control, of all of us, as if we were puppets. He *is* dead, isn't he? We broke our fast together this morning as always. I can't believe it yet. How can Walter be dead, just like that?'

My guesses about her married life, I thought, had been all too accurate. 'Rest assured that he is,' I said. 'There's nothing to be afraid of now. Sir Edward will not harass you. We will look after you. Try to sleep.'

She closed her eyes and seemed to doze, and then, for some considerable time, we watched beside her, until there was a knock at the door, and Thomas was there.

'Is my mother better?'

'Yes,' said Bridget, opening her eyes and speaking for herself. 'Yes. Is that Thomas?'

'What's happening downstairs?' Margaret asked.

'Nothing much as yet, but something important, something formal, is about to happen.' Thomas seemed different: older, more authoritative. 'It would please me if you would all come to the hall, including my mother, if she is able. My father has been laid in our chapel. Mistress Stannard, Mistress Jester, may I speak with you privately, for just a moment? Perhaps you other ladies would help my mother downstairs. We will follow.'

'I am able,' said Bridget. Thomas withdrew while her maid helped her to dress, and then, with Bridget cradling her dog in her arms, she and the others went down, while Thomas came in. He still held himself stiffly, but not so much as before. He stood looking gravely at me and Sybil.

'Your man Brockley is a blessing,' he said to me. 'He has salved my back most skilfully.'

'He's been a soldier,' I said. 'They get to know about such things.'

'I'm grateful to him,' Thomas said. 'Mistress Stannard, I wish you to know that if it had come to court, I would have told the truth and exposed the love potion story as a lie. I would have asked the court for protection from my father, though whether they could have stopped him from disinheriting me, I don't know.'

'In such circumstances,' I said, 'a petition to the queen might well have restored your rights. Fortunately, it didn't come to that.'

'I'm glad he's dead,' Thomas said. 'That is a terrible thing for a son to say, but it's the truth. I've feared him all my life. So has my mother. I think she has taken refuge in being remote, never showing any feeling except for her pet dogs. It's been as though she were frozen inside. Maybe she will thaw now, given time. That is all. I have said what you had a right to hear. Now let us go down to the hall.'

There were few signs left of the recent stormy scene. The floor had been washed, and all that remained was a patch in need of fresh polish. The rugs had been straightened. No trace of blood remained. Everyone who had witnessed the death was still there, however, augmented now by an angry Anthony Cobbold. He had apparently returned home, learned that his wife had been taken away to White Towers and come wrathfully after her, to find himself in the midst of what, to him, was an incomprehensible drama.

'Sir Edward Heron has been explaining matters to me,' he was saying to his wife as we came in. 'And he has insisted that we remain for the time being, which means I can't take you out of this house at once, as I wish to do, and none of this makes any sense. Jane, how could you let yourself just be brought here like this? Cobbolds do not go to the home of Walter Ferris, or vice versa! Nor do they speak to Ferrises – and –' he glared at Thomas, who had entered the room behind Sybil and me – 'that means *you*.'

Thomas's response to this was a smile, which clearly took Anthony Cobbold aback. 'Everything be made plain,' Thomas said. 'Ah, here is Maine with wine. Please will everyone take a goblet – I ordered our best silver goblets for this occasion, because it is formal and because, despite the terrible events of today, it has hopeful aspects. Thank you, Maine. Come, don't be so downcast. I am not going to dismiss you, I promise.'

To me, Maine looked not so much downcast as simply shattered. His usual pallor was tinged with green, and his sagging shoulders somehow changed the effect of his black gown so that it no longer looked impressive, merely mournful. His

master's death must have turned his world upside down.
Helped, perhaps, by the change in Thomas.

That change seemed to be increasing with every moment.
Thomas was now the man in charge. He had stepped into that
position apparently without effort. Even Heron had, as it were,
moved back for him. It was Thomas who marshalled us all
into seats and saw us equipped with goblets. I found a place
in the inglenook, opposite Sybil and Bridget and with Margaret
next to me. Thomas went to stand where everyone could see
him, and he began to speak.

'First of all, I have it from Sir Edward Heron's own lips
that the charges against Mistress Stannard and Mistress Jester
are dropped. They cannot be upheld. Sir Edward is satisfied
that the evidence against them was a false trail, laid, I am
sorry to say, by my father. We will not go into that now. Most
of you know all about it, anyway.

'Secondly, my father is now dead. He was my father, and
in arranging his funeral, I shall show him all the respect that
a son should show, but I cannot in all honesty say that I loved
him. He had harsh ways of enforcing his will.'

From Bridget, there came a sound like a sob, but of agreement, not protest.

'Thirdly,' Thomas said, 'because he is dead, I wish the task
that he undertook for the Countess of Northumberland to pass
into history – and something else with it. I am tired of this
absurd feud between the Cobbolds and the Ferrises. Master
Cobbold!'

'You are addressing me?' said Anthony coldly.

'I am indeed. Master Cobbold, you may well find it difficult,
in the future, to pursue a feud against someone who is determined from now on to be a good friend and a good neighbour.
Isn't it time we buried the hatchet which your grandfather and
my great grandfather raised against each other? Aren't you as
weary of it as I am?'

'There have been other offences, in later generations,' said
Cobbold grimly.

'There have indeed. My grandfather died violently and
mysteriously,' said Thomas, 'and you know well enough where
the finger of suspicion pointed.'

Anthony turned a dusky red.

'But it didn't point at you,' said Thomas. 'Only at your father, who is dead and gone. If I can now choose to forget it, couldn't you manage to forget the . . . lesser, more mischievous incidents? What are a few strayed cattle and even burnt ricks to us now that so much time has gone by? Wouldn't it be much more pleasant for us to turn our backs on the past?'

Anthony looked as though he were struggling with himself. Jane Cobbold, who was sitting beside him, stared at her feet. Jane, I thought, probably didn't care whether the old feud was kept alive or not. I only hoped she wouldn't try to start another one, with the Stannards. I couldn't see the friendship between our two families continuing on its old footing.

Thomas was smiling at Anthony. He raised his goblet. 'Shall we drink to it? To the end of a useless quarrel, and to friendship henceforth between Cobbold and Ferris? My friends and neighbours, I give you the toast – to the end of pointless strife!'

We all raised our goblets. Anthony at first put his down on the table and folded his arms, but unexpectedly, Peter Maine observed: 'It is said in Holy Writ that there is a time to kill and a time to heal. Perhaps now, since Walter Ferris is gone and a new generation are taking over, is our time to heal. Master Cobbold, will you not drink?'

Maine was clearly in earnest. He was, I suppose, following the lead offered by Thomas, who was now his new master. At any rate, his intervention had an effect. Slowly, reluctantly, Anthony picked his goblet up again and drank with the rest of us.

Emory said: 'Well, all this is very much to the good, but what about this marriage between you and Margaret? She's been as awkward and silly as a girl well can be, but if you were to set about talking her round, Thomas . . .'

'Margaret and I are in agreement,' said Thomas. 'We are not suitable marriage partners. I have other plans.'

'Are you suggesting,' said Cobbold dangerously, with the old enmity rising up again, 'that you ought to be allowed to marry Christina?'

Thomas almost beamed upon him. 'Master Cobbold, many years ago, in the days of Henry the Fifth, after England and

France had fought a bitter war but had made peace, they sealed that peace with a marriage between King Henry and Princess Katherine of France. A marriage is as good a way of ratifying a peace treaty as any, don't you think? It would be a happy marriage, sir. I promise you. I would take care of Christina.'

Miserably, Jane said: 'Who else will, *now*?' Anthony looked at her as if she had bitten him. Meanwhile, Emory was seething.

'If Margaret had behaved as a daughter of mine should,' he said angrily, 'she and Thomas would be man and wife already. Margaret, I tell you, girl, you'll not be welcome at home, after this. Stay here with Mistress Ferris and serve her, if she'll have you, or make your own way in the world. I won't take you back.'

I felt Margaret press nervously against me. Bridget, in her old cool manner, said: 'Margaret is an admirable young woman, and I like her. But I have no wish to see my son thrust into marrying her against his will. I didn't want her to be brought here to "fix his interest", as Walter called it. It made me stiff with you, Margaret. I am sorry for that.'

'Margaret can come back to Hawkswood with me,' I said. 'I miss my own girl, Meg. Margaret shall be her replacement.'

'There were moments,' I said, 'when I never thought I'd be riding home, ever again. This has been one of the most frightening days of my life.'

'The queen would have intervened, madam,' Brockley said. 'I'm sure of it.'

'I didn't want to ask her again to override a court decision for me. She saved Gladys. I am glad that I have been saved without having to ask another such favour.'

We were free and alive and going home, riding through a cold and cloudy autumn evening as dusk gathered under the trees in the wood that stretched most of the way between White Towers and Hawkswood. Our party consisted of me, Brockley, Wilder, Watts, Sybil and Margaret Emory. Sybil and I had at last had the chance to wash and do our hair, and Bridget had lent Sybil some clean clothes. I had stayed in breeches, shirt and jacket but had at least brushed them.

Thomas, very much the master of the house now, had lent
Wilder a horse and told Margaret that she could keep Blue.
He had also lent a pack mule for her belongings, and a pillion
saddle so that Sybil could ride behind Brockley on Mealy. I
had been reunited with Roundel.

The Cobbolds had left before us, and Bartholomew
Twelvetrees had gone to find a bed in Woking. He meant to
start for Norwich in the morning. Clearly, he'd had enough of
all of us. Heron and Parkes were remaining for supper, though
reluctantly in the case of Parkes. He had attempted to stroke
Bridget's little dog, which had promptly bitten him. Bridget
had dressed the bite for him, but Margaret had whispered in
my ear: 'That dog is more intelligent than I thought! I feel
almost fond of it now.'

'Brockley,' I said as we trotted along, 'you must have been
very quick to get down the ladder and away to the boundary
fence before Ferris and his dogs were after you. You must
have run like a stag! Is that when you hurt your ankle again?'

Brockley gave his rare chuckle. 'Yes, madam, though to
begin with, I didn't run anywhere. I was halfway up the ladder.
I hadn't time to get down and run for it across the grounds.
As soon as I heard those dogs, I went on *up* as fast as I could,
scrambled over the battlements and threw myself down on the
flat roof all round the attic floor. It was a risk, because the dogs
were sure to pick up my scent at the foot of the ladder, and
whether mastiffs can climb ladders or not, I don't know, but I
just hoped they wouldn't try. Mercifully, they didn't. I prayed
that their masters would take it for granted that I'd run *away*,
not rush on into the enemy's stronghold, as it were, and assume
that I *had* scrambled down and run for the fence, and I think
they did. Anyway, I heard them sending the dogs to range about
in the grounds. In the end the hunt was called off. Then I started
thinking how to get myself away.'

'Yes, how did you do it? They took the ladder down.'

'First, I looked at the attics to see if you and Mistress Jester
were in any of them and if I could get you out. But you weren't
there.'

From behind him, Sybil said: 'We were in the wine cellar.
With a warning not to get drunk.'

Brockley laughed again. 'I couldn't find either of you, so I reckoned I'd better simply escape. I remembered you saying that the towers had doors on to that roof, so I went to look at the west tower. Yes, it has a door, and it wasn't locked, so in I went. It was too dark to see much, but the room I found myself in seemed to be full of unwanted furniture. I kept banging my shins and elbows on bits of it. I've got some beautiful bruises. Quite apart from Ferris's efforts.'

'Oh, Brockley!' I said. 'Well, Dale will look after you.'

'Fran says I'm getting too old for this sort of thing,' Brockley said. 'But I'm none so feeble yet. I found a spiral stair in the tower, so down I went, groping inch by inch. At the bottom there was a door, bolted on the inside. I unbolted it and crept out, and there I was, on the ground and in the open. I prayed to God and all the angels in heaven that the dogs weren't anywhere near, and then I ran for it!'

'You were lucky,' I said. 'They were loose. They caught Sybil and me.'

'Ferris's mistake was building himself such a showy house. It's too big for two dogs to patrol properly,' Brockley said. 'Anyway, I never saw or heard anything of them. Heaven was with me. Until I got to the boundary fence. That was a different story. God's teeth!' said Brockley fervently. 'I'd swear those trees were laughing at me. They were that difficult to climb. I couldn't have done it except that I *had* to. I managed in the end by getting up one that was so close to the fence that I could stick out a foot and brace it against the fence to help me push myself up. That was when I hurt my ankle again. But I scrambled high enough somehow, got on to a branch that reached to the fence, slithered along, toppled over head first, landed in a heap, and then, thank God, I found the wagon waiting for me, so I brought it home, as fast as the horse would go, and roused up Master Stannard. The ankle let me down when I was fighting Ferris. Did you realize?'

'Yes. I saw what happened. How does it feel now?'

'It will mend if I don't damage it again. It probably saved Ferris from the rope. He wouldn't have ended up stabbed with his own dagger if I hadn't fallen on him. You could say he did himself a good turn when he killed my Berry. More's the pity! Well, we've come safe out of it in the end, and I never had to use your picklocks after all, though I made sure I got back the ones that Ferris took off you. Madam . . .'

'Yes, Brockley?'

'Were they waiting for us when we got to White Towers? Had someone warned Ferris that we were coming, do you think, or did he just guess?'

'I'm coming more and more to believe,' I said, 'that Dorothy Beale wasn't the only person he planted on us. Ferris trapped poor Jennet and Margery and little Bessie by hiding not one but two incriminating books in their house. He might have doubled his chances of information from Hawkswood in the same way.'

'We considered the notion of a second spy after I was attacked,' Brockley said. 'Do you remember? But we let the idea go. Maybe we were wrong.'

'I'm sure we were,' I said. 'Ferris fed Emory the news that Meg's Uncle Ambrose had died, but how did Ferris know? It *could* have been the Dodds babbling away in some inn or other, but what if someone in our house told him? Didn't I whisper as much to you, back there when Jane Cobbold was testifying?'

From behind us, Adam Wilder remarked: 'Joan Flood. Possibly Ben as well, but I'd bet on Joan. She was brought up a Catholic; she's the more likely tool for Ferris.'

'But Joan is so kind, so helpful!' Sybil protested.

'Yes, always going here and there, doing work that isn't hers, making herself useful, and not just to people inside the house. She slips off to the village to be helpful there, as well, and rushes off without being asked, to buy fresh cinnamon sticks,' Wilder said sardonically. 'At a guess, I'd say that Joan has a contact in the village, who passes news on to White Towers. I would recommend, madam, that you dismiss her and Ben, even if it does upset Hawthorn.'

'But Walter Ferris won't be paying for Joan's services now,' I pointed out. 'And she and Ben are such very good cooks. I shall speak to them when we get home, Wilder. If Ferris did plant them – or planted Joan – well, I fancy Brockley and I can frighten the truth out of them. There are things I still want to know – like whether there are any incriminating books concealed in Hawkswood and, if so, where. Joan might know, even if Dorothy was the one who hid them. If so, I think we can get it out of her. Can't we, Brockley?'

'Or out of Ben. I'd reckon he knows all about it, whether he's taken part in it or not. If it wasn't them, I dare say that will become clear enough.'

'But if it was, well, after we've said our say, and terrified them half to death and got rid of any horrible books that happen to be lying about, let's keep the Floods, if they'll stay,' I said. 'They're *very* useful in the kitchen, and after all, who knows, we might save their souls!'

And then we were all laughing, so much that the woods rang with it, and several indignant birds, who had just retired to roost for the night, flew off their perches and went to find more peaceful places to sleep.

All the same, when our absurd fit of merriment had passed, I remember that I said: 'I've sometimes thought of all this as the Affair of the Three Weddings, but it's been too frightening for anything so frivolous. It's the first time that either Brockley or I have had a bounty on our heads, and I hope it will be the last. I know that I've felt like a hunted animal.'

'I agree,' said Brockley soberly. 'We ought to call it the Affair of the Queen's Bounty. There's nothing frivolous about that.'

When we set foot in the courtyard of Hawkswood, most of the household was there. There were cries of relief and welcome. Hawthorn marched forward, exclaiming: 'Thank God you're safe back, madam!' and Tessie, though hanging back, too shy to speak to me, looked as though she had been crying. Dale was there, anxious for me but with her eyes straying to Brockley. I ordered him to leave his horse to Simon and pushed him at his wife.

'Dale, take care of him! He's been in a fight, and his ankle's got twisted again. Sybil, you look after Margaret. Where's Hugh, Dale?'

'He's in his bed, ma'am,' Dale said. 'What's been happening, ma'am? We all got such a shock when Roger came back and told us you'd been taken, and Master Stannard, he took on like anything! He'll be so glad to see you safe home. He's not been well at all . . . Oh, Roger! You're *hobbling*! Your ankle must be in a terrible state! How did it happen?'

'I'm going to Hugh,' I said. 'Wilder, take charge of everything.'

I hurried indoors, truly wanting to be with Hugh but hoping, too, that Dale had understood how much. It would reassure her, if she had.

I found Hugh propped on pillows and reading a book about chess. He dropped it and held out his hands to me. 'Ursula! Oh, I've been so afraid for you. I heard you ride in; I heard your voice, down in the courtyard. It was the best sound I ever heard in my life. I wanted to come down to greet you, but I didn't feel—' He broke off, as if he had run out of breath.

I sank to my knees at his bedside. 'Hugh, what's wrong? What is it?'

'It was a shock, when Brockley turned up here at daybreak and said you'd been taken. I was afraid of what Ferris might do. I didn't like what Margaret Emory had said about witch-craft being brought into the charge against Sybil. I suddenly found I couldn't breathe properly. I put myself to bed, and Gladys made me a medicine. Are you all safe? Sybil is with you, isn't she? I mean . . .'

'Yes, we're all safe. We've brought Margaret Emory back with us. It's a long story, but Ferris is dead. He and Brockley had a fight.'

'Brockley *killed* him?' said Hugh in horror.

'No, no. But they did fight, and then Ferris pulled out a dagger. Brockley tried to take it from him, but he turned that weak ankle and they fell over, and in the struggle Ferris stabbed himself. The sheriff was there and agreed it was an accident.'

'Thank God. I wouldn't want Brockley in trouble with the law. I'll hear the details later. I'm too tired just now.'

Trying to lighten the atmosphere, I said: 'We've all come through safely, me and Brockley and Sybil. Oh, and Thomas is sending the Dodds' ladder back tomorrow. We won't even have to buy them another one.'

I was rewarded with a chuckle. 'But best of all,' said Hugh, sobering, 'you're safe, and you're here with me. I'm so thankful.'

'Everyone is, touchingly!' I said. 'Even little Tessie looked as though she'd been shedding tears!'

'That was only partly about you,' Hugh told me. Having news for me seemed to stimulate him, and he sat up straighter. 'The whole house has been at sixes and sevens. Meals served late, Hawthorn in a temper because some milk he wanted to use went off, and then when Tessie went to feed the fowls this morning, the black cockerel wasn't there. There's been a fox about, apparently . . .'

'Yes, I've seen it. But why was Tessie feeding the fowls? Phoebe does that. Tessie's so scared of the cockerel.'

'Apparently, Phoebe was busy, and Tessie offered.'

'That was brave of her.'

'She's a good lass. Joan Flood says the girl is trying not to be so timid. If we're kind to her, Ursula, and let her grow out of her nervousness, she'll probably end up either as a respected matriarch with hordes of respectful grandchildren, or else as someone's head housekeeper with all her underlings terrified of her. Such things can happen! But she's still easily frightened, and I think you'd better have a word with Wilder.'

'Why?'

'When he heard that somehow or other the fox got the cockerel in the night, he accused her of either not locking the chickens up properly last night or leaving it too late. He shouted at her – they were outside, just under my window and I heard everything – and I could hear Tessie bursting into tears and saying it wasn't true, she *had* locked them up properly and at the right time, and then, I'm sorry to say, Wilder slapped her. He'd been as upset as anyone by Brockley's news, but that's no excuse for bullying Tessie. I wanted to get up and protest, but when I heard you'd been seized . . . well, it knocked all the strength out of me.'

His brief spurt of energy faded. He sank back against his pillows. I studied him concernedly. His lips once again had the bluish tinge that worried me. I said: 'There's nothing to fear any longer. I'll let you rest now. I shall look after you. Just as Dale, by now, is probably putting ointment on

Brockley's bruises and a cold poultice on his ankle. It's all right, Hugh. I'm here and I'm with you, and Hugh . . .'

'Yes, my love?'

He looked so very far from well. And now, finally, I realized how bleak the world would be without him. I said: 'Even if Matthew de la Roche really did walk into this house, in person, I would choose to stay with you. I mean it.'

After a time, when he had relaxed into sleep, I went down to the hall, where I found Sybil, Margaret and Gladys deep in a discussion about the end of the Cobbold–Ferris feud and whether Thomas would, one day, succeed in marrying Christina.

'I think he will,' Margaret was saying. 'I've seen them together, and we all heard what Mistress Cobbold said. She doesn't think anyone else will want to marry her daughter. Poor Christina. But Thomas still loves her, and I fancy he'll get his way, if her mother is on their side. Or maybe the two of them will just run off together. I wouldn't be in the least surprised.'

There was something just a little wistful in her voice. I smiled at her and said: 'One day, Margaret, you'll meet someone who will feel about you as you obviously think Thomas feels about Christina. If you stay with us . . . My dear, you come of a Catholic family, but this is not a Catholic household. If you would rather we found Catholic guardians for you . . .?'

'I don't care about that,' Margaret said. 'I have never thought that there was enough difference for the fuss that everyone made about it. And it feels strange, being whisked from one house to another, twice in such a short time. I'd rather stay put for a while. If I may.'

'You certainly may,' I told her. 'And we shall see that you meet plenty of suitable young men, and one day, the lightning will strike for you. Yes, it will! You'll see.'

Margaret flushed but smiled. Sybil put an arm round her. 'Mistress Stannard is right. You're still young. Just wait a while.' She glanced at me. 'Brockley and I have been talking to Joan Flood. I thought you'd like to know straightaway. Just now, Joan is Flood by name and flood by nature – I never saw such a flow of tears. She was Ferris's spy, all right. Brockley had the truth from her in two minutes. She's told us where to find the books on witchcraft, and we fetched them. One was pushed to the back of a shelf in the master's study, and the other was in a drawer in Mistress Meg's old chamber. They were foul things – I could hardly bear to touch them. We took them straight to the kitchen fire. I hope that was right. You didn't want to see them, did you?'

'No,' I said with a shudder. 'I didn't.'

Gladys said to me: 'I'd like a word. Alone, like.'

I led her out of the hall and into the small parlour where Hugh and I usually sought privacy. 'Is it about Master Stannard?' I asked. 'I think we should call Dr Hibbert to see him.'

'He's been already,' Gladys said. 'I didn't tread on his toes, don't you worry. Kept out of his sight, I did. But I'd given Master Stannard my foxglove potion, and he was better, a little, before Hibbert got here. Having you safe home, too, that'll be the best medicine of all. You came near the rope, Brockley says. If you'd hanged, that would have killed Master Stannard, I reckon.'

'So do I, Gladys. He needs a quiet life, and from now on, I mean to see he has one. I can't believe I was nearly taken up for a witch. It feels like a bad dream.'

'It were no dream, and I know what it's like,' Gladys said grimly. 'And it were my fault, or almost – I've been nearly hanged myself, and that's the peg they damned near hanged *you* on! Think I don't care?'

'It's all over now, Gladys. Ferris is dead, and Sheriff Heron knows I'm innocent.'

'Ah. Ferris is dead. Yes, Brockley told me that.' Gladys grinned, her dreadful grin, which glittered in her black eyes and displayed her brown, unlovely fangs. 'Well, so he should be. Witching ain't all nonsense, Mistress. I've always known that. When Brockley come back, just as the sky were showing grey in the east, I woke up and I got myself up too, look you, and I was down in the hall listening while he told the master that you'd been taken, at that White Towers place. So I went out quick and quiet and crept to the fowl yard. Lucky it's not easy to see from the windows. I opened the fowl house and grabbed that vicious old cockerel round the neck and yanked him out. I pushed the door to and latched it with me elbow, and then carried him off to the herb garden, where no one would see or hear. He flapped and tried to squawk and peck me, but I held his beak shut tight. It's said midnight's best for this sort of thing, but I reckoned dawn would do.'

'Gladys, what are you saying?' A dreadful suspicion had started up in my mind.

'Sky were clear, just then. First lift of the sun in the east, that's magical enough, I said to meself, and that'll be any minute. So when it come, I held him up to it and then cut his throat and poured out his blood on the earth that's mother of us all and what we're made of, and I cursed that man Ferris.'

'You . . . *what*?'

'Cursed him. Cursed him for real. Cursed him out of this life and into hell if he meant harm to you. I tossed the old cockerel over the fence into the wood. Fox will have had him by now. Got Tessie into bother, and that I'm sorry for, but there was you to think of. Everyone's saying it was the fox as snatched him. But it was me,' said Gladys, grinning more horribly than ever. 'And it worked, didn't it?'